BROKEN

A Cade Ranch Novel

GRETA ROSE WEST

eBook ISBN: 978-1-955633-01-7
Print ISBN: 978-1-955633-04-8

PUNK ROSE

PRESS

ALSO BY GRETA ROSE WEST

Wild Heart: Welcome to Wisper, a Cade Ranch Short Story prequel

Join the newsletter for this short introduction into the Cade Ranch world and for extra goodies and scenes! Check out my website to join.

gretarosewest.com

BURNED: A Cade Ranch Novel

BROKEN: A Cade Ranch Novel

BUSTED: A Cade Ranch Novel

BRAVED: A Cade Ranch Novel

BLINDED: A Cade Ranch Novel

Coming Spring 2022

To you:
I know that wall; I have that wall. You were my wall.

To warriors of anxiety:
I feel you, and I'm here with you.

Dear Reader,

I didn't like Dean at first. He made me mad. He frustrated me, and he scared me. But with a little help from my editor and a few friends, I came to understand him better. He finally let me in, and this story is the result of that angsty get-to-know-you period.

I have never been a lover of Country music, but this book led me to it. I hope you'll take a few minutes to check out the playlist on my website, if you're into that kinda thing. The songs will inspire you too. gretarosewest.com. Don't worry, they aren't all Country. I'm not that far gone ;p

I've said before that these books, this series, is a labor of love. This book hurt my heart and healed me little bit too. And it opened me up to so many new characters.

Dean's book is the one that brings me back home, the one that reminds me home is where your heart is, and your heart is where you're always home.

Thank you for reading it and for coming on this journey with me.

Love always,
greta
greta@gretarosewest.com

ACKNOWLEDGMENTS

To my boys, as always, thank you for supporting me and putting up with my endlessly repeated playlists. Sean, I don't think you complained once. That takes some *serious* patience. I know me. I love you both.

Thank you again, Christy, for reading every single version of this book and for telling me, "It's too flowery. Dean doesn't talk like that. He's too broody." I know I can always trust that you'll say what I need to hear. Keep doin' that!

To Peter Senftleben, my editor: You and Christy should meet up for drinks. I'm sure, by the end of the night, you'll have my life and career planned out for me. You are never allowed to retire. Got it? I can't live without ya. Dean would still be a stalker sans you. Thanks for helping me turn this book into one I LOVE, when, in the beginning, I so did not. You made me believe in this process of revising, killing my darlings, but coming up with new ones I love even more. You helped me believe in me.

Thanks again to Joanne. Why must apostrophes be turned backward for slang only at the beginning of a word? WHY???

Tracy, your friendship and that you believe in me grounds me and makes me remember that we can do this. We can do what we love, have what we love. We can be someone we love.

To my Betas, again, thanks for reading and giving your feedback. Jackie, for your military guidance. And Cece, just you wait for the next book's acknowledgements, my Dutch guru. I bet when I reached out on GR, you were like "Deze Amerikaan is gek!" Thanks for putting up with my whiny insecureness and for correcting my horribly attempted Dutch emails. I'm getting better!

Thanks to every single person who read this book, friends, family, ARC readers. I appreciate every single comment and piece of feedback.

And to the real Carolyn: Thanks for reading and for being my Wyoming go-to, and for being the subliminal inspiration I never knew I had, little ducky ;)

PROLOGUE

Dean

You don't need her. You have me.

I crouched below the open window of a fallin' down buildin' somewhere in Baghdad. Or Mosul. Or one of the thousand gateways to hell we'd been. The old mud-brick house fell in pebbles and stones. Fell from above, shot up from below, flew sideways at my face, stingin' my skin like the rain whippin' in the Wyoming wind. Bombs. Gunfire. It pounded all around me and nothin' but her voice would break through.

She was seven and I was eight. My world crumbled then too. I held onto her hand that day, in my meadow, the little-boy-adventures meadow where my brothers and I played every day of our lives. I held onto the softest hand, lookin' in the prettiest brown eyes. Even at eight years old, I knew Oly Masterson was special. A little girl with the fight of some obstinate woman from a black-and-white movie, one without sound, and she scrunches her face and stomps her foot, poundin' her fist in the air. She gets her way. You don't mess with that woman.

That girl.

You don't need her. You have me.

She held my hand that day, but really, she held my heart. I never got it back. I figured it was why I could hear her now. Miles and light years and countries and smiles away. Long lingerin' caresses from her ankle to the soft curve of her neck —lazy—a summer's breeze of a touch away. But still, I heard her when my heart beat so fast 'cause I thought I might die. Alone. Separated by worlds from my family.

From her.

You don't need her. You have me.

I wished I did.

I pushed her voice outta my head. Improvise, adapt, and overcome. There was no room in a Marine's head for a girl. A woman. For regrets. There was only the mission. Only honor, courage, commitment. Country.

She wasn't part of my mission. She wasn't part of my life anymore. Hadn't been for a long time.

But still, even through the fallin' down rubble and the earsplittin' sound of the helicopters and gunfire, the punch of bullets into old sun-dried mud stone, I heard her voice.

I wondered, wherever she was with my heart still in her hand, did she feel it throbbin' and racin', tryin' to figure a way out of the mess, tryin' to find its way back home?

1

DEAN

"Sonofabitch. Kevin, get outta the way!"

The midnight-black, seventeen-hand stallion reared up, and my brother, if he didn't move his ass quick, would most likely find himself in the back of my truck on his way to the damn ER again. Jack heard the ruckus, ran from the arena, and jumped in with me, tryin' to calm Mad Max and get him back down onto four feet. Kevin hopped outta the way in the nick of time, but the horse kicked out, attemptin' to get at him. He stuck his leg through the fence, and I actually heard the skin of Max's leg tear.

I cringed. "Damn."

"Call Doc," Jack said, and he sighed, pullin' Mad Max around in a circle to walk it off.

"Kevin, do you annoy this horse on purpose, or is it just your natural charisma?" I asked my accident-magnet brother.

"Oh, shut up, Dean. All I did was walk by him. Stupid horse is scared of everything."

My younger brother, in all his wisdom, had irritated and promptly been pummeled by a pregnant mare a few months back, and she'd broken his leg. He'd just graduated from a hard cast to an air cast and boot, and the stallion must've been spooked by it. Damn horse did startle at everything.

"That leg's bleedin' like a bitch," he commented.

"Thanks for that shrewd observation. Will you be useful for once and call the vet? And go get somethin' to wrap it with."

"Yeah, yeah, I'm goin'." Kevin hobbled into the barn, and five minutes later, Doc P showed up.

"You're damn lucky you didn't call a few minutes later and that Cade Ranch is on my way back to the clinic. I had a big emergency up the mountain, but I'm by myself, boys. I got a clinic fulla patients waitin' on me. This horse woulda bled to death. He tore a big ol' blood vessel." He sighed and wiped at his face, smearin' blood on his cheek. "I'll stitch it up. He'll be fine. Didn't get the tendon." My brothers and I had lived and worked on the ranch all our lives, and Doc Prittchard had been our vet since before I was born.

"When you gonna get some help, Doc?" Kevin asked, limpin' to the fence and climbin' up to sit. "You been runnin' the clinic on your own now over a year."

"Damn, this horse is big," Doc said, appraisin' massive Max. "Jack, get over here, do your thing. I can't work on him if he won't stand still."

My older brother walked over, grabbed Max's halter, and murmured to him in a soothin' voice. He had a way with horses, seemed to be able to speak to 'em somehow to calm 'em. Max relaxed a little, but he still stomped and bristled. Stallions were notorious for bad behavior.

I'd known one other person who could talk to horses like that, could calm a horse just by touchin' its skin, could infuse the love and peace inside herself into the horse.

"I'm gonna have to sedate him a bit. If I don't and he

kicks while I'm workin', I might make it worse. Hold him steady. I'll get the injection ready."

Doc P released Max's leg and went to his Jeep to prepare the anesthetic. When he came back, it took a minute to get the horse quieted enough to inject him, but we finally did and Max dipped his head and relaxed. Doc numbed his leg with a little bit of lidocaine and got to work.

"Help is on the way, boys. I got a new doc comin'. You remember Oly Masterson? Carolyn?"

I closed my eyes. Did I remember Oly Masterson? Hadn't been a day in the last seven years I didn't remember her. If she'd been here, she probably coulda looked Max in the eye, and he'd stand still just to please her.

I remembered her in my arms, in my bed, remembered lookin' at her with the sunset at her back as she smiled at me and crooked her finger. And I remembered her as a teenager, when she'd become so serious and studious, and stupid childhood love fell away to make room for dreams and plans. I remembered her sittin' next to me in the meadow when I cried as a boy, when she said, "You don't need her. You have me," after my mama up and left, and nothin' in the world made sense, and the pain of adulthood seeped in and bled away the edges of my innocence.

"Yeah." Kevin looked at me with squinted eyes, searchin' for a reaction. "Thought she moved away."

I kept my eyes on the doc.

"No. She went away to school but she's done now. She's my new vet. She'll be back from London in a couple weeks, and I'm puttin' her to work just as soon as I can."

"Cambridge," I said. It just slipped out while I reeled from the new information. I'd had no idea she'd be comin' home.

"Oh yeah, that's right. You two were friends, huh?" Doc

asked, narrowin' his eyes a little against the midday sun and lookin' up at me from where he'd been bent, almost upside down, stitchin' Max's leg.

I inclined my head a little.

Oly was the only woman I'd ever loved. Probably ever would. I missed her every day. I mourned her every day. She was alive and well, but I'd killed any hope of ever bein' with her again. I'd lied and pushed her away.

"Well, she'll be here soon. She'll probably stay in the clinic mostly, at first. I'll still do farm calls."

Relief flooded my body and I sighed. I dreaded seein' her again. I *wanted* to see her, wanted to wrap her up in my arms, look in her beautiful eyes, make her laugh, kiss her. Make love to her—what I wouldn't give to make love to her again. But since there was no chance of any of that happenin', it would be much easier—and a hell of a lot less painful—if she didn't have to stop by our ranch to treat the horses every few days.

"Alright, boys," Doc said, snappin' the gloves off his hands. "That does it for this one. Got anything else for me?"

"No, sir," Jack said. "That's it for today."

"Okay. Antibiotics for ten days. You know the drill."

We finished up our work for the day, and I took off. I'd been thinkin' about Oly all day, and I needed to get her outta my mind. I drove straight to Manny's Bar in downtown Wisper, Wyoming, and ordered shots of whiskey. It didn't help. The color of the liquid reminded me of the color of Oly's eyes—rich, warm brown, with little flecks of burnt orange that danced and sparkled when she laughed. I sighed and threw back another shot.

"That's your fourth shot, son, and I ain't even countin' beer," Manny said. "Hand me your keys."

A Gulf War and Iraq veteran, the guy was tough and demandin'. He held out his big mitt of a hand for my keys, and I dropped 'em in. I knew I couldn't win in a fight for dominance with him.

"So, you have a bad day or somethin'?"

"Or somethin'."

"Hm." He tossed my keys into a jar by the cash register and planted his hands on his hips. "This is what, the third, fourth time I've seen you in here in the last week? Don't get me wrong, I'll take your money, but seems like you might need a hobby. Lucky for you, I got just the thing."

"No, thanks. I got plenty to keep me busy," I mumbled, twirlin' a cardboard coaster on the bar top with my finger. "Just needed some time alone."

"Well, 'scuse me for sayin' so, but I think that's the last thing you need. 'Sides, you ain't alone. This bar's fulla people."

I looked around at all the people packed into Manny's Bar congregatin', dancin', laughin', and enjoyin' life. Huh. How long had I been sittin' in my local dive bar, drownin' my sorrows? I was disgusted with myself.

"You know Lloyd Barlow over at the Veteran's Center in Jackson?" Manny asked.

"No, sir."

"No? Well, he's a friend of mine. He was just sayin' the other day he needed some help over there. He's got a few new vets on his hands. Young guys who could use a mentor. A pal. I think you're just the guy for the job."

"Oh no, sir, that's probably not a good idea. I'm not much of a talker."

"You're talkin' to me just fine. I remember you talkin' to a certain young lady just fine. Couple years ago. You hear she's comin' back home?" He eyed me, looked me up and down in my chair at his bar. "Maybe that's why you're here tonight, sittin' in my bar, drownin' yourself in cheap whiskey." I looked up, and he tipped his head and raised his eyebrows.

I didn't answer.

"Mmhm. Welp," he popped his lips, "perfect. You need a distraction." He grabbed a piece of paper and a pen from next to the register and wrote somethin' down, then slid it in front of me. "Here. Call Lloyd in the mornin', or better yet, just stop on by the VC. You'll be doin' me a favor, and I think you might be able to help some soldiers havin' a hard time in life. And while you're there, have a look at some of the stuff they offer veterans. Won't kill you. Now, I'm callin' your brothers to come pick your ass up."

———

So that was how I ended up walkin' into the Veteran's Center in Jackson, Wyoming two Tuesdays before Thanksgivin', and that was how I met the biggest pain in my ass, Bigsy Jones.

Ten or fifteen men and women milled around the big open room when I walked in. Some played pool, some sat watchin' a big flat screen. Others talked or worked on a bank of computers set up on a far wall. It was quiet and awkward, and the walls looked a dingy sad yellowed shade of white, and you could barely see the sun shinin' outside through the grimy window.

Bulletin boards lined the wall next to me with flyers of different services offered at a discount to veterans, nearby college programs, and job opportunities. One whole board offered sign-up sheets for groups where, I assumed, people sat around cryin' about their lives.

That was harsh. Veterans could have any myriad of issues, and none of 'em were unimportant. It just wasn't for me. I'd been one of a few of a select breed of Marines. These people wouldn't understand the thoughts in my head.

I didn't understand 'em.

I didn't like to think about my time on active duty. In fact, I never did. So walkin' into the place made me nervous. My heart beat in double time as I worried I'd see someone I knew from my unit, even though I knew it was ridiculous.

It skipped into triple time as I worried someone would look at me and know what I'd done.

I *never* thought about what I'd done in the military, if I could help it. Or what I'd found.

"Look at this big cowboy motherfucker. Walking in here like he owns the damn place," a little man muttered. He didn't get up from the chair he slouched in, like he'd been poured into it. He didn't look military, and I wasn't sure if he was talkin' to me, but there hadn't been anybody else walkin' in the door, so I guessed he was.

I looked behind myself at the door just to be sure. Nope. Nobody else. Why did everybody call me a cowboy? I rarely wore my Stetson.

Definitely a little guy, the man was skinny and kinda short, maybe five-foot-nine—though it was hard to tell since he didn't get up—with dark skin, dark eyes, and a dark expression on his face.

"'Scuse me. You know where I can find Lloyd—"

"You Dean?" a big boomin' voice asked, and I turned my head to see a white version of Manny comin' at me full force. He thrust his hand out and we shook.

"Yes, sir."

"Good. Glad to meet you. Manny wasn't sure if you'd show up."

"I try not to piss him off, sir."

"Good fucking idea." He laughed, but it sounded more like a bark. "I'm Lloyd." He released the grip he had on my hand, and I resisted the urge to shake it out. Jesus, the guy was strong. Bigger than me by a good three inches, the guy was built like a tank—tall, wide, and indestructible.

"C'mon back to the office. I wanna get your stats."

"My stats, sir?" I noticed, outta the corner of my eye, the little guy sneerin' up at me.

"Yeah, you know, name, rank, all the good stuff."

Followin' Lloyd back to a tiny box of an office, he barely fit in it, let alone the two of us, but I squeezed through the door, stood at parade rest, and waited.

"At ease, man. Relax."

"Yes, sir." I wasn't much for relaxin'. Never had been, and that hadn't gotten better since I'd been home. I stuffed myself into a little gray foldin' chair in front of his desk.

"So, Manny seems to think you can help me."

"Uh, yeah, I dunno why, sir. I'm not sure what you need."

"What are you, Marines?"

"Yes, sir. Scout sniper. I was."

"Oh, a hotshot, huh?" He chuckled.

"No, sir. Just a good shot."

"I'm Army. Colonel. How long you been home?"

"Six months."

He bobbed his head a few times, open curiosity on his face. "You adjusting okay?"

"Yes, sir."

"That's good. I hear you got horses."

"My family owns a ranch, yes."

Sittin' back in his chair, he sighed. "Well, I'll tell you, I've got a new guy here. I think you might've met him out there. Bigsy."

"Oh, the guy sittin' at the—"

"Yeah. The little guy. The smartass." He sat forward, straightenin' some papers on his desk. "He's probably terrified of horses, but I was thinking, maybe you could make friends with him. Take him out to your ranch."

"Uh," I hedged and winced. "He doesn't seem—"

"No, he doesn't. But that's what happens to some people when they come home. They forget how to be good people, or they just forget to live. Bigsy's had a hard time of it. He's had some injuries. His wife called, asked me to help. They just moved here. She took a job at the hospital, and Bigsy's just kind of flailing around. Going nowhere. He could use some comradery. Whaddya say?"

Dammit. I wanted to say no and make a run for it. Like I needed another smartass in my life—I already had two at home—but I couldn't say no to a superior, and I couldn't say no to Lloyd, even if he hadn't outranked me. He pleaded with me in his eyes. The guy, Bigsy, must've really needed help.

"Yes, sir. I'll give it a shot."

"I knew you would. You *are* a sniper." He barked a laugh at his own joke. "Good, 'cause I already told him you're his new 'buddy.'"

Great. I had to work really hard not to grumble and roll my eyes.

He stood and led me back out to the main room. A couple people looked me over, but mostly, they just focused on whatever they'd been doin' before I'd interrupted the sad quiet day at the VC.

The vets in the big open room all looked lost. They all had that thing. An air about 'em that said, "What am I doin' here? What do I do now?"

I was lucky. I had the ranch at least.

"Bigsy."

Bigsy turned in his chair, lookin' up at me as we approached him. "Dammit. I knew the minute this douche walked in you were gonna dump him on me."

"Nice, Bigs."

"What? It's the truth."

"Stand up and introduce yourself, dumbass. Where are your crutches?" The colonel looked all around then boomed, "Martin!"

A young guy, didn't look more than twenty, came runnin' over carrying a set of forearm crutches and handed 'em to the colonel.

"Sorry, sir. Just having some fun." Martin sniggered.

"Do it again and you're on latrines."

"Yes, sir," the kid said and bowed. I stifled a laugh.

Bigsy didn't stifle his as the kid slinked away. "That kid smokes crack. He has to."

"Bigs," the colonel warned, handin' him the crutches.

Pushin' himself up, he leaned on the crutches and stuck his hand out for me to shake. "Marcus Jones."

I shook his hand, noticin' the extra-hard squeeze he added. "Dean Cade."

"You are a cowboy. I can hear the twang already."

"No cows. I work with horses."

"Oh, *and* he's funny. Thanks, Colonel. This should be a blast." Bigsy rolled his eyes.

"All right, well, I'll leave you to it," the colonel said, and he walked away! Uhh…

"Well, you gonna sit down, or you wanna make me stand here all day?"

"Uh, no. Sit. Please." I held out my hand like a hostess.

"Oh, gee, thanks." Bigsy rolled his eyes again, lowerin' himself into his chair, balancin' his crutches against the table in front of us. I took the chair next to him and we both sat, stiff, lookin' at nothin' for about a minute.

"So…" I looked all around the depressin' room, puffin' out my cheeks. I blew the air out. "You wanna get outta here?"

"Fuck yes. Let's go."

We made our way out to my truck, and I winced, watchin' him tryin' to climb up into my passenger seat. I wanted to offer my help, but I didn't think he'd appreciate it.

"You gonna stand there all day watching me, or you maybe wanna give me a hand?"

"Oh."

"Yeah, yeah, I know. Big tough Marine shouldn't need any help. Well, my leg don't work, so sometimes, I need a shove. Get over it."

"It's fine, man. I just—"

"Yeah, I know just what you thought," he said as I leaned in, and he pushed off my shoulder, hoistin' himself up into the seat.

I shut his door, walked around the back of my truck, and took a deep breath. I had no idea how to talk to the guy. He seemed pissed at the world. What could I offer him? I didn't have any answers. I wasn't so much pissed at the world— only myself. I climbed in my truck and started it up.

"Uh. So—"

"Look, man, just drive. I don't give a shit where we go, as long as I don't have to sit in that depressing loser clubhouse all day. But don't you go thinking you and me are gonna be some macho, good-looking"—he paused, peerin' at me with narrowed eyes—"well, on my end—Thelma and Louise, I'd-give-my-life-for-you BFFs."

I had no clue what he meant, but I'd skipped breakfast and thought, maybe if he had a mouth fulla food, he'd shut it.

"You hungry?"

"I could eat."

We drove back to Wisper mostly in silence, and I took him to José's Diner. But as we sat in a booth across from each other, and he stowed his crutches against the seat next to him, he spoke.

"So, this is where you live?"

"Uh, not in town. 'Bout fifteen miles that way." I poked my thumb to the west.

"Hm. So what does one do around here to entertain oneself?"

"Uh…"

"Dude. Are you really that boring?"

"I work a lot. I guess I go to the bar some." I rested my hands on the table, then pulled 'em back. God, I hated talkin' to people.

"Thrilling."

"Well, what do you do?"

"Nothing. I do nothing, cowboy. That's how we ended up in this predicament."

"Right. What'd you do before your tour?"

"HVAC tech." He looked out the window, seemin' to stare at nothin'. He sighed. "I can't do that anymore."

Mona, the old cranky waitress who had worked for José for as long as I could remember, cocked a hip next to our table. "Whatcha want?"

"You haven't even given us menus yet," Bigsy said, scowlin' at her.

"You like eggs?" I asked.

"Yeah."

"Bring us two huevos rancheros please, Mona. All the fixin's. Coffee."

"Fine," she intoned and walked away, and Bigsy stared after her.

"She always so friendly, or is it just me?"

"Nope, this is her havin' a good day."

He eyed me. "You know everyone in this town?"

"Probably."

"Ever live anywhere else?"

"No."

"Ever been anywhere else?"

"Not really." Even I could hear how boring I sounded. "Well, I mean, apart from Iraq. Syria. A few other places with the Corp. You?"

"Same. My old lady and me just moved here from Baltimore. Lived there my whole life."

"Kids?"

"She wants 'em. I'd be worthless to 'em, so what's the point? You?"

"No."

"You got a woman?" he asked.

I sighed. I hadn't meant to, just couldn't help the reaction.

"Oh good." He scoffed. "Something else to bore me with besides my own pathetic existence. Start talking, cowboy."

And that was how Bigsy and I became friends. He listened as I moaned and complained about my worthless excuse of a life, and I... I talked about my *feelin's*.

2

CAROLYN

Wyoming.

Home again.

Well, technically, I was still in Utah, but I'd be in Wisper, Wyoming, my hometown, soon enough. Four and a half hours. Maybe five and a half. I still had to wait for my luggage at baggage claim, and my dad would be driving.

So maybe, like, six hours.

I waved as my parents appeared outside the security checkpoint at the end of Concourse D in the international terminal of the Salt Lake City airport.

"Oly!" my mom squealed, and my dad teared up and blinked really fast, hoping I wouldn't notice. I laughed and shook my head.

Home again.

"Hi, Mom!" Dropping my carry-on, I threw my arms around her.

I'd just seen them a few weeks earlier when they'd come to Cambridge, England to visit me after I'd been in fender bender and hurt my wrist. It had just been a sprain, but you would've thought I needed an arm replacement, the way my mom acted.

My dad hugged us both and spoke into my hair. "It's so good to have you home, baby girl. We missed you so much."

"Guys, I just saw you. It hasn't even been a month," I said, laughing and soaking up their love. I'd missed them so much too.

"Yeah, but it was in another country. Doesn't count." My mom kissed me on my lips, and my dad swooped back in after lifting my backpack to kiss my cheek.

"Happy to be home, Ols?" he asked.

He'd given me the nickname Oly when I was four after I'd spent the ten minutes he'd been on a work call decorating our living room with a full bag of baking flour. My mom tells the story all the time. Apparently, he'd been too exasperated to use my full name, Carolyn, so that day, I became Oly. Like "ollie ollie oxen free," just spelled differently. Everyone called me Oly. Except for anyone who wanted to irritate me. Those people knowingly called me Carrie. I didn't think anyone actually called me Carolyn, except maybe teachers on the first day of school.

My best friend from vet school called me Carolina for some odd reason, but he was Dutch so I let him have it.

I had one other nickname. Duck. Or little duck. But I wasn't going to think about that. Or the man who'd given it to me.

"Of course I'm glad to be home. It's been a while, huh?" My dad followed behind my mom and me as she led us to baggage claim.

"Yes. Too long," she said. "I can't believe you missed three years of my Halloween parties, Thanksgivings, and Christmases."

"I know, Mom, but it's such a long plane ride. And don't tell me you didn't love the excuse to travel. Besides, when am I gonna have another chance to experience Christmas in another country? Didn't you like the gifts I sent from Prague last Christmas?"

"Of course, sweetie, but I would much rather have had you home."

"Well, I'm home now. You'll probably never get rid of me, especially when I can't find a job."

"Now, Oly, you know you have a job with Doc P. He's been waitin' on you for weeks," Dad said, trying to keep up with my mom and me. The woman never slowed down.

"I know. And I'm grateful. It's just, you know how much I wanna work with horses. A general clinic isn't exactly what I had in mind. Don't get me wrong, it's good experience. I know that. It's just not where my heart is, you know?"

We stood around the carousel at baggage claim, watching all the suitcases drop down and rotate, like yellow plastic ducks swimming in their little table river at the county fair, just waiting for some three-year-old to pick them up and claim the prize associated with the number underneath. The only prize in my suitcases was dirty clothes.

"We know," Mom said, stroking my hair, examining it like she'd never seen hair before. "At least you'll get some horse cases at All Animals. You could be in the city some-where, cleaning cats' teeth all day long."

All Animals was our only local veterinary clinic. Dr. Harvey Prittchard had owned and operated it for more than thirty years. He used to have a partner, Doc Gee, but he'd retired last year, and Doc P had been on his own since.

"True. Those two, Dad." I pointed to my two overstuffed, hunter-green suitcases banging together and stopping the flow of all the others.

"Crimeny! What the heck you got in here, Oly?" He grunted, hoisting them over the lip of the carousel and dropping them on the floor.

"Watch your back, Glen! Remember what Dr. Whitley said."

"Oh, hush. I'm fine. Fit as a fiddle."

"The doctor said he needs to exercise more and try not to lift stuff like a dang cowboy," Mom whispered in my ear while my dad attempted to stack one suitcase on top of the other.

"Dad, here. Let me—"

"I got it," he snapped, then smiled victoriously as he maneuvered the bags but grimaced, pulling on the handle of the bottom one. "Ah, see. No problem. And I heard you, Susan. Not my fault I can't keep up with Dean Cade. Have you seen that boy? Kid's muscles have muscles."

And there it was. How long had it been? Ten minutes? If that, and they had already mentioned the one person I didn't want to hear about. And 'boy'? Uh, no. Dean was *all* man.

"Dad ran into Dean and Jack Cade at the farm supply store last week and thought he'd help them load those heavy bags of horse kibble onto their truck. I don't know why he goes there. He's not a farmer," she whispered again, well, whisper-yelled, and in my dad's direction so there could be no way he hadn't heard her. "Needless to say, he ended up on the couch for two days 'cause he couldn't get up the dang stairs to the bed."

"Mom, horses don't eat kibble."

"Well, what do you expect, dear?" Dad argued. "I work in an office all day. Those boys use their muscles for a livin'. Besides, I've got twenty-five years on 'em, easy."

Mom shook her head. "You're no spring chicken. That's

all I'm sayin'." She flicked her hand in the air as if sending her comment out into the world for all to hear.

"Yes, dear," Dad conceded, smiling at me with sympathy because he knew what would come out of my mom's mouth next.

I was an only child. My parents wanted more, but my birth had been difficult and they learned then more children would have been a big risk. So they loved me enough for eight kids, and our little family of three had been the happiest. I'd never known another family like mine. A lot of the people I knew were the products of divorce. My parents were happy. They loved each other more than any two people I'd ever met. And that love had rubbed off on me.

My parents' marriage had been the thing I aspired to my whole life. I wanted the same thing: stable, steady, dedicated love.

But my mom was a housewife. She volunteered, baked, sewed, and organized till she was blue in the face. She spent her life doing everything to take care of my dad and me and just about every other resident of the small town we called home. Making other people happy made her happy, but I knew that could never be me. I wanted it all: career, then marriage and kids.

I knew I was lucky and fortunate, and I never took either of my parents for granted, but being the only object of their collective affection could sometimes be a little stifling, even at twenty-seven years old.

Case in point—I counted down in my head. *Three, two, one, and…*

"You know, Dean's still single. I asked."

"Mother! Who did you ask?"

"Oh, relax, Oly. I asked Evvie. I'm not completely embarrassing."

"Who?"

"Jack's girlfriend. The woman who rented your house? I told you about her. Remember? She and Jack are coming for Thanksgiving."

"Evvie? Oh, Everlea." Another nickname. "How's she doin'? I mean, she's better after…?"

"Yeah, that girl's a fighter," Dad said. "We went to see her when we got back from visiting you. She's the happiest thing. After everything that happened, she's like a different person."

"Your dad's taken a shining to her. She is sweet though. I hope you won't mind, but she asked me to help her learn to cook."

"Why would I mind?" I asked as we exited the airport into the cold western morning air and headed into the parking garage.

I inhaled through my nose and felt the crisp air expand my lungs. I'd missed the humidity-free air. I'd also really missed mountains. When you grow up with them surrounding you on all sides and then live somewhere they don't exist, you feel weird, like you're naked somehow, vulnerable, open to the elements with no shelter.

"Oh, just 'cause Dad treats her like she belongs to us. But you always wanted a sister."

"I don't mind at all, Mom. Sounds like she could use a mama. You're the best one in the world, so I'm happy to share." She wrapped her arm around my shoulders and I kissed her cheek, soaking up her motherly aura and breathing in her subtle perfume, fresh-baked-cookies, and sunshine smell. It relaxed me and reminded me of every Christmas and birthday I'd ever had. "I love you guys. Thanks for pickin' me up."

"You're welcome, baby girl," Dad said, popping his trunk as we approached his car. "Oh, hey, have you talked to Jules?

I saw her at the gas station yesterday. She said somethin' about the Christmas market. Opening day is tomorrow. I swear it starts earlier every year."

"Yep, talked to her last night. We're goin' to the market tomorrow afternoon. She wants to look for somethin' for her dad for Christmas."

"That'll be fun. I think your best friend missed you." My mom smiled, tugging on the ends of my hair. "You need a haircut. Ronnie Evans will get you in real quick. I'll give her a call."

I chuckled under my breath.

Home again.

———

Approximately ten minutes into our drive, during my mom's all-things-Wisper gossip monologue, I fell asleep. I tried to keep my eyes open, but they'd refused to obey. I'd never been able to sleep on a plane. Something about strangers being able to see me drool.

When I woke, we'd just passed into the Wisper town limits, and I sat up in the back seat of my dad's sensible sedan, wiping at the corners of my mouth with my coat sleeve.

Everything looked the same as it had when I'd left for vet school in England over three years ago. The Grand Teton mountains, rugged and dark in all their majestic glory, surrounded us on all sides, near and far, dusted in snow. The whole town had been decked out for Christmas already even though Thanksgiving was still two days away. Pine boughs wrapped every lamp post. All the stores on Main Street dripped with Christmas lights, and flags donning "Christmas in Wisper, Country Christmas Market" flapped and waved in the air all over downtown.

"There you are, bright eyes," Dad said, smirking at me in his rearview mirror. "You know, I'm not sure I ever noticed just how loud you snore, Oly."

"I do not snore."

"Oh, honey, you really do," Mom said with just a tinge of pity in her voice.

"It's just 'cause I was all kinked up. This back seat sucks, Dad."

Dad snorted. "Sure, keep tellin' yourself that, darlin'."

"Oh, look, Oly." Mom pointed out her window. "There's Mrs. Whitley. Wave."

I pressed the button to roll mine down as my dad slowed the car a little.

"Hi, Mrs. Whitley!"

She turned when she heard me, looking all around in confusion, like she just couldn't fathom someone would yell hello from a moving vehicle, but when she saw my head sticking out of the car, she smiled and waved her delicate hand. She wore one of those floor-length puffy coats, a dusty mauve color.

"Oh, hello, dear! Back from school?"

"Yes, ma'am."

"Stop by the clinic. Can't wait to catch up."

"I will. Say hi to Doc for me. You look great. So good to see you!"

She flicked her wrist to dismiss my compliment, then continued up the sidewalk to her front door with her mail.

I rolled up my window, and as I turned, gasped, squeezed my eyes shut, and slumped in my seat, hoping not to be seen as a big black truck passed us on Main Street.

"Oh, there's Dean right now," Mom chirped.

"Mom!"

She turned to see me practically melting onto the floor of the car and clicked her tongue in disapproval as my dad honked his horn.

"Dad!"

Mom rolled her eyes. "Oh, Oly. You can't avoid him forever."

My heart stuttered into a sprint as I peeked up over the back seat and through the glass to see Dean's arm wave out his window.

"Are ya sure? 'Cause that's my plan."

"Not a very good plan. If you're wantin' to work with horses, that's the place you need to be. Cade Ranch. Best quarter horses around."

"Yes, Dad, I know."

"Why don't we just invite Dean to dinner with Jack and Evvie?" Mom reached between the seats to pat my knee. "Get it over with. You'll feel better."

"No! You didn't invite him already, did you?"

"Ugh, Oly, no, I didn't." She faced forward again, and I huffed out the gallon of air I'd been stockpiling in my lungs, in case my body forgot how to breathe when I saw him. "I should," she mumbled, knowing full well I could hear her. "Two morons avoidin' each other like the plague, when it's clear as day to the rest of the world they belong together."

"Well, it wasn't clear to him, Mom. It wasn't me who ended it. Besides, you didn't always feel that way. You guys didn't like him the whole time we dated."

"I get a pass for that. I'm your dad. I don't like anybody who dates my daughter, but now I want grandbabies."

"We did too like him, honey. It's just, you were so hot and heavy, and we worried you'd get too caught up, get married too young, and forget about school."

"Doesn't matter now," I grumbled, sitting up and swiping non-existent lint from my coat. "And it's been years. We're different people."

My mom sighed and I closed my eyes.

It hurt, even just seeing Dean's arm. His truck.

I'd loved Dean Cade so much. We'd loved each other our whole lives. I thought we'd always be together, like my parents. I thought we'd get married, have a family. Build a life together.

But he'd thrown it all away.

Seven Years Ago

"Oly, stop."

"What? Why? Am I hurtin' you?" I asked as I grasped Dean's extremely hard erection under his unbuttoned jeans, rubbing and pumping a little, but his whole body tightened, like I'd caused him pain. I thought guys liked girls to give them head. I hadn't even started yet, and already, he didn't like it? "Am I doin' it wrong?" My cheeks pinked and my stomach flipped as embarrassment washed through my whole body, but I wanted to know. I wanted to be good at it. I wanted him to like what I did to him.

Since the first time he'd kissed me in tenth grade, we'd become increasingly physical. Now, a year after graduation, we had sex a lot. But he never let me go down on him. He was always hard, and he went down on me all the time. But he never let me return the favor.

He was too reserved. Careful.

And ever since I'd told him I'd been accepted into the University of California Davis, things had gotten worse. He didn't touch me like he used to, and when he did, he wasn't really in it.

"Just… stop. You shoudn't— You don't have to do that."

"I want to," I purred, trying to assert my sexy side while I kissed his neck and sucked his earlobe.

"Just, Oly, stop."

"You don't want—? Oh, okay. Sorry." Crawling off his lap, I sat back against my parents' couch. They'd gone shopping in Idaho Falls and decided to stay overnight. I'd been so excited to have the whole night with Dean alone. But I was mortified. How embarrassing! "Dean?"

"Yeah?" He stuffed himself back into his jeans and zipped his fly, the sound a final nail in the coffin of my horribly failed attempt to give him a blow job.

"What's wrong? You've been… I dunno, different lately."

"Nothin'. Just, you don't need to do stuff like that. You're not— I don't need you to do it."

"Stuff like what? I thought we were loving each other physically. Is that bad?"

"No. It's not bad. It's just you're— It's not somethin' you should do."

"Why not?" I shook my head in confusion. "But that's not what I'm talkin' about. You've been so quiet. Are you mad at me about UCD? I'll come home all the time. We'll still see each other."

"Mad at you? No. Oly." He scoffed. "College is where you belong. Not here, with— No. Look, I need to tell you somethin'." Pulling his knees up, he wrapped his arms around them, hugging himself so I couldn't. "I joined the Marines."

"What?"

Wait. What?

I laughed. It wasn't funny, but just out of the blue, he announced he'd joined the military? Like it wasn't a major life decision? Like it didn't matter to him, or to me?

"What?" I asked again. "Dean. What?" I shook my head

furiously. "I'm confused. I thought you were gonna stay here, work the ranch. Where did this come from?"

"My pops was a Marine. It's a good job. I can send all the money I make back to Jack, to put back into the ranch. My dad— It'll make my dad happy."

"Your dad? How can he be happy if you're leavin' the ranch? I thought— I mean, he gets mad when we go to the movies 'cause he doesn't want you to spend so much time away from your work. Why would he be happy about you goin' away? To another country?"

"Well, he won't be happy at first, but the money will help."

"But what about us? How will we see each other if you're—"

"We won't."

"We… won't?" I released my breath in a sharp exhale. "That's what this is? You're breakin' up with me? You're leavin'."

"Yeah."

I laughed. "Well, that's— I-I don't even know what to say. I thought… I thought you loved me. I can't believe you'd do this without talkin' to me about it."

"You're leavin' too. Classes start in, what, a month?"

"Yeah, but I've talked to you about it every step of the way. You helped me with my applications. We spent the whole last year tryin' to get me accepted into school. You're actin' like this is some sudden decision I made. But, Dean, the Marines? You've never even been out of Wyoming. You could be killed!"

I'd taken a year off after graduation, and Dean and I had spent every moment we could together, in the evenings, after he'd finished his chores at the ranch and when I wasn't working at All Animals Veterinary Clinic. I couldn't even *imagine my life without him in it. We'd been connected at the hip since grade school.*

"Oly," he said, turning to face me finally. He grabbed my hands and held them, looking in my eyes. "I do love you. But college is where you belong. You shouldn't be thinkin' about comin' back here all the time for me. You've worked so hard to get where you are. You deserve to make the most of college. You won't do that if you're comin' home every other weekend, wastin' your time with me."

"Wasting my time?"

"Yeah. This is a good thing. You'll be free of this place. You deserve the world."

"Wha— I-I— What are you sayin'?"

"And I don't wanna end up like my dad."

"You're not like your dad. You're good. You're kind, the most loving person I know. You're not like him at all. You don't have to join the Marines to prove it."

"If I stay here, if I keep you here, I'll be just like him…"

It took me years to figure out what he'd really meant that day. I'd been so blindsided, it hadn't occurred to me. He didn't want to trap me in Wisper like his mother. He believed, if he'd stayed with me, if we'd stayed together through college, gotten married like we'd always talked and dreamed about, had a family, he would be trapping me like his mother had been trapped, and I would leave him like she left his dad.

He kept saying I deserved so much, but what about him? Hadn't he deserved to be happy too?

My dad pulled up outside my parent's two-story, river-stone, middle-class house, and I quickly swiped away the tears that had snuck out of my eyes as I remembered the day Dean broke my heart.

My mom had turkeys, stuffed and ceramic, still in every window, but I saw the boxes of Christmas lights and decorations, ready for implementation, waiting for my dad in the garage when we pulled in.

Home again.

Now, time to put my plan into action. I *would* avoid Dean Cade like the plague. I had to.

The survival of my heart depended on it.

3

DEAN

Bigsy and I'd made plans to get together again. The colonel had been right. Bigsy just needed a friend. It seemed I did, too, and we got along pretty well. Two Marines and all. He had other issues, things holdin' him back from livin' his life, but I couldn't hope to fix any of those. I thought I might just be able to be around for him if he ever needed somethin'.

I picked him up from the VC on Wednesday mornin' and brought him out to the ranch. I'd given him a little bit of a tour, and as we made our way to the end of the first aisle in the barn, we saw Evvie with her little foal, Ruby.

"Who's this? Hi. I'm Evvie."

Evvie smiled at Bigsy as she tied Ruby to the holds on either side of the aisle, preparin' to groom the filly, then walked over to shake Bigsy's hand.

"Evvie, this is Marcus Jones. Uh, I guess I never asked. You wanna be called Bigsy?"

"I don't give a shit what you call me," he said, leanin' on his crutches.

Evvie laughed.

"Sorry, ma'am."

"Ma'am?" Evvie shook her head and giggled. She stepped forward to hug Bigsy, foregoin' the handshake. "Just call me Evvie. It's nice to meet you, Bigsy."

When she backed away to begin curry combin' Ruby, Bigsy looked at me with his eyebrows raised almost off his face.

I shrugged. Evvie loved everybody, and she wasn't shy anymore about showin' it. "This is my oldest brother's girl-friend. And this idiot walkin' into the barn is one of my broth-ers, Finn."

"How many brothers you got?"

"Four, unfortunately," I said as Finn walked up to us.

"What, you got sasquatch blood running through your veins?" Bigsy joked, starin' up at Finn.

Finn rolled his eyes. "Ha ha. Sooo funny."

Stickin' his hand out to Finn, Bigsy introduced himself, "Marcus Jones."

"Nice to meet you, man, but watch it with the tall jokes. I'm sensitive." Pretendin' to sniffle and walkin' away, Finn turned, flippin' Bigsy the bird. An instant bromance formed in that moment, and I knew I would regret bringin' Bigs to the ranch every day after because of it.

We tried, without success, to get Bigsy onto a horse, but he'd been dead set that he couldn't ride 'cause of his injured leg. He'd been shot in his thigh three times at close range. The bone had been shattered and the muscle left in tatters. After several surgeries, he'd healed as much as his body would allow, but he'd been left with less than a third of the muscle and a weak and fragile thigh bone, with plenty of metal to hold it together. I knew horse ridin' could help him —there wasn't a better way to condition leg and core muscles and build more. But he was adamant. And, I thought, maybe a little afraid.

He seemed to like the animals, though, and enjoyed feedin' 'em hay. We spent the rest of the mornin' in the barn and the house, eatin' and talkin', and my family took him in, made him feel welcome.

That afternoon, Finn and I took Evvie and Bigsy to the Christmas Market in downtown Wisper. Jack, Kevin, and Jay were workin' on a surprise for Evvie at home, so we needed to distract her for a couple hours.

Bigsy made fun of the country bumpkin atmosphere, but he bought a bunch of gifts for his wife, Annie.

I could tell he was gettin' tired, even though he'd never say it, so we called her and asked her to meet us at Manny's Bar after we celebrated Evvie's surprise at home. My brother was preparin' to ask her to marry him. Bigsy came along, and after, we went to get a drink. Finn came too.

"Well, for a buncha white guys, I guess you're not all that bad," Bigsy said as Manny slammed three shot glasses down in front of us. "That was pretty cool what your brother did for Evvie."

Finn snorted. "Yeah, if you're into all that romantic bullshit."

"Watch yourself, Finnegan. I forget nothin'," Manny warned, kiddin', kinda.

"Finn, man, maybe you should wait outside. I don't think the big dude likes you." Bigsy laughed.

"He's just sore 'cause I dated his daughter in the first grade," Finn said with a straight face, and Manny growled.

"What kind of backwards place is this? Is she your cousin?"

I laughed. We all laughed. Once Bigsy relaxed, he was a riot. I'd almost forgotten the reason I ended up chaperonin' Bigsy in the first place until I stood to use the men's room.

When I turned to walk in that direction, I bumped right into the reason.

"Oh. 'Scuse me, miss, I'm sor—"

"Jeez! Watch where—"

Reachin' out to steady whoever I'd bumped into, I realized too late it was Oly. I held her arms in my hands and our eyes met. I froze.

Finn and Bigsy turned in their seats, and I heard Finn whisper, "Oh, man."

"Who is that?" Bigsy whispered out of the side of his mouth, and I dropped my hands to my sides. They felt like they'd been tasered.

"Uh, Bigsy, this is Carolyn Masterson. Oly, we call her Oly," Finn said, and Oly tore her eyes away from mine to smile politely at Bigsy. "Oly's our new town veterinarian."

I stood there, starin' at the side of her face, thankful to Finn for fillin' the silence since I'd been struck stupid. I couldn't think of one thing to say. I couldn't think.

She was so beautiful, and it felt like my chest filled up with water while I stood there towerin' over her. My heart raced. My hands sweat.

Her hair was longer than it had been the last time I'd seen her three years ago, but it was still that shiny, wavy, chocolate cascade I couldn't stop myself from imaginin' shovin' my nose into so I could inhale the cinnamon scent of her. Or wrappin' my fist around it so I could...

I'd gone so long without touchin' her, when I saw her, it was all I could do not to pick her up and pin her to the nearest wall. Onlookers be damned. I just wanted to hold her, feel her body against mine. Kiss those poutin' lips.

I wanted to tell her I was sorry, and I was wrong, and I still loved her. I never stopped.

It seemed funny to me she came home now. She always

smelled like Christmas to me, cinnamon, vanilla, and ginger-
bread cookies, probably from some fancy soap she'd used. I'd
missed her so much, missed huggin' and kissin' her, lyin' next
to her while she studied her animal anatomy books.

She'd always wanted to be a horse vet, and now she'd
gone and done it. I supposed it meant she was Dr. Oly now, or
well, Dr. Masterson. I was so proud of her. But I was
confused. I thought she'd be anywhere other than Wisper,
chasin' her dream to work with horses. I figured she'd end up
workin' with some big fancy vet clinic for the Kentucky
Derby or somethin'.

Why'd she come back home? There wasn't anything here
for her.

I'd loved Carolyn Masterson since I was five years old,
since the first day of kindergarten. She walked into our class-
room with her shiny shoes and chocolate hair, and I was a
goner. Somehow, after years of bein' best friends, I mustered
up the courage to formally ask her out. It only took me until
halfway through high school, but she'd said yes, and we spent
the next few years mad for each other until she went away to
school.

I pushed her to go then 'cause I knew she needed to experience life without some poor rancher holdin' her back. I tried
to move on, enlisted in the Marines to get myself as far away
from the memories of her as I could. To be a better man than
my dad. To find some semblance of control in my life so I
didn't walk around breakin' every single thing I touched.

I hadn't seen her again until four years later, after she'd
graduated with her bachelor's degree. I'd been home on
leave, and we'd come back together for one night. One
amazin', heartbreakin', scaldin'-hot night.

But I'd come home different. The Marines had changed

me, and I'd tried to keep that from her. She started vet school in England soon after, and I went back to finish my service.

"Hi. Marcus Jones," Bigsy said, holdin' his hand over the back of his chair.

"Nice to meet you, Marcus."

Oh, the sound of her voice. It was small—she was nervous—but just that tiny sound from her made my heart race faster.

They shook and she looked back up at me. I took one step back.

"Excuse me, I, um, I was just leaving."

"Oly, need me to call someone to pick you up?" Manny asked from behind the bar. All eyes were on us while we stared at each other. I wanted to look away, let her outta the trap I had her in with my eyes, but I couldn't.

"No, thank you, Manny," she said without lookin' away from me. "Jules was supposed to meet me but she just texted. We're meeting at my house instead. I'll walk."

"May I walk you out?" My voice sounded weak and I cleared my throat.

"I really wish you wouldn't," she whispered. She was still angry with me. She would never have walked away in the middle of a conversation like that if she hadn't been upset. She stepped around me, and Finn and Bigsy faced forward in their chairs while I followed her out the door. She said she didn't want me to, but I couldn't stop myself.

"Oly."

"Good night, Dean. Great to see ya," she called over her shoulder. "Let's do it again in another three years."

"Oly, wait."

Whippin' around, she said, "Please, Dean. Just stop it. I get it. You're tryin' to be polite. The consummate cowboy.

But I don't need you to do that. I don't *want* you to do that. Okay?"

I nodded. It wasn't what I was doin'. There were so many things I wanted to say to her, but clearly, she didn't wanna hear 'em and I couldn't blame her.

She huffed a breath that turned to steam in the cold air and shook her head, then turned and kept on walkin', and I watched as she disappeared around the side of the buildin'. I waited a few seconds but then followed.

Her little house was just down the street, four blocks away, and I knew she could get home on her own just fine, but it felt like my heart had ropes attached to it, and she held 'em, pullin' as she walked away. I couldn't stop my feet.

Roundin' the side of the bar, I stopped in my tracks. I heard the stupid bongo drum sound from *Scooby Doo* in my head when he tries to stop runnin' but keeps slidin' in the wrong direction, arms flailin'—which is weird since he's a dog— until he collides with whatever it was he was trying to avoid.

Oly bent forward with her backside against the brick wall, breathin' heavy, with her hands on her knees to hold herself up. When she saw my boots on the ground in front of her, she stood and pushed off the wall.

"Dang it, Dean. I don't need your protection. The little lady can get home all by herself," she said, walkin' away again.

"Oly, that's not what—"

"Oh, it's not?" She whipped back around. "Then what is it? You know what, it doesn't matter. I'm a big girl now. I don't need you." But she stepped toward me. I wasn't sure if she realized she did it 'cause when she looked up at me, she seemed surprised. She held her breath, and her eyebrows dipped up as her eyes opened wide and round.

"I know you don't. You never did," I whispered, steppin' closer. I took one more slow step closer still.

We stood a foot apart, and she placed her hand on the middle of my abdomen and pressed, fisted her fingers around my shirt, and I felt the heat from her skin even through the fabric.

She shook her head. "Why would you say that?" She closed her eyes. "Please. Dean." Barely a whisper.

"I'm sorry, little duck. I-I can't seem to make myself walk away." The use of the nickname I'd given her when we were kids practically burned my tongue on its way outta my mouth, and she pushed against me and took one step to the side. Her breath came out in a hard puff.

"No? You've done it before. I'm sure you remember how."

She didn't walk away then, she ran.

4

CAROLYN

I ran all the way to my house. It was only a few blocks, but still. I called my best friend Jules on the way, and by the time I stepped foot on my little front porch, I was hyperventilating. She arrived a few minutes later, and we collapsed on the old green couch in my living room.

"Oly, what is the matter?" she asked, pulling the strands of hair I'd been inadvertently attempting to swallow from my lips. "Oly, oh my God, breathe, ya freak."

"Dean." I gulped for air. "I just saw Dean." I couldn't catch my breath. The pain in my chest was constricting my freakin' lungs.

"Oh, Oly, what's the big deal? You knew you'd run into him eventually. Wait." She narrowed her eyes, glaring at me. "Carolyn Masterson, are you still in love with Dean Cade?"

Jumping off the couch, I paced my little living room. "No!"

"Oly, c'mon, it's me, talk to me. I thought he was old news. You haven't talked about him in so long."

I stopped and faced away from where she still sat, dumb-

founded, on my couch. "Whatever, Jules. He's just— I just—
I've dated plenty of guys since Dean."

"Yeah. 'Cept, that's not what I asked."

Turning back around, I stood my ground. "Dean Cade is
no longer part of my life. He made that decision all on his
own when he joined the Marines and took off without one
glance back in my direction. I don't care about him."

"So then, why you shakin'? Looks like you can't catch
your breath. Did you develop asthma while you were in
England?" Jules smirked and I scoffed. "Or maybe you were
thinkin' about that night. What was it, three years ago or two?
The night you slept with him and fell in love with him all
over again? That why you can't breathe?"

"I don't like you."

"Mmhm."

"Oh my God, Jules. Seein' him again, just the sound of
his voice, brought it all back. Yes, from that night, and from
every other night we ever spent together. I tried to move on.
But I compared every guy I met to Dean. I couldn't help
myself. I-I just wasn't prepared to see him so soon after
comin' home." I crossed my arms over my chest, trying to
protect my stupid still-lovesick heart. "God. Have you seen
him lately? Is it possible I forgot how sexy he is? He's, like,
twice as big as he used to be! The muscles— ughhh."

I stomped into the kitchen. Jules followed, and when I
turned back to her, the pity on her face broke me down even
further. "Of course I'm still in love with him, Jules! I've
loved him my whole life. I will *always* love him." I groaned,
leaning over the sink. Maybe I could puke Dean out of my
system and wash him down the drain, like bad food poison-
ing. I was a mess. "Jules, what am I gonna do?"

She wrapped her arm around my shoulders and pulled me
up. "C'mon, let's get some wine in ya. You'll feel better."

"No. He doesn't get to do this to me again." Straightening, I gently pushed her away. "I'm a freakin' doctor. I refuse to act like some stupid little girl, pinin' over someone and somethin' I can't have. I'm movin' on. Finally." I stepped back, cut the air with my hands, and took a deep breath. Reaching for the bottle of cheap red wine sitting on my counter, I pulled hard on the cork until it dislodged, then gulped it.

"It's gonna be okay, Oly."

"Yep. I know. I'm not lettin' him get to me. But I start work with Doc P on Monday, and I just know I'm gonna get called out to Cade Ranch. Doc said I can stay in the clinic, but he gets so many after-hours farm calls. It's the main reason he needs help. There's no way I can avoid Dean once I start doin' those."

"Know whatcha need?" Jules asked, wiggling her perfectly thick, dark eyebrows.

"What? A different life? A knock upside my stupid head?" I slumped back against the counter, clutching the bottle of wine in one hand. "What?"

"You need a date."

"No." I scoffed, chugged more wine, and wiped my mouth with the back of my hand. "Oh, no. You are not settin' me up with some jerk from high school. Nuh uh." I took another gulp.

"I wasn't thinkin' of a jerk. I was thinkin' of Brady Douglas. He just moved back home."

"Brady Douglas? No, Jules! He's probably divorced with a dad bod and no hair."

"Hey, dad bods are all the rage right now. But no. Brady still has all his thick dark gorgeous hair and his trim figure. No wife. Or ex. His dad is sick and Brady came home to help." A frisky grin spread across her face. "He's a lawyer. I just ran into him at the Stop and Go."

"No, Jules. There must be something wrong with him if he moved back home at his age. I mean, he's never been married. That's a red flag."

Jules snorted. "Oly, *you* just moved back home. *You've* never been married. Gimme that," she said, swiping the wine from me, taking a swig of her own.

"Yeah, and I'm a freakin' disaster. Look at me. I'm a mess. Besides, if he's so great, why don't you go out with him?"

"You know I'm obsessed with Finn Cade. I can't give up on him now. I've almost worked up the courage to actually speak more than one word to him. By the way, did you see the way he smiled at me today at the Christmas market? But maybe it was just indigestion... Anyway, I was thinkin', you and Brady, a veterinarian and a lawyer. The new Wisper power couple. Think of the beautiful dark-haired babies you'd have."

I melted down to the floor. "But I want beautiful blond-haired cowboy babies, Jules."

"Oh, Ols, I'm sorry." She sat next to me, wrapping her arm around my shoulder, and handed the wine back to me. "That's it. You need a distraction. I'm callin' Brady. We'll all go out. It won't be a date, just a get-together with friends. You'll see. It'll be fun."

Jules went home after another hour of me moaning and worrying about seeing Dean again, and I called my parents to let them know I'd be spending the night at the little cottage my grandparents had left me on West Street. I hadn't moved in yet. I'd shipped all my belongings from Cambridge to my house, and they'd just arrived earlier in the day. I wasn't even sure if I had toilet paper in the bathroom, but I knew if I went home, my mom would take one look at my face and I'd never hear the end of it.

There weren't even any sheets or blankets on my bed, but I didn't care. I crawled in, covered myself with a folded towel from a stack at the end, and passed out.

At one in the morning, I woke to strange sounds outside my house.

Listening for a minute, I thought I heard the side door to my garage opening and some kind of pounding noise, so I grabbed the baseball bat my dad had left in my hall closet, inching closer to the side door in my kitchen to hear better. It was probably just a raccoon.

I tiptoed back to my front door. If it were something more sinister than a raccoon, I could sneak up behind without alerting whoever lurked outside to my presence with the squeaky kitchen door hinges.

It was freakin' cold outside. The air was still and quiet, and I could feel a storm coming on. Yet another thing I'd missed about home. There was a peacefulness before a big snowstorm, especially at night when the pressure changed and the temperature dropped. The whole world became quiet and calm.

Taking a deep breath, I inhaled the clean, earthy mountain air.

The side door to my garage stood wide open when I got to it, and I listened for thirty seconds more but didn't hear any further movement. If it were a raccoon or a cougar sniffing around for food, I'd hear something, breathing at least, but I still prepared myself to run like hell.

Stepping into the doorway, I gripped my bat hard and held

it up, then flicked my fingers inside the door and switched on the garage light.

I should have run.

I didn't. But what I found inside my garage was far more detrimental to my safety than any starving cougar.

"Dean! What the hell are you doin' here?"

He lay on the concrete floor, sprawled out, legs spread eagle, with an empty bottle of whiskey cradled to his chest like a baby.

Walking over to him, I pushed on his side with my bare foot. I hadn't even thought to put shoes on when I made the wise decision to attempt to sneak up on the animal or serial killer potentially invading my garage. Smart. *Way to be prepared, Oly.*

He rolled a little but didn't wake up.

"Great. Are you kiddin' me?"

I stomped back inside and grabbed my phone, thinking too late I should have taken the stupid thing with me. I didn't have any of Dean's brothers' phone numbers programmed into my cell, but I remembered the number to the ranch, and I knew someone would answer.

Dean's oldest brother, Jack, did answer, and his younger brother, Finn, showed up ten minutes later in Dean's truck. He walked into my garage and laughed.

"It's not funny, Finn. He's *out*."

"It's kinda funny." I swatted his arm. "Sorry. I been lookin' for him. Marcus' wife picked him up from the bar, then Dean stole that bottle from Manny when I was in the john and took off. Left his truck. Didn't occur to me he'd come here. I figured you were stayin' at your folks' place. I been drivin' 'round town for an hour. When'd he get here?"

"I don't know. Twenty minutes ago, maybe. But why would he come here?"

"Oly." Finn shoved his hands in his pockets. "He's been messed up since you left after high school. The Marines didn't help any. And then all that stuff happened with Evvie. And last week, we heard you were comin' home. Honestly, I'm surprised he didn't end up in your garage sooner."

"What does Evvie have to do with anything?"

"Just, you know, it was fu— messed up." He stared at the floor, kicking at absolutely nothing. "I guess it messed us all up a little, everything that happened." He looked at the wall, Dean on the floor, the ceiling—everywhere but at me. "Oly?" Still, he didn't look at me, just waited for me to answer. I got the feeling I wouldn't like what he might say.

"Yeah?"

"When Dean came home last spring, things here didn't… go so well."

"What does that mean?"

"He, um, he kinda shut down. He doesn't think we noticed, but… he took off for a couple weeks. Didn't tell anyone where he was goin'. I didn't know about it at the time, but now I think he probably went up to our pop's ol' huntin' cabin. It's where everything happened with Evvie. It's gone now, burned down." Closing his eyes, he sighed. "Oly, I'm pretty sure Dean still loves you, and after everything that happened, you bein' here— I don't think it's gonna be good for him."

"What? Finn!" What the eff?

"I'm sorry. I'm not tryin' to be a dick, but I'm kinda worried about him." Finally, he turned his head to look at me, and I saw a little kid, a baby brother scared for his big brother.

But my mind was reeling. Dean still loved me? Was he serious?

"I'm sorry. I'm not tryin' to change the subject, but I'm

confused." I really didn't want to cry in front of Finn, but my throat was tight and I could feel the tears coming on, so I gritted my teeth, pinching the inside of my cheek, and blew out the breath I'd been holding in like a hoarder. "Finn, your brother does *not* love me, and what does Evvie have to do with me?"

"After he came home from the Marines, and then wherever he'd gone to hide out, he had this look, this feelin' all around him. He was... far away. Sad, angry. It was just startin' to go away when Evvie showed up.

"Then, I kept seein' that same look on his face and felt him cringe when Jack and Evvie were together, when they touched each other. Most of the time, he couldn't even be in the same room with 'em, and I think it might've been 'cause of you. After you left tonight, his whole demeanor changed. I'm fairly sure he planned on drinkin' himself into the abyss. Probably did."

"But *he* dumped *me*. He broke my heart, Finn. Broke it, stomped on it, he incinerated it!"

This was all my fault? Was that what Finn was telling me? Poor Dean? What about me? I'd been devastated. I was still devastated! It was still hard to breathe sometimes when I lay in bed at night thinking about him. Missing him.

Clenching my fists so hard that I thought I might pop my knuckles out of their sockets, I looked away so Finn couldn't see the anger and frustration on my face. Or the tears. I wiped them away with my sleeve.

"Wait, you didn't break up with him when you left? I thought—"

"No! I thought we'd just do the long-distance thing, but he pushed me away. God, I'm still so angry with him." I growled, looking at Dean on the floor. I wanted to kick him and wrap him up in my arms. "I've missed him so much," I said in a small voice. "Seeing him isn't easy for me either. It's so stupid. It's been years."

"It don't make a lick a' sense. If he walked away from you— Why? Why would he do that?"

Like I knew. I scoffed and shook my head as we heard a loud truck clunking into my driveway. I hit the switch on the wall to open the garage door, and we saw Jack stepping out of his old red pickup, slamming his door shut. Dean didn't even twitch an eye.

"Hey, Oly," Jack grumbled. "Sorry 'bout this. We'll have him outta your hair in a minute."

"Great. Thanks."

Jack took two steps toward Dean and his cell phone rang.

"'Scuse me. It's Jay. Jay, what's—" I heard Jay shouting through the phone. "Shit. Okay, we're on our way back. Start shootin', Jay, scare those fuckers off. We'll be home soon as we can." Jack hung up and bent to lift Dean by himself. "C'mon, Finn, we got a pack of wolves circlin' the property."

"Oh, man. Okay— Damn, he's heavy." Finn grunted, lifting Dean's feet while Jack pulled him up by his shoulders. "Let's put him in your truck. His is too high up."

They both strained under Dean's weight, and as they shuffled him toward Jack's truck, his eyes popped open and he flailed around, pulling his arms and legs out of their grasp and falling onto his butt on the driveway.

"Dammit, Dean, I ain't got time for this shit," Jack growled.

"I'masthay here. Needa talka Oly when theecomzhome."

Jeez.

"Um, Dean, I'm right here," I said, stepping in front of him. He looked up at me, flashing me a goofy, cross-eyed grin as fat, wispy snowflakes fell from the sky. They landed on his face and melted, but one stuck in his dark blond eyelashes, and I wanted to rub it away with my finger. He blinked it away.

"Haducky. Can ya tell Oly I'mere?" he slurred as he passed out and fell backwards. Luckily, Jack was quick enough to stick his boot under Dean's head so he didn't smack it on the concrete.

Rolling my eyes, I sighed. "Just put him back in the garage, guys. I've got a couple space heaters, and I'll get some blankets. He'll be fine while you go deal with the wolves."

"Goddammit," Jack grumbled and yanked Dean, with only the strength of his annoyance, by the neck of his coat back into my garage. He stood with his hands on his hips, peering down at Dean for a moment. Jack would never say it, but he was worried for his brother.

"I promise I won't leave him, and I've got lots of blankets."

"Fine. We'll be back as soon as we can. You lock up this garage after we're gone and keep your phone on," Jack commanded.

"I will. Go. Take care of your animals."

"Finn, just ride with me. Give her Dean's keys in case she needs to move the truck or somethin'," Jack ordered. "Dammit, Finn, move it!"

"Yeah, yeah, I'm comin'." Finn recited his cell number, and I sent him a text so he'd have mine.

"We'll be back, Oly," he said, tossing me Dean's truck keys. "I'll call when we're on our way. Thanks for lookin' after him." He winced, climbing into Jack's truck. "Sorry."

5

CAROLYN

I shut the garage door, plugged my two small space heaters in and turned them on, then went into the house to get blankets and warm clothes. The storm was heading toward Wisper quickly, and the snow had already begun to fall faster. I wouldn't have been surprised if the guys couldn't get back until morning if it kept up its relentless descent. Fortunately, Evvie had left some granola bars and canned goods in the kitchen when she'd moved her stuff out, and I noticed some bottled water my dad had probably left in the corner of the garage, if it hadn't frozen yet.

I used the bathroom (I did have toilet paper—looked like my mom had stocked essentials for me before I came home) and changed my clothes, dressing in thermal underwear under thick sweatpants and a sweatshirt. I shoved my feet into heavy wool socks, pulled on a pair of warm Sorel snow boots that had been sitting in my hall closet for years, and grabbed hats and gloves and blankets.

When I got back to the garage, Dean was curled up into a ball on the floor, snoring. I put a couple old yoga mats down and laid several thick blankets over them, then tried to roll him.

As I grunted and groaned and pushed his body with all my might, he mumbled, "I juswanna talkher, tellherthorry," and rolled himself onto the makeshift bed.

Covering him up with all the blankets I had left, I put a pink winter hat on his head and made sure I had my house phone and cell within reach. I sat down, pulled my knees up to my chin, wrapped my arms around my legs, and stared at him.

Sorry about what? Dumping me? Leaving me? Breaking into my garage in the middle of the night? Existing?

This was so not how I saw my night going. Seeing Finn and Evvie downtown at the Christmas market, worrying about seeing Dean, and then actually seeing Dean at the bar, and now here, in my garage—I'd been so hopeful just this morning I could continue to avoid him. Now what?

I didn't know how long I sat there looking at his beautiful face as he snored in all his drunken glory, but the whole time, I fought the urge to wrap myself up in his body, warm and strong as I knew it would be.

I wanted to touch his face, rub my palms over his cheeks and jaw, feel his stubble. Remembering what that stubble felt like between my thighs, heat flooded my body. I wanted to drag my hands down from his shoulders to his wrists, wanted my hands on his chest, my tongue. I wanted to touch and lick and kiss every inch of him.

Dean had been my first. He'd been *everything*. I'd had a string of boring and failed relationships through college, and I went on a few dates while I was at Cambridge—another vet student, a Dutch guy my friend Luuk had introduced me to, and a professional British soccer player. The last guy had been just as big and strong as Dean, excessively good-looking, kind and funny, but no one compared to Dean. No one could love me the way he had. He'd ruined me for the rest of my life. I tried to get over him. Move on.

I failed.

I couldn't help but compare any guy I dated to Dean.

Sex, though. I'd had sex with four men since Dean. Not one of them made me stupid with desire the way he had. But I'd learned something about myself since Dean too.

Dean had always treated me like some fairy princess. I'd loved that he protected me, was careful about not hurting me, but sex with other men had shown me that I didn't mind a little danger. A little pain. I liked to be dominated by men a little. Not like BDSM or anything too severe, but it made me feel powerful.

If a guy was wishy-washy, my vagina dried up like the freakin' Sahara. Yeah, okay, so there was something to be said for a guy being all politically correct and expecting the woman to take charge sometimes. But in bed, I hated it. I longed for someone to hold me still and give me a good, stiff *fucking*.

I wanted to be vulnerable enough with someone to allow them to do that to me. It was what I fantasized about. Masturbated to.

It turned me on like nothing else could, and I knew why. Knew exactly where that particular fantasy came from. One night—just one—three years ago before I moved overseas and Dean was home on leave, we'd come together one last time.

It was the single best sexual experience of my life so far.

We'd both been drinking a little. The spark, the can't-keep-my-hands-off-you thing that had always existed between us, came to life that night, and I still thought about it.

Dreamed about it.

Dean wouldn't talk to me before he left for the Marines or before I left for Cambridge, and I had no expectation he would now that I'd moved home. We used to be so close. I'd never understood how he could've gone from being with me every day to not talking to me in pretty much seven years.

He'd rarely talked about his feelings, showed emotion. But *that* night, I'd known something dark simmered beneath his surface.

He didn't tell me what it was. We hadn't had that kind of relationship anymore. We didn't have any kind of relationship at all then.

But he'd shown me.

I was a little tipsy but, for the most part, disappointingly sober because I was the designated driver for the night. I'd been having a good time with Jules and a few friends who were home for the summer, bar hopping in Jackson, but then we'd come back to Wisper, to Manny's Bar, so we'd be closer to home when we ended the night. I could just walk to the little cottage my grandpa had left me when he passed the year before.

I was rewarded with two Snake Bite shots when we arrived at Manny's Bar, and I downed them both. But things were winding down, and my friends were quickly scattering to the wind around me. Jules had cornered me, begging my permission to abandon me so she could leave with Jacob Dunn, a guy who'd been a year ahead of us in school. Of course I said yes. Who was I to block her cock? So I said goodbye to Manny and headed home.

But as I placed my hand on the big wooden door to push my way out, it swung open and Dean Cade appeared in front of me.

I'd been home for a month and hadn't seen him once. The town gossip mill had informed me he was still away on his tour with the Marines. Somewhere in the Middle East. He'd become a sniper and, according to my dad, some kind of big deal for the Marines. It hadn't surprised me. He always did like to shoot, and he'd always been good at it. It was something he'd done with his pops.

So when I saw him, nearly walking right into him, I was dumbfounded and tongue-tied.

He looked so different than he had before he'd left. His body seemed even bigger. Taller. And he'd definitely been working out. Hard muscles dripped off his body.

"I— Um, excuse me," I muttered.

He didn't say anything. He stared at me as I gaped up at him in the doorway. His chest heaved up and down with quickened breath, but still, he said nothing. Didn't move. Until two men walked into the vestibule behind him, wanting entrance to Manny's. Dean stepped forward and wrapped his arm around my waist, lifting me out of the way.

It hadn't been a sexual thing, but just the heat from his arm around my back and his hand flat on my stomach felt so good. And the possessive, bossy action made my core clench. I hoped desperately he hadn't heard me moan.

Setting me on my feet, he took a step back, and I ran. I ran all the way home. I hadn't seen him in four years, hadn't spoken a word to him in all that time, even though there were a million things I wanted to say.

But I just ran.

When I got to my house, I changed quickly into a tank top and boy-short undies with shaking hands, trying not to cry. The air conditioning had gone out, and my dad had scheduled a repairman for Monday, but it was Saturday night. I opened all the windows, turned on a box fan, and washed my face and brushed my teeth. And just as I had been about to lie down and (hopefully) pass out without thinking about Dean Cade, my doorbell rang.

Figuring it would be Jules wanting to spill after a quickie or a disastrous encounter with Jacob and/or to drink more—the girl could party—I flung my door open, and my jaw dropped onto the floor.

Dean stood on my porch looking like the brooding and tortured man he most certainly was.

Still, he didn't speak.

I suppose he hadn't needed to. The look in his eyes said it all. He wanted me. The older, stricter Marine, wanted the older, more confident me.

And I wanted him. I'd never stopped.

Arching a brow, I opened the door wider and stepped back, and he stepped inside my house slowly. But once the door had closed behind him, slow flew out my opened windows.

He lifted me—I mean, can I just say how much it turned me on that he lifted me like I weighed no more than a book!—and turned to press me up against the wall next to the door. I wrapped my legs around him and ground myself against his erection. Jeez-o-pete. Had that grown too?

I whimpered at the contact, and he closed his eyes, rasping a breath like he'd been holding it in for four years.

"Stop," he commanded and I froze, hanging from his body like a freakin' over-sexed sloth.

I gasped and jumped up to my feet. Nope! Not goin' there. Hopping up and down, I shook my head and flapped my arms, trying to dispel the horniness taking over my whole freakin' body. I paced the garage, using all of my measly self-control not to look at Dean.

When all my ridiculous attempts to quell the desire didn't work, I went out into the falling snow and attempted to freeze it away. Finally, after fifteen minutes of forcing myself to think about pus-filled abscesses on cows and green eye infections in cats, I lost the overwhelming urge to hump Dean in his sleep.

I guzzled a freezing bottle of water and lay down as far away from him as I could on the makeshift bed, and it only took a few minutes then to succumb to sleep.

But apparently, my subconscious hadn't had enough of Dean either.

"You want this?" Dean asked, still holding me against the wall, and a light—a fire, a burning—flared in his gray eyes.

"Yes," I almost begged, breathlessly.

"I don't think I can be gentle."

"I don't want gentle."

"Oly."

"Dean. I'm not the same girl you knew."

"Yeah, but—"

"Dean. Make me come. Please." The alcohol had given me the courage I'd never been able to grasp before, and I'd never wanted him more. I took the risk.

He gasped and took my lips in a brutal kiss, exhaling again into my mouth and owning it with his tongue, his lips, his whole face. Untangling my legs from the death grip they had around his body, he pinned me to the wall with his hips, then lowered my feet to the floor and dropped to his knees.

Pushing my tank top above my bare breasts, he palmed one, twisting and pinching my nipple and nuzzling his nose into my belly. He breathed for a minute, inhaling my skin like he worshipped me, but then he hooked his fingers under my panties and dragged them down my legs, following the fabric with his nose, inhaling everything. Pushing them to the floor, he lifted my bare feet out of them, then spread my legs with his strong hands between my thighs, spread my pussy lips with two fingers, and speared my clit with his tongue.

I cried out, trying to grab his hair for something to hold onto, but it had been cut so short, high-and-tight for the Marines, so I dug my fingers into his scalp and pushed his head into me.

I writhed and whimpered as slick, hot juice nearly poured out of me, and he pumped two fingers inside me, licking and sucking my clit like he'd been starved for the taste of my body.

It hadn't taken long. I came so fast and hard that I slid halfway down the wall in the middle of my orgasm.

"Little duck?" Dean's deep, rich, resonant voice pulled me grudgingly from my sweet—and seriously erotic—dreams until, finally, I realized where I was and with whom. I shot up off of the little makeshift bed and out of Dean's big warm strong arms, and the separation was physically painful.

My stomach clenched and my heart ached.

"Oh!" I yelped, and Dean sat up holding his head in his hands.

"Oly, what the— What're you doin' here?"

"This is *my* garage, Dean." He looked around, confused. He probably had no memory of even coming to my house.

"Oh, well then, what am I doin' here? Ohh, we didn't— Oly, I didn't—"

"No, Dean, we didn't *fuck*."

The word sounded so wrong coming out of my mouth, like a betrayal. Dean had never just "fucked" me. He'd made love to me or we'd had sex, but he would never let go enough to "fuck."

Except for that one night.

Not that I had been some wanton hussy, begging for coarse, raw, hard sex back in high school, but, I mean, doesn't every woman want that sometimes? To know the man you love wants you so much he loses control, becomes wild?

Can't hold back.

Yeah. Dean didn't do that. At least, he never had with me.

"Oly, that's not what I—"

"That's not what you meant? What did you mean then?" When he didn't answer, I decided to let him off the hook. "You stole a bottle of whiskey from Manny and wandered over here, drunk. You wouldn't let Finn and Jack lift you into the truck. It was starting to snow and Jay called, said there were wolves at your place, so they left you here. They were gonna come back for you, but Finn called and said the whiteout stopped them. I turned on my space heaters and covered you with blankets. I must've fallen asleep." I turned away from him so he couldn't see the pain on my face. *Dammit.* I'd found myself in the exact situation I'd been trying so hard to avoid.

"Wolves? Shit. Oh, sorry, 'scuse me. Okay, um, I should go. I'm sorry, I didn't mean— I don't know what I was th—"

"Yeah, whatever. It's fine." I heard him shuffling around behind me, but I kept my back to him. If I faced him, I'd cry. I knew I would. The tears were already filling my eyes.

"Oly—"

"Just go, Dean. Please. Happy freakin' Thanksgiving."

He did go, and just like the first time he'd left me, I found myself on my knees, crying the agony out of me.

6

DEAN

Sittin' in my truck as it warmed up, I realized I couldn't make a fast getaway. I knew Oly wanted me gone, but several feet of snow blocked my exit. I watched as she left her garage, trudgin' through the mounds of the stuff to her front door. We must've gotten three feet; it reached past her knees.

She didn't look at me and she went inside.

Sloggin' back into the garage, I found her snowblower and shovel and got to work. It took a while—plus I had to clean off my truck then shovel all that snow—but finally, after throwin' road salt over the driveway and shovelin' in front of her mailbox, I finished.

She was just inside the house, and fifty times at least, I stopped what I was doin' to stomp up to the door so I could hold her and hug her and tell her I still loved her. I still wanted her. But I stopped myself every time. It took every ounce of strength I possessed and every last drop of self-disgust.

I was sure she'd moved on since I'd last seen her. Maybe she had a boyfriend now. It didn't matter. She would probably never forgive me for leavin' her for the Marines.

It was what I'd wanted. For her to live her life, to move on, to find somethin' better than the sad life she'd have with me. Fightin' for my country hadn't made anything better. Hadn't made me a better man.

It made things worse. Now, I was even less deservin' of Oly than I had been back then, before the awful things I'd done, when the only thing I'd been guilty of was bein' a bad son. And even if she would forgive me, I couldn't let her do it. I wouldn't let her throw her life away.

I wanted to tell myself I did it for her, but it was just another lie I tried to make myself believe.

The truth was that I felt pretty sure she *would* forgive me. I saw it in her eyes. It had been in her touch last night outside Manny's. But if I gave in, let myself be happy, she would quickly realize she'd shackled herself to a broken man. She'd resent me, and I'd be too weak to let her go again. And when she did go, I'd be devastated.

I didn't think I could live through that again, and it scared the fuck outta me. I'd been through a lot in my life. I'd been hurt and I'd done some hurtin' myself. I'd ended lives. I'd held men in my arms as the life bled outta their eyes.

But losin' Oly Masterson, once and for all, disappointin' her like that…

It would kill me.

Back in my warm truck, I sat there, starin' at Oly's little house. I'd finally talked myself into backin' outta her driveway when I noticed I'd left the side door to the garage open, so I got out to shut it, and when I was standing next to my truck again, turned for one last look in her direction. She stood in her big front-room window, lookin' out at me. There was no expression on her face, not sadness, not anger.

Nothin'.

Clutchin' at the pain in my chest, I watched as she closed

her eyes and turned away. The curtain fell back into place and she disappeared.

She had already moved on. I told myself again it was what I wanted, but it hurt so fuckin' bad. I tried my hardest to hold back sobs as I reversed outta her life and drove three miles an hour down West Street for a minute, then pulled over and threw up in the snow.

My cell phone rang, and I wiped the puke from my mouth with my jacket sleeve and grunted an answer.

"What the fuck's wrong with you?"

"Nothin'," I croaked, closin' my door and leanin' back against my seat.

"Whoa-kay," Bigsy laughed. "I believe that. You sound like you just got shot."

"Feels like it," I mumbled.

"What?"

"Nothin', man. I'm just—" I gulped air into my lungs and sighed. "It's been a rough mornin'. Need somethin'?"

"No. My wife forced me to call you, to thank you for showing me around yesterday. I kinda hoped you'd volunteer to get me out of the house again."

"Yeah, just not today. I probably shouldn't be drivin'. I think I might still be drunk."

"No shit, hotshot, it's Thanksgiving. I meant another day. So you assholes partied after I left? Nice."

"It was just a one-man party," I said, rubbin' my hand over my face. "I fucked up."

"What'd you do?"

"I never shoulda let her go. She hates me and I don't blame her. I can't take it back and I keep hurtin' her, but I dunno how to stop. She deserves the whole world, and I'll never be good enough, but I want her so fuckin' bad." I must've still been drunk to be talkin' to him like that.

Bigsy went quiet for a minute, and I thought he might've hung up on me after such a disgustin' display of pathetic. The guy barely knew me and here I was, spewin' my problems on him again. What the hell was wrong with me? I'd never talked about this to anyone, not even my brothers. Why in the world was I doin' it now?

"Sorry. I-I'm a mess. I'll let you go, man. I'll, uh, I'll call you tomorrow. We can set somethin' up."

"No. Don't hang up." He cleared his throat. "We gonna be friends, or am I just some pity project to you?"

"What?"

"My wife had a miscarriage. Three months ago."

"Marcus, I'm— God. I'm so sorry. Are you—"

"No, it's— I mean, yeah, thank you, but… I felt relieved. I still do. I'm a pariah for feeling that way, but she doesn't understand. I could never be the father any kid would need. I'd fail them both. I'm worthless with this fucking leg."

"You ain't worthless."

"No? I can't provide for a family. Can't even provide for me and her right now. She's at work while I sit here picking my ass and watching *Jerry Springer*."

"You're not worthless. You can get stronger, and I think I know a way to help. If you're serious about it—"

He scoffed. "I didn't tell you that to make you feel sorry for me."

"I don't—"

"I told you so you'd know I'm pathetic too. And so you'd trust me enough to talk to me. Maybe tell me a little more about your girl. I assume we're talking about the hot veterinarian I met last night?"

"Yeah. She's the one."

"Okay. Go home. Sleep it off, then come pick me up at the center tomorrow morning. We can get started on this

'Make Bigsy a Real Man' project, and you can tell me about your woman."

"Yeah, okay, man."

"Do me a favor?"

"What's that?"

"Text me when you're home," he said, like he was one of my brothers.

"Actually, I think I'm just gonna sleep in my truck a while."

"That sounds really smart," he said, laughin'. "Okay, text me when you wake up then."

"Okay." I waited for him to say somethin' more, and when he didn't, I said, "Bigsy?"

"Hm?"

"Thanks."

"Dude. Don't make this weird."

Parkin' my truck a mile away on a dirt pull-off next to the old, abandoned textile factory, I passed out. I had the weirdest dreams about fallin' off cliffs and avalanches crushin' me. But the dream I remembered the clearest had been about my mama.

I'd woken in the middle of the night when I was eight years old. I tried to go back to sleep 'cause I'd known, if I got outta bed and woke my dad, there woulda been hell to pay, but I just couldn't make my eyes stay shut, so I went downstairs to sneak a piece of my pop's venison jerky. He'd let me help him season the meat that year, and it turned out to be the best batch he'd ever made. He and I kept a secret stash of it in the pantry.

It wasn't a dream, exactly, more like a memory. I'd had it before but never with so much crystal clarity...

"Mama? Where you goin'?"

I scared my mama when she was just about to go out the door in the kitchen. But she turned around and looked at me, and she dropped her bag, the ugly one with the wooden handles that looked like Granny's dumb knittin' blankets. Red, orange, and brown.

"It's still nighttime. You can't feed the horses yet. Too early. Daddy'll yell atcha."

"Dean."

"Why you whisperin'? Here, you forgot your sweater." I ran back to the hook in the livin' room and grabbed Mama's sweater, her favorite. It looked like a rainbow saddle blanket, and it was warm. I took it to her, and she pulled it on over her clothes. But I didn't understand. It was still really dark out, way too early to be goin' anywhere. "Want me to make you some coffee? You goin' to the store?"

"No, baby. I'm— I-I just have to go."

"Okay, Mama, but I'll come with. Lemme just—" I turned, lookin' for my jacket. I'd left it on the back of the couch, but it wasn't there. Granny probably hung it up. She'd be sore with me later. I always forgot to put my stuff away, and she always hollered at me for it. "Dang it. Granny hung up my coat. I'll go get it. Just wait for me."

My jacket was probably in the back hallway 'cause that's where Granny hung all the jackets. Mama was actin' weird, and I didn't want her to go without me. I needed to be a man and make sure she was safe, but she grabbed my arm when I ran past her.

"Dean."

"I'll be quick, hold on a second. You can't go to the store

by yourself. It's still nighttime. I'll be your lookout. Like a bodyguard." I smiled up at her, but she didn't smile back.

My mama was the prettiest, 'specially when she smiled. All the other mamas in town were okay-lookin', I figured, but my mama was beautiful. She had the prettiest, waviest brown hair, like Jack's and Kevin's. Mine was yellow, like Finn's and Daddy's.

And my mama was the nicest, most special one. She never yelled at me and my brothers. Even when we got ourselves in trouble. Granny punished us, gave us extra chores, and Daddy used the belt, but Mama never got mad. Instead of makin' us in trouble, she'd take us for ice cream at the Dairy Dream.

But Mama was sad, and she didn't smile like she used to. I didn't know why. I asked her one day when I helped her with my little brother, JJ, changin' his diaper and foldin' the laundry, but she just shook her head and said it was nothin', and she kissed my cheeks and hugged me. I knew she wasn't bein' truthful. I told her not to let Daddy know she told a lie, or he'd be mad at her. Daddy didn't like liars. Uncle Jon lied to Daddy when I was six years old, and Daddy was still *mad at him. That was two years ago!*

He didn't like when we made up stories neither. Mama liked to tell us stories 'bout whole other countries. Like Italy and Franz. Somewhere else, too, but I couldn't 'member. And she said when you go there, they got all kindsa food that's good to eat. So good that you wouldn't be able to stop yourself from lickin' your fingers when you was done. And they had lotsa chocolate in them other countries. And somethin' called jelly lotto. I asked if it was some kinda scratcher ticket like Granny always bought at the Stop and Go, but Jack said no. He said it was like ice cream, kinda. Like sherbert. He said he ate some, but I didn't believe him.

"Dean, baby, you can't come with me. I need you to stay here, to help Jack take care of your little brothers. They need you. Okay?"

"Oh. Well, okay, I guess. But want me to wake up Finn?" I poked my thumb toward the stairs. "He could go with and I'll stay here. He's littler than me but he's taller, so I guess he can protect you. If you want."

"No, thank you, my love. I'll be okay."

"Okay. But where you goin'?"

Mama tried to tell me where, but then she got tears in her eyes, and she kept suckin' in breaths that sounded funny, and her chin started quiverin'.

"You'll be a good boy? You'll help Jack and Granny?"

"'Course I will, Mama. But just for a little while, right? 'Cause you'll be back, right?"

The tears dripped outta Mama's eyes, and she grabbed hold of my face. She hugged me and I couldn't hardly breathe, but I knew she was sad, so I didn't bellyache about it.

"And your brothers. Always help your brothers. Jack's the oldest, but you got more love in your little body than anybody else in the whole world." She leaned back to look at me, and she sounded like she always did when she chopped up the onions for supper. I was almost as tall as her, but I still had them pesky growin' pains to get through. That was what UJ said. "Promise?"

"I promise, Mama. You promise too. It's a big wide world out there. Better be careful. Then, when you get back, we can make a picnic, take it to the meadow after Jack and me do our chores. That's a good idea, huh?"

A dark look crossed my mama's face then, like on one of them scary black-and-white movies on the PBS, but she nodded and swiped the snot away from her nose with her wrist.

"Dean, I forgot my umbrella. Would you run and get it for me? It's in the back parlor. All the way in the corner by the window. Look real hard, okay?"

"Yes, ma'am. Be right back."

I ran fast as I could to get it, but I didn't see mama's red umbrella anywhere. I tried to be quiet. I didn't wanna wake my daddy 'cause he'd yell, and he'd definitely be mad at Mama for leavin' without tellin' him. I didn't wanna get her in trouble. But if I did, I could take her to the Dairy Dream. I had some quarters saved up from Pops. He paid me one each time I found him a good log for the fire.

I looked and looked but I couldn't find it, so I ran back to the kitchen. Maybe she could just take her raincoat instead.

"Mama, I couldn't find—"

I ran back and slid on the kitchen floor 'cause my socks were soft, but Mama wasn't there. I looked in the back hall, looked up the stairs, but I didn't see her.

When I turned to check in the bathroom, somethin' out the livin' room window caught my eye. I got closer and squinted, lookin' harder, and saw my mama runnin' down the lane, toward the highway, where me and my brothers waited for the school bus in the mornin's.

Wait. She forgot to tell me when she'd be back.

I ran out to the porch and said her name, but she didn't stop.

She ran faster.

I got them tears in my eyes too. I didn't yell for her 'cause then my daddy would wake up, and he'd stomp and cuss at her.

Back in the kitchen, I waited for her to come home. There was a note on the counter. It had her loopy handwritin' on the front, but it was folded in a square, and it said my daddy's name, so I didn't open it. I might get swatted for that. I left it there by the old coffee pot and pulled a chair out at the kitchen table.

It was a Saturday, so my brothers would get up at six to watch Tom and Jerry and Power Rangers before me and Jack had to get to work in the barn. I waited there till everybody got up. The clock on the microwave said 02:47. But I was sure my mama would be back by then.

I was sure, but my stomach hurt real bad when I remembered her runnin' away, and I could feel my heart thumpin' like it was kickin' me. My daddy would be so mad at me for lettin' my mama leave. Them stupid tears came back.

But I swiped 'em away so I wouldn't get in trouble for that too.

7

CAROLYN

"Mom? Whatcha doin'?" Walking into my parent's kitchen, I saw my mom foil-wrapping the steaming-hot turkey she'd just lugged out of the oven. I set my purse and truck keys on the side counter and grabbed an apron from the hook on the wall, preparing to be bossed and directed to help with Thanksgiving dinner.

"Oh, Oly honey, can you take the sweet potatoes out of the oven for me please? And there's some pies cooling in the garage. Bring 'em in?"

"Okay, but I thought dinner wasn't for a couple hours?"

"It isn't, but we're takin' it to go."

"Huh?"

"Well, now don't freak out, but we're taking this all over to Cade Ranch. Mrs. Mitchum isn't feelin' well, and Jack and Evvie would rather stay with her there, so I told them I'd bring everything over. We can all eat together. The boys made a bunch of food too."

"What? Mom!"

"I know you're tryin' to avoid Dean," she puffed out her cheeks, blowing her messy hair out of her eyes, "but it's Mrs.

Mitchum. This is probably her last Thanksgiving, Oly. And I have all this food. Please, honey, will you do this for me? I know it's not what you had in mind but…"

I whimpered in defeat.

I knew she was right. I didn't want to act like a spoiled brat, but just the thought of walking into Dean's house had my hands sweating and my heart thudding.

But it *was* Mrs. Mitchum. And it was the right thing to do, and I was proud of my mom for risking my wrath to bring some holiday joy to a dying woman.

Sighing loudly, I said, "Okay, Mama." I kissed her cheek and ran up to my old bedroom to change.

If I had to walk into Dean's house, I'd walk in looking like a million bucks, and he could eat his effin' heart out.

An almost hysterical laugh escaped my throat as my dad drove up the lane to Cade Ranch. I gripped the scalding hot sweet potatoes topped with browned marshmallows on my lap, not caring that the dish nearly burned my fingers, even wrapped under eight layers of my mom's trusty, extra-thick tin foil. If my parents had any idea what I'd done in that house, in the barn, in the meadow… Just the memories made my whole body heat, like I was sitting naked in front of raging hellfire.

I pressed my thighs together and squished my nipples (which were doing their best impression of cut diamonds in the cold November weather) with my upper arms as they attempted to poke their way through my LBD. I tried— without success—to will the nervous sexual energy out of my body. Just knowing I was about to see Dean had me all hot and bothered.

Why had I worn this stupid thing? I'd ripped through my closet at my parents' house, trying to find the sexiest thing I'd ever owned. That was why. But I was freezing and probably looked ridiculous. The guys wouldn't be dressed up. I'd only met Evvie yesterday, so I didn't know if she would, but my mom looked normal in her sensible tan sweater set and black slacks, and my dad looked very fatherly in his chinos and blue-and-green button-down flannel shirt. Compared to everyone else, I'd look like a club kid.

I just couldn't think when it came to Dean Cade, couldn't be trusted to make smart decisions. It made me angry. How dare he have such an effect on me? Still, after all these years. I felt like a nineteen-year-old girl again, in love with him and willing to do whatever it took to make him happy.

To make him stay.

When I saw him last night, besides the overwhelming urge I'd felt to strip and jump him right there in the parking lot of Manny's Bar, I'd wanted to take care of him. To beg him to talk to me, to tell me why he'd said all those things years ago, to open up.

And then watching him sleep, even drunk and unconscious, had only made me remember all the good things. Seeing him so relaxed and vulnerable, his beautiful face so open and unguarded, brought back so many memories.

It made me remember him as a boy, when we'd held hands and run through the paddocks, petting the horses and playing hide and seek together. It made me remember how much I'd loved him—what I'd loved about him, his huge open heart, his loyalty, and his shy smile.

He hadn't smiled at me like that in over seven years, and it broke my heart. I wanted to make it better. Make him better.

I wanted him to let me love him.

No! I was a doctor, an educated, professional, fierce woman. He didn't get to make me feel like that anymore. I would not be my mom, dang it.

Nope. That was why I'd worn this stupid, body-hugging, skimpy, little black dress. I intended to show him what he couldn't have. I'd show him how grown up I was, how mature, and how *not* in love with him I could be.

Except, as my dad parked the car and helped my mom with the mountain of food she'd cooked, I had another flashback of that night three years ago when Dean had let me into the hidden-away part of himself.

The brutal, guarded, broken part.

He'd let himself go inside my body. He had never been that way with me before, so raw and bold. He took my breath away. Many times that night. In many different ways.

Lifting me from where I slid down the wall after the most intense orgasm I'd ever had, Dean picked me up, alpha-cowboy style, and carried me to my dining room table, laying me down on it and spreading my legs wide open.

Watching as he pushed his jeans down and ripped his shirt over his head, I bit my lip and tried not to touch myself, but I was so turned on, so needy, even after the monster orgasm he'd just given me, and seeing his body bared just made it worse.

As he pulled a condom from his wallet and opened it, rolling it on, he lit me on fire with his eyes. I couldn't look away. I dragged two fingers through the arousal he'd caused, pushing them inside myself, and he growled and knocked my hand away.

He grabbed my hips, pulling my ass to the edge of the table, and impaled me with his hard, throbbing cock.

My whole body arched, and I threw my head back,

knocking it on the table, and he groaned and pulled out, then thrust back in.

All the air rushed out of my lungs from the force of his body pushing into mine so fast. I tried to reach for him, but he locked my wrists in his hand and held me immobile while he fucked into me with a desperation I hadn't ever known he had inside him.

The control he exerted over me made my core clamp down on his cock with a desperation of its own. All I'd been able to do was breathe and pump my hips to meet each thrust of his. His hand moved down between my legs, feeling himself moving in and out of me, and his thunderstorm-gray eyes closed to half-mast, but he wouldn't look away from mine.

I gasped when he bent his knees a little, changing the angle his cock entered my body, pounding into that spot inside, like my clit was on the inside of my vagina. Oh my God. And then he reached further down and collected my cum with his finger and rubbed it over my... back door. My eyebrows shot up, and my eyes rolled back in my head as he pushed a finger into my ass, and I mewled. Like a cat! I probably purred too.

It felt so good. The pressure from his finger as he pressed in further created resistance against his cock in my core, and the feeling of fullness was divine. My mouth popped open, but no sound came out.

My body bowed and strained, and I cried out when he pulled his finger from my ass and bent over me on the table, holding my wrists again and sucking my breast into his mouth.

He just kept fucking. He was frenzied and hard, and it worried me a little, seeing him so broken open, but I loved it too. I wanted it. I wanted all of him. I always had.

I tried to pull my wrists from his grasp, but he wouldn't

release them. I wanted to touch him. I needed to feel him under my fingers, on my tongue, but the almost painful grip he had on me made me wild. He liked it too. He moaned and lifted me, still inside me, and carried me to my couch.

As he sat, he positioned me over his cock and pushed me down. He released my wrists, and I clutched at his shoulders, rubbed my hands down his hard, obscenely large biceps as he wrapped his arms around to hold my ass cheeks in his hands.

"Dean!" Breathing in shivers, I felt every single inch of him as I pushed up on my knees and descended, over and over and over. He felt so good and I'd waited so long for him. I could barely contain the pleasure.

"Fuck, Oly," he grunted, and I kissed him. I licked and sucked and penetrated his mouth, assaulting him with my tongue while I assaulted his body with the rest of mine. Grinding my clit against his body with every descent, I'd never fucked so hard, almost violently, but I needed it.

I needed him.

His fingers dug into my skin hard enough to leave a bruise, driving me down on his rigid cock again and again, and I loved it.

"Harder," I begged, and he ripped his mouth away from mine to breathe.

Digging his fingernails into my ass cheeks, watching my breasts bounce, he commanded, "Faster."

Reaching between our bodies, he looked up at me and pinched my clit, hard.

"Come again. I'm gonna come. I can't— Oh, fuck. You're so close. I can feel you squeezin' my cock. I can't hold back anymore."

He pinched harder and bit my nipple, and some kind of reply squeaked out of my mouth as another orgasm rushed from my clit to the inside of me, exploding to the tips of my *fingers and toes. I hugged his face to my chest as I came, and he bucked up into me one last time, shouting my name.*

"Happy Thanksgiving!" Evvie chirped when she yanked the kitchen door open. I nearly dropped the sweet potatoes but fumbled and caught them before they fell onto Dean's porch. But they were freakin' scalding hot still, and the hand towel I'd been using to protect my fingers slipped away and fell to my feet.

"Oh! Ow, ow, ow. Move!" I pushed past my mom to the kitchen table, dropped the dish, and ran to the sink to douse my fingers in cold water.

"Oly? Are you okay?" Evvie asked, rushing beside me.

"I burned my fingers," I whined.

"Here." Dean's deep voice behind me raised goosebumps all over my body, and I turned to see him holding a cold pack from the freezer. "Hold onto this. Did it blister?" He reached for my hand and held it up, inspecting my fingers.

"N-no, I don't think so." I looked up into his dangerous gray eyes, probably drooling, as the flashback flared in my mind's eye.

So much for being sexy.

"Are the sweet potatoes okay?" Kevin asked, and Finn smacked the back of his head. "Ow! What? Sweet potatoes are my favorite. 'Specially the ones with the burned marshmallows." He peeked under the crumpled tin foil, poking his fingers into the orange goo.

My mom swatted his hand away. "I don't burn food, young man. Are those hands clean?"

Kevin looked at his hands and shrugged. "Kinda?"

"Ach, go wash them."

Dean still held my hand but dropped it when he realized everyone in the room was staring at the two of us standing a foot apart, staring into each other's eyes.

"I think we have some burn spray upstairs in the medicine cabinet. I'll get it," he offered.

"No, it's fine. I remember where it is. I'll go."

My mom scolded me like a ten-year-old as I jogged to the stairs. "Oly, don't be rude. You're a guest here." But I had to get away from Dean. I took the stairs two at a time, nearly bowling Mrs. Mitchum over when I made it to the top.

"Oh! I'm sorry. Are you okay?" I grabbed her arms to steady her, and her skin was cold and paper-thin.

"Honey, I'm fine. What's the rush?"

"Oh, it's not a big deal. I burned my fingers carrying the sweet potatoes."

Behind me, the stairs creaked with someone's footsteps, and I rolled my eyes. I just knew it was Dean. Mrs. Mitchum pressed her lips together and tried not to smile.

"Look in the medicine cabinet, sweetheart. There's probably somethin' in there for your burn."

"Yes, ma'am."

"Good to see you again." She smiled, batting her eyelashes. Oh. She felt fine. The devil. "Glad to be home?"

"Yeah, I—"

"Here, Ma, lemme help you," Dean said, interrupting me, and she took his outstretched hand. He helped her down the stairs and she whispered to him, but like my mom, her whisper could probably be heard in the next county.

"You should help her."

Dean grunted.

"Oh, just go help her."

"She's a vet. I'm sure she can spray her own fingers."

"Dean."

He sighed. "Yes, ma'am."

8

DEAN

Tappin' on the open bathroom door with two knuckles, I looked in the bathroom mirror, and Oly looked at my reflection.

"I'm fine, but I don't see the lidocaine spray in here." She closed the medicine cabinet carefully and looked at me again.

"Oh, hold on. It might be in the hall closet."

She washed her hands as I went in search of the spray. When I found it, I grabbed it and a clean towel.

"Sit down," I said, walkin' back into the bathroom, and set the aerosol can on the edge of the sink. It was an old can and probably far outta date, but the medicine would work.

Kneelin' in front of her as she sat on the side of the tub, I clasped her wrist in my hand, lookin' up at her as I blotted her skin dry.

"It's not so bad," I said, but it came out more like a whisper.

"I said it was fine."

She'd worn a short dress and cowboy boots, and she opened her legs a little as I inched closer to her. My attempt at first-aid had veered off track just a little. I had a feelin' it had been the reason behind Ma pushin' me to help Oly even though there really wasn't much wrong with her.

Holdin' her hand up in front of me, I reached back for the spray and popped the cap off with my thumb. I coated her fingers with the numbin' medicine and blew on it to make it dry faster, and her eyes roamed all over my face.

"Your hair's longer," she said softly.

I bit my tongue so all the things I'd wanted to say to her for seven years didn't fall outta my mouth.

"I like it. I like this beard too." She nodded to the scruffy mess on my cheeks and chin.

"Thanks." I smiled a little as I eyed her chocolate tresses. "Yours is too."

"Yeah. I was thinkin' about cuttin' it."

"There," I released her hand, "think you're all set. You might survive. I'm not sure. Better get your papers in order."

She pulled her head back, and her beautiful dark eyebrows bent up in disbelief.

"Was that a joke? You—Dean Cade—made a joke?"

I looked down and scoffed a little but then looked into her eyes.

"Oly?"

"Yeah?" she asked apprehensively, like she might be afraid of what I'd say next.

"I'm sorry about last night. I shouldn't have done that."

"It's fine. Don't worry 'bout it." But she looked away 'cause it wasn't fine.

"No, I feel like an assh— a jerk."

"It's fine." She dismissed my apology again, stood, and waited for me to stand, too, so she could get past me.

When I did, she leaned back on her heels, but then, fast as

lightnin', she threw her arms around me and hugged me. I held my arms out to the sides. If I touched her, hugged her back, I didn't think I'd ever be able to let go.

"I'm so glad you're home safe. I worried about you so much."

Slowly, I wrapped my arms around her back, but once they were there, it wasn't enough. I pressed her to my body and held on, like we stood on the edge of the Empire State buildin' in a high wind with no railin'.

I'd dreamt about touchin' her again. Holdin' her.

"I worried about you too."

"Why? I didn't go to war."

"No, but you were so far away, out in the big wide world. Away from your family. I dunno. I just worried."

She hugged tighter and I leaned into her hair, inhalin' the cinnamon scent I'd missed so much.

"I heard you're workin' for Doc P. You excited?"

"Yeah. I start Monday."

"I'm proud of you, Oly. You went out there and made your dreams come true."

"Thank you."

Her soft voice against my chest stoked a fire inside me, and I struggled not to suffocate her as I hugged her closer, as close as I could without mergin' our bodies into one. Holdin' her caused a ragin' erection—I couldn't have stopped it if I'd wanted to—and I was sure she could feel it against her stomach.

Abruptly, she released me and dropped her arms, so I did too. We both backed up a little, creatin' a distance between us, just lookin' at each other. "We," she took a deep breath, "we better get back downstairs before the rumors start."

Backin' up against the wall so she could go, I nodded,

pressin' my hands to the sides of my thighs so I wouldn't reach out and pull her back to me. She looked down at the floor, then walked outta the bathroom, and I stood there, paralyzed, tryin' not to die from the lack of oxygen in my lungs and the heart in my chest that had probably just broken in two.

Again.

Thanksgivin' went well. Ma seemed to be feelin' fine, and she enjoyed havin' a full house. She laughed and talked all night. Evvie had a ball too. She ate so much, I thought she might bust her incision open. She and Oly seemed to get along pretty well, and they sat in a huddle, talkin' for a long time.

Oly didn't speak to me again, and I didn't say anything more to her. She watched me though. I caught her peekin' at me all night. I watched her too. I pretty much couldn't look at anything else.

Jack and Evvie announced their surprise from the night before, their engagement. My brothers and Ma already knew since we'd been there, but Oly and her mama swooned, and the conversation turned to all things weddin'.

For the second time that night, my heart split in two 'cause, for the longest time, most of my life, really, I'd thought that would be me and Oly's future. I thought we'd get married, have a gaggle of kids, and be happy.

But I knew it could never happen. I couldn't chain Oly to my train wreck of a life. I couldn't drag her down the road with me, to the fucked-up mess I'd made of myself.

I wouldn't do it.

A wall came down inside my head, a thick heavy concrete

wall, and I imagined it makin' a loud thunkin' noise when it hit the ground. It blocked out sound and light and love.

The rest of the night passed in a blur. Finally, the Mastersons prepared to leave, and I lurked in a corner, watchin' Oly smile at me. I didn't smile back. She looked so hurt as her eyes dropped to her boots, and she walked out my kitchen door.

I knew if I told her what I'd done, she'd forgive me. She was the kindest, most forgivin' person on the planet—of course she would—but I didn't plan on givin' her the chance to do it.

Ma and Finn sat at the kitchen table with me, chattin', while Jay and Kevin argued and washed dishes, and Jack and Evvie snuggled on the couch, touchin' and kissin', watchin' some holiday movie.

My wall came slammin' down again till Ma tugged on my arm.

"Dean, help me upstairs? I think I'm ready for bed." I didn't answer. Carefully, I took her frail arm, hookin' it through mine, and she patted my hand. "Thank you, sweetie."

Dozens of people I'd killed with my rifle and she knew, but to her, I would always be "sweetie."

"Mmhm."

Steadyin' her as we climbed the stairs, I wondered how much longer she'd be able to climb 'em with her own strength. One of us would have to carry her, if she'd let us. Maybe we needed to set her up in Jack's bedroom. He and Evvie were still usin' the den. Or maybe they could switch with Ma and take the guest room upstairs. But then they'd be above her, and I wouldn't wish that on anyone, let alone a sick old lady. We were all goin' a little nuts with 'em livin' here with us till their house was fixed up and habitable. They fucked like animals at all hours of the day and night. Poor Ma would never get any rest.

I wasn't gettin' any anyway. I lay awake night after night just thinkin' about Oly. Picturin' her beautiful face, her lips as she smiled and laughed at me, before I'd lied and pushed her away from me.

"Dean, you wanna open the door or just stand here in front of it forever?" Ma elbowed me in my side.

"Sorry." I opened her door and led her to sit in the big puffy white chair with purple flowers Kevin had bought for her. She sat on it, and I thought she might fall in—the thing dwarfed her frail tiny chemo-ravaged body.

"What on earth is goin' on with you? You been actin' like a zombie most the night. I thought you'd be happy Oly was home." She scooted back, pullin' a blanket from the arm of the chair over her legs, and looked up at me, pity and disappointment clear on her withered old face. The kindness in her voice knocked me back into reality for a second, and when I looked at her, I noticed her cheeks were gaunt, and she had dark circles under her powder-blue eyes. She hadn't lost her hair though.

"I am happy she's home. I'm just tired. I'm fine."

"You don't seem fine. You barely spoke all—"

"I said I'm fine." *Ahh, dammit.* "I'm sorry, Ma, forgive me. I'm just tired. I haven't been sleepin' very well. Just been thinkin' about some things."

"Dean. Will you talk to me, honey? I'm here. I'll listen. You've had a lot on your mind since you got home from Colombia."

I shook my head and backed away. "Ma, I'm fine, really. Please, don't worry about me."

"Dean, when you gonna get it in your head that you're a

good man? You walk around here like you think you're not worth anybody's time."

"I don't think that," I lied, lettin' my wall fall down again. "If that's all you need, I'll leave you to rest." I didn't give her a chance to add anything more. I couldn't take any further life lessons. Backin' outta her room, I pulled the door shut with a quiet thud.

I brushed my teeth and stood starin' at my face in the mirror, thinkin' about the night Oly and I had shared three years ago or so, before she'd gone off to study in England. I pushed her away after high school, before I left for the Marines, but that night, I lost myself inside her.

Sniper work was… hard.

What a fuckin' understatement.

At first, I felt like some superman. Everybody looked to me; my "accomplishments" became known throughout my unit, then our base, then the Marines overall. I'd earned some kinda cult followin'. Soldiers congratulated me on my kills.

On the number of my kills. The distance I'd overcome and the accuracy with which I'd made those kills. But nobody ever talked about what had been on the other end of my gun. The people. The human beings. Men, a few women. Young men, recruited into sacrificin' their short lives for all kinds of bullshit. It was so fucked up.

And I'd been fucked up by it.

Yeah, I'd saved American lives by killin' those people, but who was I to take a life? I wasn't God.

But I kept doin' it.

The pain and confusion and anger it caused took hold of me, and when Oly and I had sex that night, it all came out. I fucked my pain into her, and I hated myself for it. It only lasted a night, and the next mornin', as she talked and planned and tried to make somethin' outta what we'd done, I panicked.

"I didn't get a chance to tell you—I found out yesterday—I got a spot in an amazing large animal program for grad school."

"Oh yeah?" I snuggled up to Oly, lyin' in her bed after hours of hard sex. It had been a revelation to me. Life changin'.

But not in a good way.

I knew I needed to get away from her, but I just couldn't do it. I'd waited so long to see her again. I thought about her every day. Afraid it would kill me to stop touchin' her, it felt like she was the only link to sanity I had left.

"Yeah. It's in England. Cambridge. Can you believe that? I mean, me? At Cambridge?"

"I believe it." She turned on her side and looked at me. *"You're the smartest person I've ever known. You deserve it."*

"Thanks. I'm so excited. There's a world-renowned horse vet there, and a really good large exotic doctor." She touched her fingers to my face, trailin' 'em down my neck and my arm, all the way to my wrist, and her eyes followed the movement. *"When do you go back? Are you goin' back? I just assumed you would but…"*

"Yeah. I leave in two weeks."

"Are you okay over there? I mean, my dad said you're a sniper. Is that scary?"

"No." It was terrifyin', but I didn't want her to know how much of a coward I was. I should be able to handle my job without cryin' about it, without it affectin' every single thing I did or every thought in my head.

"What's it like?"

I looked in her amber eyes, and all the shit I'd been feelin' *wanted to pour outta me, but what came outta my mouth instead was fear.*

"What the fuck, Oly? What do you mean, 'What's it like?' I kill people for a livin'." I sat up, facin' away from her on the edge of the bed lookin' for my clothes 'cause the faster I could get away from her, the less pain I'd cause.

"No. I didn't mean that. I meant what's the country like? The desert? Bein' in the military."

I shook my head. "I'm sorry."

"It's okay. I'm sorry." She crawled up behind me onto her knees and wrapped her arms around my chest, restin' her chin on my shoulder. "Listen, I was thinkin', how often do you get leave? Or, like, a break or whatever? I'll be in England. Maybe we could meet up somewhere in between? Or you could come to see me?"

Squeezin' my eyes shut, I held my breath. No. She wanted to go back. She wanted us to be the same people we'd been in high school.

But I wasn't that person anymore.

She deserved better than the guy I was then, and definitely better than the fucked-up man I had become.

"No. I can't."

"Oh. Well, maybe I could come to—"

"No, Oly." I stood, severin' her hold on me. "You can't come to a fuckin' war zone. Look, quit tryin' to make somethin' outta this. It's not— I'm not the guy you want me to be. We've changed. I've changed. And you… you have no idea what's out there. You shouldn't go to England, not by yourself. This world is fucked."

She sat back on her heels, naked, confusion all over her whole face.

"I sh-shouldn't go to vet school? The thing I've been workin' toward my whole life? Just 'cause it's in another

country? Last I checked, Cambridge, England wasn't a war zone. And why shouldn't I go by myself? What are you sayin'?"

"Nothin'." I sighed. "I gotta get to work. Jack needs my help this mornin' and I'm late."

"Okay. Can I see you later? I feel like we should talk."

"Yeah. Sure. I'll call." I didn't look at her. I walked outta her bedroom, still lookin' for my clothes.

She followed, wrappin' herself in her bedsheet. "Dean?"

"Yeah? Where are my boots?"

"Um, the dining room, I think. What's goin' on here? Why're you actin' like this? Why won't you look at me?"

"Nothin's goin' on. I just— I gotta go."

I found my jeans, yanked 'em on, and grabbed my shirt off the dinin' room floor. Stuffin' my feet into my boots, finally, I looked at her. "What?"

"What aren't you sayin'? Where is all this anger comin' from? It doesn't feel like you."

I laughed. Nothin' she'd said was funny, but it had been involuntary 'cause there was such a juxtaposition between her and me, between the guy I'd been with her and the guy I'd become. The killer I'd become. It scared me 'cause I knew I could never have her. This kind and beautiful woman I'd planned to spend my life with—I knew, now for certain, I didn't deserve her. It fuckin' hurt and it scared me so much.

'Cause if I couldn't be with her, who would I be?

But if she wanted to be with me, that tainted her. It charred her shinin' soul.

I wouldn't have that.

"You're a little girl, Oly. You been off readin' books and drinkin' overpriced coffee for years, and that's where you need to stay. In your sheltered life. You can't get hurt there. You need to find some brainiac man who makes a lotta

money, settle down, pop out some kids, and quit chasin' after things you shouldn't."

Her mouth popped open but no sound came out. The look on her face tore a hole clean through my gut. It killed me, what I said next. I had to bite a hole through the inside of my lip to stop the tears from formin' in my eyes.

I tasted blood and said, "There ain't no room in my life for an immature little girl. I live in the real world."

She gasped as I walked out her front door, and the tears fell down my face as I slammed it shut behind me.

9

CAROLYN

Thanksgiving had been painful.

My stupid heart hoped there was something to salvage between Dean and me. His face as my parents and I left Cade Ranch had popped that balloon with a big fat needle. It hurt. Bad. I should've known better, but it seemed I just couldn't learn my lesson when it came to Dean Cade.

But my new job started Monday, so I threw myself into it. What else could I do? I wanted to make a good impression on Doc and the rest of his staff: Yola, Doc's long-time clinic manager, and Amy and Joe, his two capable vet techs. They'd all worked together for years, and I was the rookie. I wanted them to feel confident when they asked me to do something, it would be done well.

It was hard to keep my mind on work though. Dean's face, his voice, and his words as he looked in my eyes that morning forever ago kept popping back into my head.

God! He didn't have any idea how much he'd hurt me. Thanksgiving had brought it all back.

And Jules called. She'd invited Brady Douglas out to dinner with us, along with another teacher from the elementary school where she worked. A guy. So, great. A double date. Or at least, Brady would assume it was a double date. I couldn't even think about it. It was all I could do just to get through my first week at the clinic.

But at least I got my first few horse cases. I got to play with some mini horses after I'd given them their yearly immunizations, and I castrated a couple feisty colts. I stitched a laceration from a barbed wire fence on the flank of a beautiful sixteen-year-old Friesian mare.

Mostly, though, I stayed in the clinic doing routine small animal appointments. It was fun meeting the clients and finding my way around, learning to be a practicing veterinarian. My mom kept stopping by, like I was five and it was my first week of kindergarten. She brought food for everyone, though, so none of the staff minded.

Thankfully, I hadn't had to go out to Cade Ranch.

Before I'd known it, the week had flown by, and I walked into my house after work on Friday to get ready for "the date." The guys were meeting Jules and me at a new restaurant in Jackson.

I tried (and failed miserably) to get into dressing up, to look forward to seeing Brady Douglas after years out of high school. He'd always been a really nice guy. Kind of quiet and a little shy, but the girls in school had all chased after him.

Not me. I'd always been too in love with Dean, even before we'd morphed from best friends to high school sweethearts. Brady had dated a couple girls from our class, if I remembered correctly, but he never had a serious girlfriend. And then we'd all graduated, gone our separate ways, and I hadn't seen him since.

"You look great, Ols," Jules praised me, tryin' to help me get into it.

"Yeah? Thanks, I guess."

"C'mon. Have fun tonight. You deserve it. Brady's gorgeous, and Evan, even though we're only friends, is pretty cute too. This is gonna be fun," she chirped as we drove through Jackson. The antler arches in the town square had been lit up for the holidays, and they nudged me a little more into the spirit.

"I'm tryin', Jules. You look nice too. Hot, actually. I pale in comparison." I sucked up, trying to distract her from her pep talk.

"I know, right?" She fluffed her gorgeous banana-blonde hair. "I got my hair highlighted the other day, and my mom and I went on a small impromptu shopping spree. I bought these jeans and treated myself to new make-up. She needed some retail therapy. She gets so frustrated with Isaac—the kid never leaves his bedroom. I swear my brother's gonna turn into a potato chip, as much as he eats 'em. I keep tellin' her to stop buyin' 'em for the little shit, but you know her. She spoils him rotten."

"How's he doin'? He still really into all that online gaming stuff?"

She scoffed. "Into it? The whole world could come crumblin' down around him, and he wouldn't notice. As long as he still had Wi-Fi. My dad tried to get him to join the football team this year. You shoulda heard the screamin' matches."

"You really need your own place, Jules."

"Yeah, I know. But I get free rent and meals. It's not doin' much for my social life but— Besides, I'm still waitin' for my knight in shinin' armor to come take me away from it all."

"Yeah, well, it's that kinda thinkin' that's gonna make you an eighty-year-old spinster. You gotta make things happen for yourself. Can't depend on a man to do it for ya."

"Yeah, yeah. Look, here we are."

We pulled up outside of a wanna-be-hipster restaurant with twinkle lights and a faux run-down facade.

"What is this place?" I asked, both of us leaning forward to look through the windshield at the ridiculous restaurant. A big boxy illuminated sign hovered over the front door that said, "Culinary COMMOTION", and lit tiki torches lined the sidewalk to the entrance.

"It's new. I've heard good things about the food though."

Jules and I had arrived a little early, so we waited at the tiki bar for the guys. I saw Brady the second he walked in. Still gorgeous, still tall dark and handsome with his russet skin and full, rich, stick-straight jet-black hair. He had an air about him that screamed heartbreaker. There was something else about him, too, but I couldn't put my finger on it.

He waved and smiled when he saw us, and I felt absolutely no physical attraction to him at all.

"Hey! Jules, Oly. It's so good to see you." He hugged us both, and the hostess showed us to our table. Jules' friend joined us a few minutes later, and all the proper introductions were made.

"So, Oly, Jules says you just finished vet school. That's so cool. Are you gonna be workin' in town?" Brady seemed just as uncomfortable as I was as he folded and refolded his napkin.

"Yeah, at All Animals. I just finished my first week. It's fun. What about you? You're a lawyer?"

"Yeah. Well, I'm taking a little break to be home with my dad. It's a risk to step out of the fast-paced dogfight so early in my career, for sure, but my parents need me right now so…" He smiled at me. He did have sexy lips and a great smile. "I'll still be doing some casework from home, though, so at least I still have a job." He laughed awkwardly.

We talked all through dinner. There had barely been a lull

in the conversation, but mostly because we listened to Jules'
friend, Evan, an elementary phys-ed teacher and also the
assistant coach for the high school soccer team, talk endlessly
about soccer.

By the end of the evening, Brady and I had developed a
silent drinking game. I'd noticed him crossing his eyes when
Evan would say the word "soccer," so I held my glass up
discreetly, spearing Brady with my eyes until he caught on.
Every time Evan repeated the word, we drank. I only had a
glass of cheap white wine and Brady only two beers the
whole night, but it helped pass the time and eased the uncomfortable forced situation. Jules had been oblivious. She was
always happy to be around people, my social butterfly best
friend.

By the time we left, Brady was laughing and hugging
me.

In my ear he whispered, "Thanks for that. I thought my
head would explode if he said it one more time. Call me. We
can drink and gossip."

Jules chattered the whole way home about Evan and how
she'd never noticed before how passionate he could be about
his job.

"That was fun, right? Brady's still gorgeous," she said.

"Yeah, I had a nice time."

"Oly, c'mon. He's to die for. What's not to like?"

"Nothin'. I liked him fine and he seems fun, it's just—"

Jules whined, "Ol-ly, come on. Don't make it so hard.
You just have to open yourself up to the possibilities. Forget
about Dean. What's he ever done for you, besides make you
miserable?"

I sighed as she pulled up outside my house. "Night, Jules.
Thanks for drivin'."

"Night. Don't listen to me. What do I know?" She smiled,

flashing me a "sorry to push" smile. "Love you. Talk to you tomorrow."

"Love you too."

When I was inside, I grabbed my half-full bottle of wine, changed into my Smurf pajamas, and crawled into bed.

Jules had been partly right. I wanted to be open to possibilities. I didn't *want* to be miserable forever, but she was wrong too. Dean hadn't made me miserable. Well, I mean, he had, but it wasn't always that way. We used to be so happy.

As kids, we'd spent every minute we could together, and we talked about our future. We'd talked about building a house on his ranch where we could raise a family and I could build my own horse clinic. We'd even picked out a spot for it in the middle of a meadow on the northwest corner of the ranch where there was plenty of room for a recovery barn and a clinic building. We'd planned it all out.

And we'd spend whole days horseback riding. He always had a new trail to show me, or a lake or a stream. He loved to be outdoors and he loved the horses, and I remembered thinking the fresh country air provided a freedom for him he'd desperately needed sometimes when he was sad or frustrated with life.

It killed me not to know what he'd gone through in the Marines. Whatever happened caused him pain, and it devastated me that he felt he couldn't share any of it with me. It took me a while to recover from the slap of his words, but eventually, I realized it had been the reason he'd said those things the morning after The Night.

It wasn't the first clue things could never last between us. He hadn't loved me enough to share the hardest things about his life. Or maybe he hadn't trusted me enough.

And maybe that had been why he pushed me away, 'cause he knew he never would.

But there was a time when he had.

I sipped the rest of the wine from the bottle, remembering…

"Hey, what's wrong?" Catching up to him after school to offer him a ride home, I hooked my arm through Dean's as we walked out of Wisper High. I wanted to find out why he'd been in such a bad mood all day.

Sophomore year had gotten off to a great start for me. My classes were going really well, and I was on track to have all my math and science requirements completed by first semester senior year. The plan was to get admission into a pre-veterinary program.

Dean was on the football team, and I'd pick him up from practice after I helped at the vet clinic a few days a week after school. My parents thought it might help me decide if I really did want to specialize in equine medicine when I eventually went to vet school. I knew I did. I'd known all my life I wanted to work with horses.

"Want a ride? I don't have to be at the clinic till four. There's no practice today, right?"

"Sure." He pulled my backpack off my shoulder, carrying it for me.

"So, what's wrong? I tried to get your attention at lunch today. I saved you a seat."

"It's nothin'. You have a good day? How'd your chem test go?"

"Good. I think I did well. Mr. Craig is such a jerk though. He's so sexist. He made the rudest comment to Hallie Bishop today. She said she wants to be a biochemical engineer, and he laughed and said, 'That's a lofty goal for a girl,' then looked her up and down. Ugh. I think I should report him."

"Oh yeah?" he mumbled, staring off into the distance. "That's good."

"Dean?" We'd arrived at my dad's old Toyota Four-Runner, and he opened my door for me.

"What? Oh, sorry. What'd you say?"

I climbed in and, when he was buckled into his seat, I turned a little, looking at him.

"What's goin' on with you?"

"It ain't a big deal. My dad made me quit the football team. He said I was neglectin' the ranch and bein' selfish. Leavin' too much work for my brothers. I'm just," he sighed, "just disappointed, I guess. I don't wanna let my team down, but you know my dad. He put his foot down." He shrugged, like that was the end of the story.

"Tell him no! You don't have to do what he says. You're not a baby. And you work so hard. You barely ever get time off. Jack didn't say you were bein' selfish, did he?"

"No. He said I should stick with it. All my brothers did. They know how much I enjoy playin'. Not like I'm any good at it, but still, it was fun. While it lasted."

"Dean, stand to up him. You deserve to have fun. You deserve to have somethin' for yourself. You are not your dad. Your life doesn't have to revolve around the ranch if you don't want it to."

He smiled, grabbing my hand across the seat of my truck. "Thank you. You're my biggest defender. Maybe, if I was as strong as you, I could stand up to my dad. But he's right. I am bein' selfish. I'm not bein' a good son. The ranch is what's important." He looked out his window.

"It's not more important than your happiness."

"It is."

"Dean—"

"C'mon, let's get outta here. I'll buy you an ice cream before work."

When we had our cones and sat on top of the old falling-down picnic table outside the Dairy Dream, I tried again. I held his hand. "I mean, what would happen if you did stand up to him? It's not like he can fire you."

He laughed a little. "No, I guess not. It's not a big deal, Oly. We weren't winnin' any games anyway."

"That's not the point."

"Yeah, I know." He smiled at me and my heart melted.

We liked each other, we had all our lives, but he didn't ask me out. I was too scared to ask him. Maybe he never would. Maybe he didn't like me the same way I liked him. Loved him.

"And you are a good son. The best. And the best brother. Why do you doubt yourself?"

He looked away and didn't say anything for a minute, then quietly, he said, "You remember that day, after my mama left, out in the meadow?"

"Yeah." I knew exactly the day he meant. My dad used to take me to Cade Ranch for riding lessons. Dean's granny had taught us both to ride, and sometimes, when my dad had his solo lessons, I was allowed to hang out with Dean and his brothers. They'd let me help with the horses, or we'd just play.

The day Dean was referring to was the first time I realized I loved him. He was eight and I was seven. It was grade-school, best-friend love then, not romantic love, but still, I loved him fiercely, even then. His dad had been such a jerk and then Dean's mom left, and I'd wanted to protect him. I used to beg my parents to adopt him so I could always have him with me.

"You said, 'You don't need her. You have me.'"

"It's still true." I threaded my fingers through his. "It was the first time you ever called me little duck."

"Yeah, 'cause your chicken impression sounds an awful

lot like a duck." He chuckled, still looking away from me. "I think about that a lot."

"You do?"

Turning his whole body toward me on the picnic table, he looked at me finally. "I know we were just little kids, but you don't know what that meant to me. I can still see your face when you said it. You're so fierce. So strong. I admire you." He squeezed my fingers.

"I'll fight for you any day."

He smeared his ice cream all over his lips, then leaned over to kiss my cheek, rubbing it on my face.

"Ach! Dean!"

He pulled away a little, inspecting his work. "It don't matter, Carolyn Masterson," he whispered. "You're beautiful, even with chocolate all over your face."

I turned to look at him, and he smacked his lips to mine. My eyebrows shot to the sky, and I squeaked but closed my eyes and sighed into his mouth.

Finally!

Lifting his hand up to cradle my non-chocolate cheek, he rubbed it with his thumb, tilted his head, and pushed his tongue into my mouth. Oh my God! I touched my tongue to his and then it was over.

Wait. What? So soon? My face turned an embarrassing shade of red, and I looked at my knees.

He pulled away. "Was that okay? I shoulda asked first. I'm sorry, I thought— But I shoulda asked." He looked at me, waiting for me to answer. "Oly? I'm sorry. Are you mad me?"

Finally, I gathered my courage and peeked up at him. He looked terrified.

I took a deep breath.

"Do it again?"

10

DEAN

"Well, well," Bigsy said, scoffin' when I called him more than a week after I said I would. I was on a break from work, stuffin' my mouth full of ham sandwiches Evvie'd made before headin' back out to the arena.

"Sorry."

"That's it? Sorry? You know, you ghost a guy like that, he might worry he said something wrong," he joked, but it sounded awkward.

"I'm sorry, man. I just… just kinda got in my head a little." I sighed. "You wanna get a drink tomorrow? I got work durin' the day but—"

"I don't know. I'm not sure I feel like hanging out with such a whiny bitch."

"Oh. Uh—"

"Like I have anything *else* to do." He sighed. "Pick me up after work."

We'd been workin' in the ring, lungin', exercisin', and breakin' horses all day. The weather was damn cold, and I was tired of bein' in it. I'd just been about to go into the office for my ninth thermos of hot coffee when Jack called over to me from where he sat astride Sammy.

"What's goin' on with that filly's leg? You see that don'tcha?"

"I do now." Ruby, Evvie's little filly, looked lame on her right hind leg, limpin' along as Finn began to walk her around the arena.

"Well, shit," Jack grumbled. "Looks like it hurts her. I'm callin' Doc."

"Finn, hold on," I called out, walkin' toward him and the filly. "Somethin's wrong with her hind leg."

"What?" Finn crouched down to inspect Ruby's gait. "Oh, shit, I didn't even see it. What the hell?"

"Jack's callin' Doc P. Take her back to a stall."

"Yep. Hey, you're gonna have to wait around for Doc. Jack and I have to pick Evvie up in town and then hit Bob's Feed. He's got an order waitin' for us."

"I'll go with Jack. You can wait for Doc." I hadn't heard Oly was takin' farm calls, but I didn't wanna risk the chance of seein' her.

"Nope, he's droppin' me at band practice after. Sorry."

Dammit. I grunted my agreement and followed him and Ruby back into the barn to start on some chores while I waited. Maybe I'd get lucky and Doc would show up.

An hour later, I'd finished muckin' stalls down the first aisle just as I heard the doc's Jeep's tires on the gravel lane. I breathed a sigh of relief, grabbin' my last bale of hay and breakin' it up, waitin' for him to gather his things, but then it occurred to me that Oly's truck would probably sound the same as Doc's. They were similarly sized, older SUVs.

"Did you call for the vet?" Oly's quiet voice filled the barn a few minutes later, and I froze. Shit. It did make sense she'd be the one to come; horse injuries had always been her passion. It was the whole reason she'd gone away to study, but — "Hellooo?" I could hear the irritation in her voice, and the nervousness. I turned to face her slowly 'cause I knew when I looked at her, it would hurt, so I attempted to brace myself.

"Yeah." Okay, so not the most sophisticated answer I coulda come up with. I sighed.

She walked down the aisle toward me, carryin' a huge pack slung over her left shoulder filled with supplies and a computer tablet in her right hand. Standin' ten feet from me, she wouldn't look me in the eye.

"Which horse?"

"She's right behind you, first stall." Oly turned to face Ruby's stall, lowered her pack, lettin' it rest on the floor, and looked in at the filly.

"God, she's gorgeous. Where'd she come from?"

"Remember Lucy?"

She nodded. "The mean old mare?"

"Yeah, last year, Finn found an appaloosa mustang out by the west property line. He'd been cut up pretty good, so he brought him in and Doc stitched him up. The next day, Kevin left the gate unlatched and the mustang got out, found his way to Lucy. The filly was just born a couple months ago. I don't know how she's injured. We just started workin' with her, gettin' her used to the halter and lead. She can be a little wild though. Got some of her daddy in her, I guess."

"Okay. Is she used to bein' handled?"

"I think she'll behave for you. You've always been good with our horses. She's Evvie's. They spend time together every day. Seems to like women best."

"Will you bring her out? I can't see much in there. I'll get a few things together. I brought the ultrasound. It's in my truck."

"Get your stuff ready and I'll go run, get the ultrasound for you." She didn't reply, so I shuffled out to her truck.

Dammit. This was gonna be painful. Everything in me wanted to go to her, to wrap her up in my arms. Inhale her. She looked more beautiful than ever. She'd gotten her hair cut. It was a little shorter than it had been a week ago, and she wore a yellow knitted hat with one of those silly, floppy balls on top, but her chocolate waves flowed from underneath, little wisps of it framin' her face.

Her cheeks had been flushed from the cold, and the pink color against the porcelain of her skin called to me. I wanted to hug her to my body, press her cheek against my own to warm it. I wanted to look in her eyes and see the beautiful smile there, the deep amber brown color like fine whiskey, with little flecks of rusty orange that danced like fire when she laughed.

She wasn't gonna laugh with me tonight or any other night.

She wouldn't even look at me. It was just as well. I didn't think I could survive seein' the disappointment and anger in those eyes anyway.

I grabbed the ultrasound machine from the back of her dad's old truck and headed back into the barn.

"Here you go—" I almost said "little duck," but I caught myself. "Doc." She whipped her head up from where she kneeled on the dusty barn floor to look at me. Guess I surprised her by callin' her that.

Settin' the machine down by her pack on the floor, I opened the door to Ruby's stall, then edged my way in, talkin'

low to the foal. I wished Evvie was with me; she had such a
sweet connection with Ruby.

"How old is she?"

"She was born the night before Jack and Evvie met, so I
guess mid to end of September. They could give you an exact
date."

"No, that's fine, so she's about nine or ten weeks old.
Wow. They've only known each other for ten weeks?
That's... wow."

"Mmhm." I watched her through the slats in Ruby's stall
while she dug through her bag, lookin' for somethin'. She
pulled her hat off and tossed it by the ultrasound machine,
then got frustrated with whatever she was searchin' for,
pullin' her yellow gloves off and tossin' those too.

The temperature had fallen to below freezin' outside, and
she was covered head to toe in winter gear, besides her face,
but when I saw the skin of her hands, instantly, I remembered
those hands roamin' all over my body, fingertips touchin' my
face, fingernails diggin' into my skin, clawin' my shoulders,
my back, my ass. I stood there like a statue just rakin' my
eyes all over her until she cleared her throat.

"Dean? Gonna bring her out or what?"

Right. I clipped the lead to Ruby's halter and led her out
into the aisle, makin' sure to be careful with the foal. She was
so young, and every pull to the rope or halter could be
stressful to her. Oly watched her like a hawk as she walked,
assessin' her gait. Ruby seemed okay, a little uneasy, but she
waited patiently when I tied her in the aisle.

Oly stood slowly, wrappin' a stethoscope around her neck,
and ran those beautiful hands over Ruby, down her back, over
her rump, under her belly, gettin' the filly used to her touch,
imprintin'. It was an amazin' thing to see her connect to the
animal. I watched as Ruby visibly relaxed, her head droopin'

down as her nervousness ebbed away. Oly moved slowly back up to the horse's head, strokin' her neck and her cheeks and nose.

"What a beautiful girl you are. You're just a baby. I know your mama. She tried to kick my head off once." She laughed real low and quiet. "But you won't do that, will you? What's her name?"

Too caught up in the sound of her voice, rememberin' when she'd talked that way to me, whisperin' low and sexy in my ear, I didn't hear her question at first.

"Dean?"

"What?"

"Her name?"

"Oh, uh, Ruby. Rubato, but Ruby."

"Hi, Ruby, it's nice to meet you. Don't be scared. I won't hurt you. I'm gonna touch your legs. You might not like it at first, but I'm gonna go real slow, okay?" Ruby nuzzled her speckled nose into the crook of Oly's arm, her breath comin' out in white puffs behind Oly's back. "Here we go, baby girl, niiice and easy."

Slidin' her hands down Ruby's chest, she murmured to her softly, then felt over to the foreleg and slowly moved down. She came back up, repeatin' the motion on the other foreleg, and worked her way back. By the time she got to the injured hind leg, the foal was practically asleep. She felt around, pulled, poked, and prodded gently, liftin' Ruby's leg by pullin' under the hock. When she finished, she stood and turned to face me, but she looked at her tablet as she spoke.

"It's just a sprained suspensory ligament. I'll ultrasound her to be sure, but I think it's just a slight sprain."

"Okay."

I had confidence she knew what she was doin'. I remembered her studyin' her anatomy books and quizzin' herself endlessly about all the different joints, ligaments, and tendons. We used to come out to the paddock so she could compare what she'd learned to Tank and Sammy's anatomy. They'd stand there while she felt all over their bodies, namin' 'em all off, and I'd sit on the grass just watchin' her. She hadn't even started college back then, but still, she studied like crazy.

I was so caught up in the memory until, finally, I heard Oly's voice gettin' louder in my head.

"Dean?"

Focusin' my eyes on her face, all I could think was how goddamn beautiful she looked standin' before me.

"You're so beautiful." I felt like I was in a trance. I could smell her hair, and all I wanted to do was bury my nose in it.

"Yeah, great. Thanks. Medication still in the fridge in the tack room?" she asked, stompin' off in that direction. I tied Ruby to the stall door usin' a quick release knot and followed. "You got Bute in there?"

When I didn't answer, she turned with her hands on her hips.

We just stared at each other.

She huffed a breath and looked at the floor, but when she looked back up, I saw that light in her eyes. Except now, it was darker and deeper, and she arched her eyebrow a little.

She wrapped her hands around my ribs under my jacket, squeezin' her fingers, and I picked her up with my hands on her hips and pushed her up against the tack room wall. I couldn't stop myself. My better judgement screamed at me inside my head, but my heart, my soul, and my body beat the shit out of it and told it to shut the fuck up.

Shovin' my nose into the crook of her neck, I inhaled her, the scent of her skin, and she gasped. The sound of her breath sent a shockwave to every nerve in my body. She moaned, and I thought I might pass out from the pleasure the little noise produced inside me.

I pulled my head back to look at her, and my eyes roamed all over her face, her neck, her hair, tryin' to soak it all in. When I finally looked in her eyes, the need I saw in 'em ignited somethin' wild in me.

She reached her head forward to kiss me, and I practically attacked her with my mouth. She went completely still for a few seconds but then exhaled hard, moaned again, and wrapped her legs around me, kissin' me back.

The kiss went on forever—I couldn't get enough of her, her taste. I nipped and licked her lips, plungin' my tongue back in to ravage her mouth with mine. At some point, I started rubbin' my body up into the notch between her legs. I could feel the wet heat from it through my jeans.

She undulated her hips against me, and I dug my fingers into 'em under her coat. She tried, unsuccessfully, to rip it off, so I helped her by unzippin' it, then pressed my chest against hers. *Oh God*. The feel of her breasts against my body was almost painful. It felt so fuckin' good and I wanted more.

So much more.

"Oly," I growled and she whimpered.

Searchin' for the bottom of my shirt, she found it and pressed her hands against my skin, draggin' her fingers all over my chest. Her touch felt like little electric shocks against my skin—electric shocks connected directly to my cock—and then she went for my belt buckle, fumblin' to unhook it, so I helped her again and pulled it free from its lock. I yanked my zipper down, and she thrust her hand inside, grabbin' me, squeezin' as hard as she could. I was ready to come at the first touch of her hot skin on my dick. I panted and silently begged my body to obey.

I pressed her harder against the wall with my chest and

unbuttoned and unzipped her jeans, and she dropped her legs to the floor so I could pull 'em down, so I did, pulled off her muck boot, freein' one leg, and she jumped back up, wrapped 'em around my ass again, and locked 'em tight.

I'd dreamed about this for so long, to feel her body against mine, to be able to smell and taste her, to be inside her. Some nights, a world away from home, it had been the only thing to get me through to the next mornin'.

The relief the anticipation of it all caused inside me made me dizzy.

I pulled my head back to look at her, in her eyes when I entered her body, just in time to see a single tear falling down her face as we heard the familiar pop and crackle of gravel under tires, and then Finn's annoyin' laugh.

Fuck.

11

CAROLYN

I froze when I heard Jack's truck pull up outside the barn. Dean looked in my eyes, and I couldn't stop the tears from falling. I'd known what it would cost me, the closeness, the kiss, the...

But I couldn't stop myself.

He stopped moving, too, his body still straining to get into me, and I felt his warm breath on my cheek and his hot, pulsing erection against my stomach. I wanted him so badly —I could've screamed it out loud. I trembled as he stepped back from me while easing me down to stand on my feet.

I just stood there. I couldn't move, couldn't look at him. My eyes focused square in the middle of his chest while he bent down to slide my jeans back up my leg and zipped and buttoned them, then zipped my coat back up. I looked away at the wall as he held my face between his hands, caressing my jaw with his thumbs, and placed a tiny kiss on my forehead. He turned, zipping and buckling his own jeans.

I still couldn't move. I couldn't believe how close I'd come to ripping my heart out of my own chest. Already, the ligaments and arteries surrounding it felt frayed and ripped. I needed to get the hell out of his barn, away from him.

Finally, I found my floundering self-control, grabbed hold of it, stomped my boot back onto my foot, and pushed past him, walking toward the ultrasound machine as Evvie, Finn, and Jack walked into the barn.

Evvie grabbed Ruby's lead and pulled the knot free from the stall door, wrapping it around her hand, and went straight to the filly. "Oh, my sweet baby. How did you hurt yourself?"

"Hey, Oly. Guess you're the doc tonight, eh?" Finn asked. I tried to smile, but the confusion I felt at what had just happened was fixed on my face. I cleared my throat and tried to blink the deer-in-headlights look out of my eyes.

"Yeah. Um, I think it's just a PSD, slight. I was just about to ultrasound it. Finn, can you hold the machine for me?"

Dean walked past Finn, shoving the bottle of Bute from the fridge in the tack room into his hand.

"Thought you had band practice," he grumbled to Finn.

"Yeah, it was cancelled," Finn called after him as Dean walked out of the barn.

"Here, Doc," Finn said, reaching for the ultrasound, and he flashed me a sad smile. My hands shook, and I hoped he didn't notice as I switched the machine on and gently rubbed and pushed the wand over Ruby's leg. I looked over at the monitor and saw exactly what I thought I would.

"Yeah, it's just a sprain, nothin' serious. Just do some cold compresses a couple times a day and give her one ML of Bute once a day for three or four days. Let me know if she doesn't tolerate it well, and we can try something else. Keep her on stall rest for a couple weeks, and then you can start workin' her. Do you guys have your own laser?" Finn shook his head. "Okay, I'll stop by every other day or so to do a quick treatment on her. Should help her recover faster, can't hurt anyway."

"I don't know what anything you just said means, Oly, other than 'it's just a sprain,'" Evvie said, frustrated.

"Oly just said it ain't serious," Jack explained, "and she told us how much pain medicine to give Ruby, and we're gonna do some cold treatments, twice a day." I looked up at them then, and the love I saw between them when Jack brushed a lock of hair behind Evvie's ear made my hands shake harder. I had to get out of there.

"Alright," I said a little too loudly, "well, I think that's it for tonight. Any questions?"

"No, thanks, Doc," Finn said, "we can take it from here."

"Okay, I'll get outta your hair then. Good to see you." I took off as quick as I could, desperately trying to seem professional while grabbing my pack and struggling to carry it and the ultrasound machine and my tablet.

"Here, Oly, let me help you." Evvie grabbed my pack from my shoulder, slinging it over her own.

The guys were unusually quiet. Normally, they would've been tripping over themselves to help, chivalrous cowboys that they were, so I assumed Evvie quieted them with a look. She must've noticed my hands shaking, or maybe I looked as desperate on the outside as I felt inside.

I stomped out to my truck, and when I got there, nearly threw the ultrasound in.

"Oly?"

"Please, Evvie, don't say anything. I just need to get outta here."

"Okay, do you want me to go with you? We could get a coffee or something?"

"Thank you, but no. I have another call," I lied. I couldn't look at her. I felt so bad lying to her, but I needed to be alone so I could scream and cry. So I could look for the claws trying to rip my heart out from behind my ribcage.

"Okay, but call me if you change your mind, anytime."

"Sure." I grabbed my pack from her outstretched arms, threw it in the back of my truck, and almost ran to the door. I hopped in behind the steering wheel and took off, trying as hard as I could not to get stuck in the snow.

I drove straight to my cottage, ran inside, and ripped apart the unpacked boxes of my meager belongings. I found BOB (battery-operated-boyfriend) wrapped in eight layers of bubble wrap in case anyone decided to look through my stuff in customs, ripped my jeans and panties off, fell down on the floor right there in my living room, and rammed it into my empty, needy, and drenched vagina and screwed myself silly.

It took about one minute of remembering Dean's hands all over me, his breath in my ear, and his raging erection, hard and straining, an inch away from entering me, and I came so hard, stars exploded behind my eyelids.

I crawled to my couch, wrapped myself in the blankets hanging over the back, and cried myself to sleep.

In the morning, I woke early to a phone call on my landline. I could hear breathing, but whoever had been on the other end never said a word. Probably a wrong number. Or maybe a bad connection. I wasn't expected at the clinic until nine but couldn't go back to sleep, so I showered and went to José's Diner for coffee and a bagel.

It seemed like the whole freakin' town was there, but I was so not in the mood to talk to anyone. I snapped at Mona when she snapped at me. I shouldn't have felt so bad since she always barked at everyone, but it wasn't normal for *me*, so I apologized. She just glared at me.

I skipped the bagel and just ordered coffee to go, and I'd almost made it out the door without having to talk to anyone when I bumped right into Brady Douglas.

"Hey, Oly. How are you? Dinner was fun, huh? You still coming out with us tonight?" He smiled such a hopeful smile. *Ughhh*. I'd forgotten about going out for drinks. I really didn't feel like going out, and I really didn't wanna be set up with Brady again. I knew I could've just said no, but then it would've been awkward.

"Hi, Brady. I'm okay. How are you?"

"I'm good. It's good to be able to get out. My dad's got ALS, so it can get pretty intense."

And now I felt guilty for groaning in my head. "I'm so sorry. That's gotta be so hard. Sure, yeah, I'll be there."

"You headed to work? How's it goin' over at the clinic? How's Doc P doin'?"

Everybody knew Doc P, even if they didn't have any pets. Docs P and Gee used to come to our elementary school every year to talk to the kids about animal care and the different ways animals could benefit our lives. I'd wanted to be a vet since I was three years old, and Doc P knew it, so he used to pull me out of class to be his assistant, and he'd let me handle all the animals he brought to show my classmates.

"He's great, as energetic as ever. You'd never know the guy's almost seventy."

"Here, lemme walk you to your car."

"Thanks," I said, ducking under his arm as he held the door open for me. He really was good-looking with his full lips and his eyebrows arched perfectly over his espresso-brown eyes.

We got to my truck, and I set my coffee on the hood, digging for my keys in my bag.

When I found them, I looked up. We spoke at the same time, and it was so awkward.

"So, um, listen, I just wanted—"

"Look, Brady, I know Jules—"

"Sorry, go ahead," he said, chuckling.

"Sorry." I forced a laugh. "Um, I think Jules is trying to set us up." I winced.

"Yeah. That's the impression I got, too, and I can see by the look of utter horror on your face that you're not into it."

"Brady, I'm sorry, I just—"

"Oly, it's fine. Really."

"I mean, we could go for dinner or something, just as friends, if you want. To catch up."

"Oly. Relax. I'm gay."

"Oh. Ohmygod. Thank you." I exhaled loudly. Oh crap. "No, I didn't mean— Oh God. I'm sorry." I cringed and he shook his head, laughing.

"Don't worry about it. I get it. My friends are always tryin' to set me up too."

"I should make my best friend from vet school come out here. You'd love him and he's gorgeous."

"Uh huh, like I just said…" He arched one dark eyebrow.

"Oh right." I laughed. "Sorry again."

"Anyway, I won't hold my breath. There's a devastating lack of gay men around here. I can't imagine your friend would wanna stay if he came to visit."

"No, you're probably right. Alright, well, I better go. I'll see you tonight. Manny's, right?"

"Yeah, Jules wanted to go to Jackson, but my mom's outta town, so I gotta stay close in case my dad needs somethin'. Hope you don't mind."

"Not at all. I didn't really feel like gettin' dressed up or anything anyway. We could wear pajamas to Manny's. No one would care."

"That is so temptin'." He chuckled. "You ever notice, as soon as you step foot back in Wisper, your accent comes out?" I nodded enthusiastically before he'd even finished his sentence. "Mostly, I work in an office, but I've litigated a few times. I'm supposed to sound professional. Here, I just sound like every other country bumpkin."

"Me too. And it's only gonna get worse. I'll be goin' on a lot of farm calls soon, so I'll be around all the local farmers and ranchers. I can feel the thick drawl comin' on already."

"Speakin' of ranchers, you still talk to D—"

"No. And I don't wanna talk about it."

"Oh. Okay then. You can tell me tonight. Bye!" he sang in his thick Wisper accent, winking and backing away.

I shook my head, laughing.

Whew. Bullet dodged.

The day quickly passed, and I found myself looking forward to going out. Now that the pressure had been taken off, getting out, seeing old friends, and forgetting about Dean seemed like a great idea.

I even dressed up. Well, for Wisper it could be considered dressing up. I wore tight black skinny jeans and a florescent pink peasant top. Underneath my ugly puffy coat, of course. Snow boots. I kept muck boots in my truck for farm calls, but I decided to walk to the bar in case I actually enjoyed myself and had too much to drink. Doc P said he'd take any calls so I could have a little fun.

We'd been finding our way into a good rhythm working

together. I still mostly stayed in the clinic doing all the non-serious injuries and vaccinations, spays and neuters, and yes, cleaning teeth, although I'd found it could be a little satisfying, and it felt good to know I'd helped an animal feel better and prolonged their health.

Doc took the farm calls and the more complicated surgeries, though I watched and assisted if I had time. He was a great teacher, endlessly patient with me. It was one thing to learn about all the procedures and techniques in books but quite another to see them done and to do them myself. And I picked them up quickly. Things were taught a little differently in England, but the basics were the same.

I went on farm calls if Doc had another emergency or just sometimes so he could have a break. I'd taken the call to treat Ruby so Doc could take his wife, Luci, out for a nice dinner for the first time in years.

But tonight was my night and I planned to enjoy it.

I walked into Manny's bar and was greeted with the biggest bear hug ever from the biggest bear—a teddy bear—Manny himself.

"Good to see you again so soon, Ollie Ollie Oxen Free!"

"Manny, you been drinkin'?" I hugged him back, laughing.

"Well now, maybe just a little. I'm off tonight. Dierdre's runnin' the bar."

"Is she new? I don't think I've met her."

"She is new. Yola made me hire her. She used to run a bar up in Fairbanks, Alaska, but she moved here about three months ago. She's a lifesaver. Dede!" Manny yelled over the music coming from speakers in every corner. It had to be Dede's influence 'cause Manny had always refused to replace his ancient jukebox—in his opinion Merle Haggard, Johnny Cash, and Elvis never went out of style.

"Yeah, boss?"

"This here's Oly. She never pays for a drink in my bar, hear me?"

"Yessir."

Dede winked at me, looking me up and down, and I blushed and focused back on Manny.

"Manny, you don't need to do that. I can pay just like everyone else."

"Hogwash, young lady. Your mama and daddy have been good to me. You know I woulda lost this bar to hospital bills when Yola was in that car accident if it weren't for your daddy. And your mama? She took care of my Yola after all those surgeries, like they was sisters. So you never pay for a drink in my bar. Hear me?"

"Yessir," I imitated the new bartender, standing on the tips of my tiptoes to kiss his cheek. "Thank you, Manny." I wouldn't argue with him—nobody in their right mind would.

I'd forgotten just how big Manny was. He had to be six-foot-six in height, and thick—the guy was made of muscle. He had short ebony hair and big dark brown eyes, and he always had the kindest smile on his face. If you didn't know him, you'd probably be intimidated or scared of him, but if you did, you knew he was the sweetest dad around.

Manny's wife, Yolanda—aka Yola—had been the office manager of the All Animals Clinic (and all-around town badass) and had worked for Doc P for years. I'd known the Perez family since I was a little kid, so working with Yola every day felt like hanging out at a family barbeque sometimes.

They had two daughters, Karen and Tracy. Tracy married right out of high school and moved to Iowa. Karen and I had been friends all through school, and we'd been in the same class every year since kindergarten. Currently, she lived in

Toronto with her wife, another girl from our class, Elizabeth Tillerman, who wrote seriously erotic and wildly successful straight romance novels and traveled with Karen for her job as a fashion model.

Manny had always been the fun dad, taking all us little girls to princess and mermaid movies in Jackson. He'd taken us shopping at the mall when we were pre-teens and sat with us in the diner (several tables away) after school dances, listening to us gossip, when we were teenagers.

Manny Perez was an amazing father, a huge part of the Wisper community, and a wonderful friend, and I realized I'd missed him. I'd missed Wisper and all its wacky characters. But it hadn't been why I'd come back. I could've chosen to stay in the UK to work, or anywhere really, but I'd come home because I'd known Dean was back in Wisper, and my pathetic heart hoped desperately he'd want me. It was stupid, I'd known that, too, but—

"Oly!"

I turned to see Brady and Jules, arm in arm, coming through the door.

"Ready to have some fun?" Brady asked and winked.

"So ready."

12

DEAN

I lay in bed every night, awake, my mind goin' round and round in circles. I kept thinkin' about Oly—when we'd first become friends, how carefree and young we'd been, how naive. And, over and over, I replayed the day in the meadow. The day she'd given me a lifeline she probably had no clue she'd given.

I thought about all the dreams we'd had, plans we'd made.

I thought about the first time we had sex.

Oly had been my first, and she would always be the only woman I'd ever love. There could never be another. We'd been fated to be together.

Maybe that sounded silly comin' from me, some gruff, dirty Marine, but I knew I loved her long before we'd dated. From the very first time I held her hand in kindergarten, I knew she was mine. And when our relationship turned into a physical one in high school, it only cemented my belief in fate.

We were young, but it had been so good. We wanted each other just as desperately then as we did now. It may have been a little uncoordinated, but we'd fit together like two puzzle pieces and had quickly become addicted to each other. We'd made love every chance we got, anywhere we could, 'cause when I was inside her, lookin' in her eyes, givin' her pleasure and takin' my own, our souls had connected.

There'd never been anyone or anything that could even come close to makin' me feel what Oly made me feel.

Then my thoughts would skip forward to the last several weeks. To seein' her again for the first time since the night three years ago. To last night when we'd come back together for a few minutes. I'd been so consumed with need for her. It felt like if I didn't get inside her, I would die. My heart beat so wildly for a second, I'd worried I would have a heart attack.

But it was just Oly.

She was my home, and my body recognized hers and wanted back in, wanted to be connected to her soul again.

There was an ache inside my chest I couldn't get rid of no matter what I did. Sometimes it lessened in intensity. Most of the time, though, it felt like it increased in intensity. I could always feel it.

I wondered what she was doin'. Did she sleep peacefully, or was she up every night, like me, rememberin' my hands on her body? Maybe she just lay awake hatin' me.

Or did she worry about her new job at the clinic? She'd always been destined to be a great vet. I was so goddamn proud of her. My chest puffed up every time I thought about it, and I wished I could help her. I didn't know what I could do, but I'd do anything, even if it was only liftin' dogs up onto the exam table at the clinic and holdin' cats while they scratched my eyes out. Or maybe I could go with her on farm calls, help her wrangle cattle or horses, pigs.

But no, I couldn't do any of that. It had been clear—bein'

around me brought her pain. I'd seen it in her eyes last night when we heard the truck pull up outside the barn and had been pulled out of our frantic, desperate, searin' rush to get underneath each other's skin.

It felt like my body cracked in half when I saw the tears in her eyes, the pain. It felt like a chasm opened up inside me, and nothin' but cold air remained, freezin' me from the inside out.

No, I needed to stay away from Oly. It was the only way I could help her. I couldn't trust myself not to climb right inside her and burrow into her body just to keep the cold away.

The ache was there to stay. I had no expectation it would go away, ever. I would just have to live around it.

When Oly had still been overseas the ache had almost worked its way to the back of my mind, most of the time anyway, but now she was home, it had come back, front and center.

It had probably started its relentless assault on me when Evvie'd shown up a couple months back. Seein' her and Jack together was painful, to say the least. Then, when I'd learned Oly would be comin' home, the pain reared up. It tried to work me from the inside out, so I'd let my guard down.

So I'd let myself be free again to love her.

But there was a reason I couldn't. A reason I needed to keep her at arm's length. There wasn't anything more important to me than protectin' her, even if the thing I needed to protect her from was me.

I had to concentrate real hard on breathin' and listenin' to the ticks from the clock on my desk at night, countin' each one, sometimes into the thousands, when the anxiety liked to take over.

I picked Bigsy up at seven the next evenin'. We got some barbecue from a food truck in Jackson and drove a while. We'd planned to get a drink, but we got to talkin', so I kept drivin'.

"So, you were a sniper, huh?" Bigsy asked as we drove west on Highway 20, back toward Wisper.

"Yeah. Always liked shootin'. What about you?"

"Infantry."

"That's rough, man."

"Yeah. First to Fight and all that. Spent some time in Kuwait, but mostly Afghanistan."

"Sounds familiar," I said.

"Yeah, but I bet you got some *other* stories."

"Not so many I can tell you though."

"Classified?"

"Couple."

"That's cool though," he said.

"Not really."

"Well, how many kills you got?"

I sighed. I hated that fuckin' question.

"That bothers you," he said. "I'm sorry. I get it. It's loss of life even if those assholes were evil."

"Yeah." I didn't say anything for a few minutes, and Bigsy didn't either. I thought he woulda filled the silence with jokes or bluster, but he didn't. "Do you... you ever have guilt... about, I mean..." I shook my head. It was stupid. I didn't know where this sappy bullshit came from, but I was a United States Marine. We didn't get sappy. We didn't cry and blubber. We did our job. We fought for our country. I fought for my family's freedom. For Oly's. That wasn't wrong.

So why did I wanna scream and rail anytime I thought about it?

"Yeah. I got guilt," Bigsy said. He probably felt the desperation in the truck. It was all around me. "Maybe I'm a hypocrite, but I got faith too. I can't seem to find a ton of it lately, but I think my God put me right where I was supposed to be. With Annie. The Marines. Here.

"Maybe he got a little confused, and that's how I ended up shot and living in a cowboy romance novel gone wrong, but I don't know, man. I think the good things I've done far outweigh the bad. And I think, if God can forgive me, and Annie can, maybe I can too?"

I looked at him. "I don't believe in God."

"I don't think he's pissed about it. And I still think he's looking out for you."

"Maybe." I tried to smile. "It's just— I think about all those people. So many people. And they had families. They were somebody's son. Daughter. Child." I looked out my window and tried so fuckin' hard not to cry. "I killed a kid."

Bigsy didn't say anything, and I pulled my truck to the side of the road and put it in park. My heart raced so fast it hurt.

"A teenager. I dunno, fifteen, sixteen, maybe. He aimed an RPG into a market where there were people everywhere. I prayed to your God, to his, to any who'd listen, to make that boy turn around. Go home. Not do the thing he was about to do. I *begged* God. He didn't hear me, or maybe he just didn't care to listen. God didn't do shit. I still killed that kid. I had to."

"Maybe it was what needed to happen. Maybe that kid would've grown up to be the next Bin Ladin. Worse."

"He was a fuckin' kid, Marcus."

"Yeah." He took a deep breath. "You know, everybody

always asks snipers about their kills, like it's a video game. But… have you ever wondered how many people you saved?"

I shook my head. "No. 'Cause all I can see are the bloody ones at the end of my scope." I smoothed my hands on my jeans. "Sometimes, I think the guilt will eat me alive. It's so fucked up. I know I did my job. I did it well. I know I saved people. I *know* that. But… it's like I'm cracked right down the middle, and I can't fit the pieces back together, no matter how hard I try."

Huffin' out my breath, I inhaled through my nose, tryin' to get a handle on it. On the panic.

"Dean. Now, don't you dare clock me for saying this, but there's a group of guys at the center. They meet every once in a while. I think a lot of them feel how you feel. I know it's probably not the brooding cowboy way, but maybe we could go to that group. Just once. See what we think of it?"

"Yeah, I dunno about that kinda shit." I scoffed. "Brooding cowboy way? Cowboy romance novel gone wrong? What is the matter with you?"

"Aww, you do listen to me." He crossed his hands over his heart and swooned in my direction.

"You're such a dick."

"Yeah, but I'm your favorite di— Ooo, bleach that out of your head."

I laughed and wiped the mess off my face with my sleeve.

"C'mon, broody, take me for that drink. I fucking need it now after you just poured your girl juice all over me. Jesus. Sorry. I swear, I'm not trying to make these jokes creepy and sexual."

I snorted a laugh, puttin' the truck in gear. "Oh my God, shut the fuck up."

We drove to Manny's Bar, and the whole time, Bigsy

joked and poked fun at me. It eased the tension a little, and the panic quieted and moved to the back of my head.

"I did get to see some cool places with the Marines," I said, holdin' Manny's heavy wooden door open for Bigsy. He crutched his way inside, and we took the first seats at the long, dark, wood bar top. "We went to South America. I was overwatch for some guys there workin' reconnaissance on cartel activity. That was… interestin'."

"The jungle? That sounds so much better than the fucking desert."

The new bartender noticed us, and I held up three fingers. Kevin was supposed to meet us for a beer.

"Yeah. Learned Spanish while I was there. Well, I took some classes in high school but got way better in Colombia. Man, the ocean down there is somethin' else. I never seen colors like that before. The water? It's like another planet or somethin'."

"Oh, look, it's the whiskey thief," Manny said, glarin' at me as he walked behind me and around the end of the bar.

I winced. I felt bad about stealin' from Manny.

"Whiskey thief? What the fuck's going on with you? You disappeared. You're stealing other people's alcohol. You don't strike me as a hoodlum."

I sighed. "I'm sorry, man. I just—"

There was a loud group of people in the back of the bar. I'd noticed a few people I recognized when we walked in, but nobody I wanted to talk to, so I didn't think anything of it. But just as I was about to apologize for bein' a dick to Bigsy and Manny, I heard it—I heard Oly's laugh. I jerked my head around to see her at the back of the group of people, huggin' and dancin' with some fuckin' guy!

Her hands were on his hips while she gazed up at him, laughin', and he wrapped his arms around her back, liftin' her and twirlin' her around. They stumbled a little, and he leaned against a table to stop their momentum. He was drunk, and he had his hands on my—

It took all the self-control I had, but I turned my head away. She had every right to go out with some other guy. She had every right to look for happiness.

But *fuck*.

It hurt. I couldn't even describe the feelin'. I thought I would die. I sat there, heart poundin', hands sweatin', waitin' for Bigsy to start yellin', "Call an ambulance! He's bleedin' all over the bar!"

How could she move on? Hadn't she been drownin' in her misery just like I'd been? Wasn't she devastated just like I was? Wasn't she in pain just like I was?

"What the hell's wrong with you?" Bigsy asked, but his voice sounded light years away.

"C'mon, come with me," Manny said, pushin' me to my feet. He grabbed my arm and pulled me behind the bar to a little room beside the kitchen. I shoulda punched him for grabbin' me like that. He wasn't gentle, but I followed him 'cause I knew I had to get outta there. I knew I couldn't look at Oly in that man's arms again, or I'd die. Or kill him.

"Sit down." Manny motioned to a hard-backed wooden chair next to a desk, and Bigsy poked his head around Manny. They looked like a cartoon—General Giant and the Grunt. "Put your head between your knees or somethin'. You look like you're gonna puke or pass out."

I felt 'em watchin' me as I hyperventilated myself into the chair and tried as hard as I could to stop my heart from rippin' itself into shreds. It felt like the walls of the little room were closin' in on me and all the light was leakin' outta the world.

I couldn't get the images of all the people I'd killed outta my head, and when I saw Oly with that guy, it was like she could see 'em too, and that was why she was with him. She knew all the bad I'd done, and she'd already found someone worthier.

"Dean!" Manny yelled my name and I looked up. "Get a grip." He must've seen the panic in my eyes, and he squatted in front of me. "You ever have a panic attack before?"

"Is that what this is? I can't breathe. It hurts." I felt so weak sayin' this to Manny, a Gulf veteran, two tours in Iraq, this beast of a fuckin' guy, but I couldn't stop the words comin' outta me. "You sure? Feels like my heart's tryin' to rip its way outta my chest."

"Just breathe slowly. I know it's none of my business, but what the fuck, man?" He stood up, plantin' his big hands on his hips. "You love Oly, she loves you, so why ain't you doin' somethin' 'bout it? If that were my Yola out there, I woulda thrown her over my shoulder and made love to her till she forgot the other guy's name."

He made it sound so simple. But I didn't have the right.

"If you're not gonna come to your senses, then you need to let her go. You want her to be in pain? Sad?"

"Fuck you," I spat, standin' up toe to toe with Manny. I wanted to beat the shit outta him for even suggestin' I wanted Oly to hurt. I hurt myself, every second of every single day, just to stop that very thing from happenin'.

Bigsy poked my chest with the end of his crutch. "Whoa, whoa now. Come on, cowboy. Just breathe. Sit down."

"Fuck you, too. Now go talk to her," Manny ordered.

"I can't."

"Why the fuck not?"

"I just can't."

"That's just Brady Douglas. She don't love him. He just moved back home, been in town five minutes."

"Brady... Douglas?" I gulped in a breath, tryin' to place the name.

"Yeah. You remember, from your football team? The quarterback, I think he was. Not a very good one. Wasn't he the same year as you? His daddy's sick, so he came home to take care of his family. Think he's a lawyer."

I hung my head. The ache in my chest swelled, and it felt like it consumed my whole body. My mind.

A lawyer? I couldn't compete with that. But maybe that could be a good thing... She could fall... in love... with...

"Oh, shit, he's goin' down," Bigsy said, but he sounded like he was underwater. Or I was. "Ooooo."

Ah, shit.

13

CAROLYN

"Oly, I got a situation," Manny whispered in my ear, pulling me away from Brady, Jules, and the group of people who'd joined us as the night went on. Mostly young women hoping Brady would take them out. Oh boy, were they in for a rude awakening.

"What's goin' on, Manny? Thought you were leavin'. Everything okay?" I asked when he led me behind the bar to the door beside the kitchen.

"Be gentle, Oly. He's hurtin' pretty bad," he said before he opened the door and pushed me inside the little room, then pulled the door shut, closing me inside.

"Dean!" He lay on the floor with a black leather jacket shoved under his head, passed out. I dropped down to my knees beside him to check his pulse. It was fine, a little high, but fine. "Dean, can you hear me?"

"Ahem, I'll just, um, I'll leave you two alone."

"Oh!" I jumped when Dean's friend spoke. I hadn't even seen him. My eyes had gone straight to Dean. Always to Dean. "Marcus, you scared me. What happened to him?" He stood in the corner of the office, leaning on his crutches.

"Uh. Maybe just ask him," he said, shuffling out the door and closing it again.

"Are you okay? Dean? Wake up."

He didn't open his eyes, but he said, "Hmm, little duck, I love the sound of your voice. It feels like tiny little hugs all over my body when you talk."

I snorted. Great, he was completely wasted and talking nonsense. You know what, nope, I refused to do this again. Last time didn't end so well for me. I moved to get up, but Dean's big grabby hand tugged on my arm, pulling me back down on top of him.

"Don't go, Oly. Please?" He opened his eyes, and we lay face to face while I held my body up with my hands on his chest. Bottomless, deep, smokey-gray eyes stared back at me. Hunter-green rings surrounded the black pupils, and it felt like they had some kind of supernatural effect on me, like they froze me in place. I could get lost in his eyes. I had been lost in them. I was still. God, just his eyebrows, thick and blond, turned me on.

"I'm not doin' this again. You can nurse yourself back to sober this time. Jeez, Dean, this is becomin' a habit for you."

"I'm not drunk. I just got here."

"Then why are you passed out on Manny's floor?" I looked around the little room where Manny did his books. An old metal desk and chair took up half of the small box of a room, with another wooden chair across from them. A calendar hung from a rusty nail on the wall behind the desk (open to the month of June, six years ago), with a file cabinet underneath, and a few empty wooden crates, but not much else.

"I just got a little dizzy. I'm fine now."

"Why'd you get dizzy? Did you eat today?"

"Yes. Bigsy and I just had barbecue. I always forget just

how beautiful your eyes are until I'm lookin' right in 'em. It's like they shine just for me. At least, that's what I tell myself." He smiled, but he looked so sad.

"I can't do this." I tried to get up again, but he held me tight.

"Oly, it's okay. I… I just wanted to tell you that I—"

Dean was interrupted by the sound of the door swinging open, and I looked back to see Brady's shoes and the bottoms of his jeans next to my leg.

"Oly, is everything okay? Oh. Shit, sorry, I didn't mean —" Brady slurred a little. "Well, what's goin' on here?" he joked, and Dean lifted us both up, growling. Freakin' caveman.

Pushing me behind him, he stood face to face with Brady. Brady had the funniest look on his face, like he was terrified and turned on all at the same time. He only stood a few inches taller than Brady, but Dean's impressive size had more to do with the bulk of his muscles and the anger emanating off of them.

"Dean, you remember Brady Douglas?" I said, rolling my eyes. "From high school?"

Brady held his hand out to shake Dean's, but Dean stomped out of the room, and Brady backed up to let him pass, looking at me with his eyebrows rising and teeth gritted in a grimace.

Kevin poked his head in the door after Dean stormed out. He looked from Brady to me, and back to Brady. "Oly," he rasped as he murdered Brady with his eyes, then walked away.

"Good goddamn, Oly. Was that Kevin Cade?"

"Yeah."

"Whoo." He blew out a long breath, and I smelled the alcohol in the air. "It's not fair. That whole family is hot as hell," he said, leaning and sagging against the door to Manny's little office. "I'm way too drunk to be thinkin' the thoughts I'm thinkin'."

"Let's get outta here. We can go to my house. Where's Jules?"

"Uh, I dunno. Maybe the little cowgirl's room."

Pulling Jules from the line waiting for the restroom, the three of us hurried from the bar all the way back to my house. When we'd made it into the warmth of my little cottage, I changed into my pajamas. The temperature still hovered below freezing outside, and we'd become veritable popsicles by the time we hit my front porch. I think the cold sobered Brady and Jules up a bit. Probably me too.

Jules went straight for the loo, and Brady plopped down on my tiny sofa, taking up most of it with his long limbs while I grabbed three bottles of water from my kitchen.

He took the bottle I held out to him. "Soooo…?"

"So what?" I asked, pretending not to know what he was after.

"So, what was that about?"

"What happened? What'd I miss?" Jules asked, emerging from the tiny bathroom in my hallway. She chugged half a bottle of water when I handed it to her, then lowered herself to sit next to me on the floor in front of my couch.

"I'm not sure. I found Oly lying on top of Dean Cade in the back room of the bar. He was not pleased to see me, though I can't imagine why. He and I always got along in school. We weren't friends or anything but…"

"I dunno. He passed out, I guess, and Manny pulled me back there. To check on him."

"Yeah, but how exactly did you end up on *top* of him, Oly?" Jules asked, clearly not buying my recalling of the night's events.

"Oh, please, Jules. I was checking his pulse and he pulled me down."

"Well, why did he pass out? Was he that drunk? I didn't even know he was there."

"No, he wasn't drunk. I dunno. All he said was he felt dizzy."

"And what about his brother?" Brady asked.

"What about him? Which one?" Jules asked, confused, and probably dying to hear Finn's name. She really was obsessed with Finn. Had been since, like, junior year.

"Kevin," Brady said, swooning, eyelashes fluttering, eyes sparkling.

"Brady!" Jules gasped. "You're gay?"

He laughed. "Sorry, Jules. I know you had hopes for me and Oly." He slid down to the floor. "Sorry to crush your dreams."

"Ugh, and here I was tryin' to set you two up." Jules swatted Brady's leg, and he kicked at her playfully.

"That'll teach ya," I admonished. "Brady, you know Kevin's not gay, right?"

"Nuh uh," Jules grunted. "No way."

"Oh, no? Hm," Brady mused.

I cocked my head. No. But no. He couldn't be gay. Kevin had always been the player of the Cade family. He chased every girl he'd ever met. Everyone knew that.

"No. You're bein' ridiculous," I decided, shaking the thought from my head.

"Yeah, well, I wasn't the one sprawled across a seriously gorgeous man, not even thirty minutes ago. Who's ridiculous now? You should be back at his place, screwin' his brains out. Did you hear him? He actually growled at me."

"It's complicated."

"Seriously, since when are you gay?" Jules whined, crossing her arms over her chest.

"Jules"—he rolled his eyes—"since I was born," he said, elongating each word. "Start talkin', Oly. What's goin' on with you and Dean?"

"Nothin'. Nothin's goin' on with us. There hasn't been any 'us' for years now. But then I came home and I see him everywhere. And we want each other still, but he's just so freakin' confusing. I've loved him my whole life, but he just keeps pushin' me away. I don't freakin' know." I groaned, lying back on the floor, noticing how dingy my old carpet was, thinking I should probably replace it and wishing I could punch Dean, or maybe just wrap him up in my arms.

"She just has to get over him. That's what I was hoping *you* would help her do." Jules scoffed.

Brady opened his mouth to say something when my house phone rang.

"Might be an emergency, be right back," I said, jumping up and jogging to the kitchen to answer. All the pranks and hang ups I'd been getting were really starting to annoy me. I would've just canceled the landline, but since I had become one of the town vets, I figured I should keep it.

"Hello? This is Dr. Masterson."

"… … …"

I could hear someone on the line, but they didn't say anything.

"Hello? Is anyone there? Hello? … If you're there, call back. I think we have a bad connection." I hung up and waited by the phone, but it never rang.

"Everything okay?" Brady asked, walking to the counter to deposit his empty water bottle.

"Yeah, I guess. I think it was a bad connection or somethin', or maybe just kids lookin' for some cheap fun."

"Alright, well, I need to get home. Jules called her brother. He's gonna pick us up. Why don't you try talkin' to Dean? Maybe there's somethin' goin' on with him you don't know about. Couldn't hurt."

I sighed. "Oh yes, it could."

It could hurt a lot.

When I woke in the morning, I felt kind of refreshed, which was weird since I drank so much the night before, but I slept well through the night. I showered, ate some toast, and started loading up on my caffeine intake for the day, but when I got out to my truck to leave for the clinic, I had two freakin' flat tires!

What the hell? My tires had been fine last night.

Great. I called Mike Williams, my dad's mechanic, and he said he'd tow my truck to his shop a little later in the morning.

After that, I rang Yola. She came to pick me up, and by the time we got to the clinic, it was nearly nine thirty, but two of my patients had also been late, so only two others sat in the waiting room twiddling their thumbs while I got organized. Doc had already left to do farm calls, so I was by myself and I felt rushed and annoyed.

Finally, I called my first patient back to the exam room— a pregnant shelter rescue stalled in the middle of labor. Yay! Puppies to start my day after a really crappy morning. Administering a small dose of calcium gluconate and oxytocin to speed up her labor, a couple fingers full of Nutri Paste for some extra calories and vitamins to help boost her energy since she'd been at it so long, and lots of snuggles, the dog's owner and I made a little nest under the counter, turned the lights off in the small exam room, and left the old girl to do what nature told her to. I checked on her frequently, and by lunchtime, we had eight multicolored puppies squealing, wiggling, and trying to nurse.

Mike called while I ate my veggie wrap for lunch and told me my tires had been slashed. I was stunned. Who would slash my tires? I couldn't think of one person in Wisper who disliked me that much. He said he called Carey Michaels, the local sheriff, and I'd be hearing from him. He also told me he called my dad.

Well. Wonderful. I'd barely had a chance to hang up the phone, and my parents were barging into Doc's office, freaking out.

"Oh, honey, are you okay? Mike called us," Mom said, beside herself with worry. She leaned down, hugging me and patting her hands all over my body. I wasn't sure how she thought it would help, but she was anxious, so I didn't complain.

"Dad, why aren't you at work?"

"I left the hospital as soon as Mike called me," he said, hands on his hips in his favorite fatherly stance.

"Guys, this is really unnecessary."

"I'm callin' Dean," he said. "I'm gonna ask him to keep an eye on things while I'm at work, and then I'll come pick you up when you're done for the day."

I stood up, knocking my bottle of water off the desk. "Don't you dare," I warned, then tried to soften my voice. "Dad, Mom, I'm fine. Really. It was probably just some kids messin' around. I'm sure it's nothin'. Please don't make a big deal outta this." I felt bad for snapping at my dad till I heard Dean's deep voice behind me.

"No need to call."

I let out a long, loud sigh, glaring at my dad, and Dean cleared his throat.

"You already called, didn't ya?" I accused my dad, hands on my hips too in my own daughterly pose, watching as his face went from concerned parent to guilty conscience. I turned around slowly to see Dean looking at me with a guarded expression on his face.

"The sheriff's on his way over, and I'll stay here until Oly's ready to go home."

"Thank you, Dean. I really appreciate this." They shook hands and I stomped my foot.

"This is ridiculous. I had a freakin' flat tire. It's not like someone tried to break into my house. You're all overreactin'."

"You had two *slashed* tires, Ols. That's unusual. You have to admit it, and after what happened to Evvie a couple months ago—"

"Dad, that was completely different and you know it. That man followed her here. He wasn't from around here."

"Still, I'll feel better knowin' you have a little backup. I know you're not gonna be happy about it, but I've asked Dean to keep an eye on you, and he's agreed to do it."

I looked around the room at the faces staring back at me and finally threw my hands up. "Fine," I growled and stormed out of the office. "Yola, next case!"

"Now you're soundin' like the doc 'round here," she mumbled, handing me my next patient file when I marched past her desk. "Room three."

I heard my parents saying goodbye to her and Dean as I knocked and opened the door to the exam room. I introduced myself to the woman and freckled, red-headed little boy holding a kitten with a clear case of respiratory infection, but

I couldn't focus until I'd said my piece to Dean. He thought he was gonna just waltz into the clinic and own the place?

Nuh uh.

"Excuse me, I'm sorry. I forgot something. I'll be right back." Turning around, I closed the door softly, then stomped back down the hall, pushing Dean with my hands on his chest backward into Doc's office as he walked out of it, closing the door with my foot.

"Fine, you stay here and 'protect' me, but you stay outta my way. You hear me? And stay away from the patients. I don't want you scarin' 'em with your whole 'I'm a big bad armed cowboy' routine. That's right. I saw the gun stickin' out your ass crack. Everybody 'round here's used to Doc. They ain't expectin' me, and it doesn't help that I'm a woman. I don't need 'em to see me as some weak damsel in distress who needs her man to take care of things for her. Got it?"

"Got it."

"Oh, you got it? You're just gonna agree?"

"Yes, I know your dad's probably overreactin', but I'm takin' this seriously. I won't be in your way. I promise."

"Fine."

"Fine," he said.

I narrowed my eyes, glaring at him. "If you're takin' this so seriously, why're you smilin'?"

"I'm sorry. I just forgot how feisty you can be."

"Oh yeah? Well, don't forget this: I know how much sedation it would take to drop your ass. Whaddya weigh? Like two-twenty? Two-thirty?"

I smirked back at him, turned on my heel, and stormed back out of the office, slamming the door against the wall on my way. I heard Dean chuckling behind me, and the sound put that old burn in my gut. Ugh. That just ticked me off more. My body was a traitorous trollop!

Standing outside the exam room I'd so rudely exited before, I tried to collect myself. After a minute of deep breathing and some serious emotional compartmentalizing, I opened the door. "I'm so sorry. Please excuse me. So, who do we have here? What's goin' on with your kitten?"

Twenty minutes later, Carey Michaels showed up. The sheriff stood in the crowded waiting room, causing a freakin' commotion.

When I walked out of Exam Room Four and saw him, I caught his eye. "Office," I ordered, realizing too late I'd probably scared the clients. I turned back down the hallway, still carrying the puppy suffering from a broken leg who I'd just examined, and marched back into Doc's office. Dean and Carey came in ten seconds later.

"Yola, will you take this puppy please? He needs an X-ray, hind left leg. Joe, will you help her?"

"Sure thing, Doc," Yola said, taking the dog gently into her arms, murmuring to him. Joe smiled awkwardly and followed Yola out of the office. When they'd gone, I shut the door, and the thin wood rattled in the doorframe from the angry energy in my hand.

"Thank you for comin', Sheriff, but it's really not necessary."

"Sheriff? Really, Oly? We've known each other for years. You don't have to be so formal."

"I was trying to be professional."

"Well, that's fine, I reckon. Look, your tires were slashed. Not just punctured but slashed. It looked aggressive. I took pictures and documented it, but until we know who did it, I'd like you to be cautious, keep your eyes open, okay? This is pretty unusual for Wisper. I don't know who the hell coulda done this to you."

"Fine, but is it really necessary for me to have a body-guard?" I nodded toward said annoying bodyguard standing next to Carey. "You have to admit it's over the top."

"Well, now, that's got nothin' to do with me. That's between you, your dad, and Dean. I don't think it's a bad idea though."

I scoffed, shaking my head. "We done? I've got a clinic full of patients, and I'm by myself."

"Uh, well, Dean said you got a new boyfriend?"

"What?" I looked at Dean and he arched an eyebrow.

I rolled my eyes. "That's none of your business." Huh. Well, if Dean thought I was dating Brady, he could keep on thinking it. Maybe it was wrong of me to omit that Brady and I were only friends, but it served him right. And a little part of me hoped it hurt. "Brady Douglas—from high school, Carey? —did not slash my freakin' tires."

"Okay, well, I'm still gonna call him. Maybe he noticed somethin'. Who else were you with last night?"

"Ughhh. Jules. Markham? My best friend. You think *she* slashed my tires?"

"No, Oly, I'm sure she didn't. But I gotta talk to her."

"Fine. Have at it. We done now?"

"Yep, that's all for now. Go ahead, I'll be in touch. Call me if you think of anything I should know. I'm just gonna talk to Dean for a minute, and then I'll get outta your hair."

"Fine," I grumbled and walked out of the office. I left the door open on my way out, but Carey shut it behind me. Rude. They were probably in there discussing how to keep the "little lady" safe.

What-the-eff-ever. I didn't have time for any of this.

14

DEAN

Oly's dad picked her up at five forty-five. He waved as I sat in my truck, watchin' her go.

She wouldn't talk to me or even look at me, but it didn't really matter.

It hurt though.

Every time she'd look away from me, avoid my eyes, it felt like she was squeezin' my stomach with her fist, tightenin' her fingers slowly. But she was in danger, or possible danger, and even if she'd cursed at me the whole time and covered me in cow shit, I woulda stayed to look after her.

She wasn't happy about it, though, so I kept my distance.

The afternoon went by with nothin' outta the ordinary goin' on. The clinic had been busy with people comin' in to get their animals looked at before the Christmas and New Year holidays. Oly handled the chaos like a champ. She never got overwhelmed, just took it one patient at a time.

I spent the day walkin' the perimeter of the property, cruisin' the roads surroundin' the clinic in my truck, and I drove over to Mike Williams' auto shop to see the tires. It looked like someone tried to gut the damn things. The knife, or whatever had been used to tear jagged foot-long gashes in each tire, probably hadn't been very sharp.

I'd worked a few security jobs after returnin' to civilian life in May, and Oly's dad knew that, so he'd called me this mornin' to offer to pay me to look after her—her parents could be a little overprotective. I wouldn't take his money, and Oly had probably been right about the tire slashers bein' teenagers, but I figured it couldn't hurt to stay alert, especially after seein' the evidence.

I planned to drive by her place a couple times before she went to bed, but first, I needed to run home to eat and shower and talk to my brothers about this Brady Douglas.

I did remember him from high school. We'd both played on our high school's football team. I remembered him bein' a decent guy. Kinda quiet, but he'd been popular. Girls fawned over him all the time. He was the quarterback. He wasn't particularly good at football, but none of us had been, really.

But then we'd graduated and he'd gone off to college, and I hadn't seen him again until last night. I didn't remember Oly bein' friends with him, but maybe I'd been wrong. Or maybe she was just gettin' to know him now. They were both adults, both professionals. Probably perfect for each other. Just thinkin' about it made me feel like throwin' up.

Wasn't that what I wanted though? For Oly to find someone better? For her to be happy with a man, someone who could give her all the things I couldn't—a good person. So then, how come all I wanted to do was bust his mouth open with my fist and rip his dick off?

Jay, Kevin, and Jack were in the barn when I got home.

"You guys remember Brady Douglas? He was in my year at school," I asked, maybe a little too aggressively, when I marched into the barn.

"Yeah. That was the guy with Oly last night, right?" Kevin asked. "Used to play football."

"Yeah."

"What about him?" Jack asked, untanglin' endless feet of lunge rope while Jay and Kevin watched.

"What do you remember about him?" I asked as someone pulled up outside the barn.

"I don't remember him at all," Jack said, hangin' the now neatly wound rope on a hook outside the tack room door.

"I do." Kevin shrugged. "But, I mean, he was just a guy. Normal or whatever. He looks different now."

"How?" I demanded. "What do you mean 'different?'"

Carey walked in the barn, and I turned to him right away. "What do you know about him?"

"Who?" he asked.

I scoffed like a teenage girl. "Brady Douglas."

"Oh, Dean, he's the nicest guy in the world. He didn't slash Oly's tires."

"Somebody slashed Oly's tires?" Jay asked. "What the hell?"

"She alright?" Jack asked.

"She's okay. That's where I was all day. Her dad called me this mornin', asked me to keep an eye on her at the clinic. I'm gonna head back into town. I just came home to grab some food and change. What'd he say when you talked to him, Carey?"

"Who?"

"Seriously? Brady Douglas." I rolled my eyes.

"Nothin'. He didn't see nothin'. He don't know nothin'."

"Maybe he's lyin'," I said, and even I could hear the whine in my voice.

"They ain't datin', Dean." Carey stuck his hands on his hips.

"Bullshit. He was all over her at the bar last night." I put my hands on my hips, too, until I realized what an idiot I probably looked like.

"Careful, I can see the green monster dancin' in your eyes already." Carey chuckled, and I resisted the urge to strangle him. "But I'm tellin' you, they are *not* datin'."

"Maybe you just ain't as a good a detective—"

"Dean. Brady is gay."

"He is?" Kevin asked, shocked.

"Yeah. Now don't go spreadin' gossip. I'm only tellin' you so I don't have to throw your ass in jail after you the beat the stuffin' outta him."

"Brady Douglas is gay?" Kevin asked again and Carey sighed.

"Yes, Kevin. It ain't a big deal."

"No. I-I know. It's—"

Jay stared at Kevin, and Kev looked away, his eyes focusin' on the wall behind Carey's head. I couldn't figure out what the expression on Jay's face meant, but it didn't matter.

I looked at Carey. "You sure 'bout that?"

"Yep. Told me himself. He don't seem too shy about it. 'Course, he ain't lived around here for a long time. Historically, Wyoming ain't the most hospitable place for the LGBTQ community."

"Yeah, that might just be a little bit of an understatement," Jay said, shakin' his head.

"C'mon." Jack walked outta the barn. "Finn texted. Dinner's ready."

"I got a weird feelin' about all this." I had no idea why, but I didn't like the knot in the pit of my stomach.

"Dean. Get over it. They're not datin'."

"Yeah, I heard you, Carey, but it's not about him. I dunno.

Doesn't matter anyway. Oly's love life has nothin' to do with me anymore. Don't mean I ain't gonna worry about her." I said the words, but it felt like I was garglin' broken glass as they came outta my mouth.

A whole chorus of sarcastic "uh huhs" sounded behind me as I stomped up to the house.

An hour later, I'd eaten and showered and was headed back to Oly's place. She'd be pissed at me for lurkin' about, so I decided to knock on her door to let her know. That might make her madder, but I figured I'd risk it.

I texted her dad to let him know I was there and then looked around. All the lights were on in her house, and I could see into her livin' room a little. It looked like she was watchin' TV, and occasionally, I could see Oly or Jules get up and move around. I was happy Jules was there to keep her company. She acted tough but I knew better. She would be at least a little freaked out by the tire thing.

I did a perimeter check but didn't find anything, then sat in my truck for a few minutes, tryin' to calm my heart. The anxiety thing was getting' worse, seemed to have pitched itself off a ledge since the day she drove back into town.

Sittin' outside her house brought up all kinds of memories of the past. Memories of the night we spent together before she'd left for England and the awful things I said to her the next mornin'.

But another memory kept tryin' to break through. I kept hearin' my dad's voice in my head. I'd been away when he died. I hadn't been able to get home in time, but I talked to him on a satellite phone a couple months before, sittin' in the middle of Jordan durin' a trainin' operation with Jordanian soldiers.

Jack had called, hopin' to get a hold of me, and finally, I got the message and called back...

"Hey, brother," Jack said, *the bulky SAT phone I held carryin' his chuckle to my ear.*

I smiled. "Brother, it's good to hear your voice."

"Where you at? You allowed to say?"

"Yeah. I'm in Amman. In Jordan. We're trainin' with some of their soldiers. Me and some other HOGs."

"Hogs? What the fuck?"

"HOGs. Hunters of Gunmen. It's a nickname, I guess, for snipers."

Jack laughed.

"How's everybody? You called 'cross the world. Somethin's goin' on."

"Yeah. The guys are fine. It's Dad."

"I figured. Cancer's worse?"

"Yeah. The doctor's talkin' about hospice, but you know Dad. He's gonna die in the barn. But, um, he wants to talk to you. The fucker's been houndin' me for days. You got time for that?"

I took a deep breath. I could face enemy forces, terrorists, insurgents, but it took way more courage to talk to my dad.

"Yeah. Put him on."

"Hold on. Hey, if he hangs up— You stay safe out there. You hear me, Dean?"

"Yeah, brother. I hear you."

"You come home."

I nodded like he could see me sittin' on my cot in the barracks on the other side of the world. "I will."

It was probably the closest I'd ever get to hearin' my older brother tell me he loved me. We didn't relate like that.

We loved each other plenty, all my brothers. We just didn't say it. Well, maybe except for Finn. Weirdo.

"Here's Dad." I heard shufflin' and Jack's voice as he held the phone out to my dad. "Jesus, ol' man. Take the phone."

"Is it your mama?" my dad asked. He sounded confused and so weak and fragile, his voice so different from the loud boom he normally spoke with, usually to tell me how I'd failed him.

"No, Dad. It's Dean. He called to talk to you."

"I don't wanna talk to him."

"Dammit, you asked to talk to him. Take the damn phone. You might not… get another chance." I heard the sadness and frustration in Jack's voice. Our dad was a dick, but he was still our dad. The only parent we had left.

There was more shufflin', then my dad's voice as he cleared his throat. "Dean."

"Yeah. I'm here."

"Where? Where you at?"

"I'm overseas. Trainin'."

"Oh." He scoffed. "You takin' it up the ass, huh? Takin' orders?"

"Jesus, Dad."

"Well, you ain't in charge."

"Nope. I'm not the President of the United States. Sorry to disappoint you."

"Don't get smart with me."

"Yes, sir. Look, Jack said you wanted to talk to me."

"Yeah. You do what I asked?" His voice was muffled, like he'd covered his mouth with his hand.

"What?"

"You find your mama?"

"Dad, I told you, that ain't my job. I don't… I don't have access to do stuff like that."

"You probably got some sissy friends, sit behind a computer all day. They could look."

"That's not— It don't work that way. She's gone, Dad. She ain't comin' home. It's been almost nineteen years."

"Maybe she's just lost."

"Dad—"

"Dean. Do this for me? Please?" He was silent for a minute. "Please?"

"Dad, I-I can't." What I wanted to say was that I didn't want to. I didn't care where my mama was. She abandoned her family. She was probably lost all right, but she wasn't lookin' to be found. If she cared about her family at all, after all these years, she woulda reached out. Called. Sent a letter. A fuckin' postcard. Somethin'.

"Son," he said, breathless. The cancer all through his lungs, spreadin' through the rest of him, didn't let him beg. *"Dean, please. I need her. What have I ever asked of you?"*

Was he kiddin'? Blood, sweat, tears, dreams, love, life.

But what I said was, "I'll try."

"Good. That's good. You do that for me."

Yeah. Sure. Why not?

"Call when you find her," he said and hung up.

I never looked and he died soon after.

He'd never know I did find her a year later, by pure coincidence.

I'd been sittin' in front of Oly's place, starin' out through my windshield, but when I saw Jules leavin', my memories faded away. I nodded to her and climbed outta my truck when she pulled away.

When Oly opened her front door, I opened my mouth to apologize for annoyin' her, but she wore pajamas, a thin silk pair that came down low on her chest. I could see her nipples through the damn thing. I stepped over her threshold, liftin' her so her toes dangled over the floor, then set her down a few feet back and shut the door.

"What do you want? Hey! What're you doin'?"

"Oly, you're practically naked. The whole neighborhood can see you."

Rage simmered in her eyes, and I stepped back against the door.

"Oh no," she laughed, but it sounded a little... edged. "No. You did *not* just say that to me."

"What?"

"You better run, Dean Cade, or I'm gonna castrate you like a dog!"

Oh shit. What'd I say?

15

CAROLYN

"You better run, Dean Cade, or I'm gonna castrate you like a dog!"

The nonplussed look on his face was comical, and I would've laughed, but I was so mad and I was not kidding. I saw red. And the fact that he didn't even know what I was so mad about just made me madder. How dare he come into my house and order me around like some... like some... little woman? I could show my body to anybody I damn well pleased.

"Oly? You're kinda freakin' me out. What'd I say?"

"You don't like this?" I slapped my hands against my chest like a neanderthal. "Screw you."

Pushing past him, I threw my front door open, stepped out into the freezing freakin' cold, and ripped my top off. I wasn't wearing a bra, and I felt like a deranged flasher, but I didn't care.

"Oly," he gritted through his teeth, "get back in here."

"No," I taunted.

"Dammit, Oly."

"What, Dean? What is it you wanna say?" Turning to face

him, I held my arms out to my sides, exposing myself as thoroughly as I could. My phone would be ringing any moment 'cause my mom would be calling, just as soon as Mrs. Wilson called her, since she was, no doubt, watching me from her living room window across the street.

"Get. In. This. House."

"No. You don't own me. You lost the right to your opinion about my body or what I do with it when you dumped me. No, scratch that. You *never* had the right to an opinion. Hashtag female autonomy!"

"Maybe so—what? Female what?—but I ain't gonna stand here and watch you expose yourself to the whole town. What're you thinkin'?"

He stomped toward me and I ran down my porch stairs, barefoot and bare breasted, into the snow. I didn't get far, of course. His long, muscular legs caught up to me in a couple strides, and he lifted me up and literally threw me over his shoulder while I punched and pummeled his stupid sexy freakin' biceps, which was about as effective a defense strategy as throwing jellybeans at Thor.

"Put me down, ya big lug. Dean! Put. Me. Down. I'm a freakin' doctor, not some stupid little girl." I kicked and struggled and dug my fingernails into his skin under his thick Carhartt jacket.

"You're sure actin' like a little girl. Cut it out, Oly."

"Ugh. I hate you!" I screeched while he carried me back inside, slammed the front door shut, and bypassed my living room, heading straight for my bedroom. "No. You're not allowed in there. That honor goes to my *boyfriend*, Brady." Hmph. Let's see how he liked that. I knew I sounded like a brat, but years of pent-up anger and need and want and heartache converged inside me, and I couldn't stop the petulance coming out of my mouth.

"You mean your gay boyfriend? I think he might be much more honored in my bedroom." Pulling me from his shoulder, he dropped me onto my bed.

I scrambled up to my knees. "How do you know that?"

He cocked an eyebrow with his hands on his hips.

"Ach. Freakin' Carey. Is nothin' private in this stupid town?"

His eyes traveled from mine down my neck to my breasts. The hunger I saw in them turned me on so much, and I tried to rub my thighs together to stop the ache between them without him noticing.

Yeah, right. He noticed.

Eyes focused between my legs, he shrugged his arms out of his jacket and let it fall to the floor.

"What do you think you're doin'?" I climbed up to my feet so I towered above him for once, planting my hands on my hips.

His mouth hung open as he stared at my body, and I wanted to shove my tongue in it, but I refused to let him treat me like—but then I looked down his body.

Dean had never been one to don tight jeans. He wore bootcut Levi's or Wranglers, but they were tight now as they stretched and molded around his erection. My mouth watered and I couldn't look away.

"Go away," I whispered, begging silently for him to strip me bare and ram himself inside me.

His chest rose and fell so fast, but he stepped back.

"Really want me to?" he asked, looking up into my eyes, and I knew what he saw in them.

Need. Naked, blatant need.

I shook my head in tiny jerks and reached for him, pulling him to my mouth with my hands clutching his T-shirt.

"Oly," he breathed when I tried to kiss him, but he pulled

away. He rested his forehead against my shoulder, then lowered his head and sucked my breast into his mouth. The whole freakin' thing! I gasped and arched, and he lowered us to the bed. I moaned and clutched the perfect hard globes of his ass through his jeans with my fingernails.

"Maybe this isn't a good idea," I said, my voice sounding pathetic, even to myself, as I moaned and panted and undulated underneath him. "Oh God, take off your pants."

He kissed down my stomach to the waist of my pajama bottoms and sat between my legs, pulling them out, one at a time, then threw my pants to the floor and stared at my pink panties.

"Dean."

He looked up. "Tell me to stop, Oly. If you don't want this, tell me now. I can't make myself leave. It has to be you."

I wanted it so much it hurt, my vaginal walls squeezing in on themselves, empty, longing for him.

I couldn't even imagine the pain I'd feel in the morning when he walked away again, but I thought my barren weeping core would dehydrate, shrivel up, and fall out if he didn't put his body inside mine in the next five seconds.

But I didn't want him to be sweet.

"Oly?"

"Fuck me," I said, breathless but bold, or as bold as I could muster, and he closed his eyes for a moment, then backed off the bed, stood, and removed his boots and jeans.

I watched as he revealed his body to me. Oh my God. I'd missed his body, dreamed of it—his thick, strong thighs covered in soft blond hair. He left his boxer briefs on, though, but pulled his shirt over his head, and when I saw his chest and abdomen, I moaned, scraping my teeth over my bottom lip. I watched his bulging biceps as he pushed his underwear down, and I whimpered.

I couldn't take the ache anymore.

When he moved his hands so I could see his whole body, I gasped. Just looking at him, hard and huge and aroused for me—I was desperate for him.

"Please. I can't take it anymore. Fuck me. I need it."

He growled and descended, spreading my legs and spearing me with his tongue, reaching as far up inside me as he could. I bent my knees, planting my feet on the bed, and ground and pushed myself against his face. He added two fingers and licked up to my clit, and I sobbed and came and strangled his head with my thighs. (Gimme a break. It had been years!)

I shuddered and shook through my orgasm, and before I could even open my eyes, he thrust his cock into me—hard—forcing the breath from my lungs in a very unladylike grunt.

He spit a condom wrapper from his teeth as I opened my eyes.

Throwing my arms around his shoulders, we both groaned. He felt so good inside me. All around me. So good. He filled me but not just my body. Everything felt full. My heart, my head. Everything.

And then he *fucked* me.

I gasped as he pushed in and pulled out over and over and over. It felt so good, each thrust of his hips so hard. His arms shook on either side of me, and I grabbed onto them for something to hold onto as I rolled my hips against his.

But not just his arms, his whole body trembled. I reached with my mouth, my lips and tongue, to bite and lick and suck his arm.

Looking between us, he watched himself inside me, and he became frantic. He pulled out and flipped me. I wasn't expecting it, and I felt like a boneless rag doll, my arms and legs splaying out, but he grabbed my hips and yanked them up, then rammed back in and pummeled my freakin' cervix with his cock.

"Uhn. Oh God. Oh my fucking God, Dean." I didn't think I'd ever cursed like that in front of him, and he never did in front of me. He had always been so careful. Too polite.

He wasn't polite now.

He growled, and every punching thrust of his hips forced me further up my bed to my headboard, my arms and legs scrambling to keep up. Cupping his hands over my breasts, he pulled me up to my knees, and I threaded my fingers through his, over them.

Grunting and groaning in my ear, he licked and sucked my neck, digging his chin into my shoulder, then lifted my hands to the top of the headboard, and we both held on as he fucked up into me from behind like a man possessed.

When he pulled his hand from mine and reached down between my legs to rub my needy wanton nubbin of pent-up sexual frustration, a sound came out of me I'd never heard before. It was some kind of squeak/growl.

"Open your mouth."

He hadn't needed to ask. My mouth popped open as I gasped for air, and he pushed two fingers inside, and I sucked and licked them, lavishing them and tasting them with my tongue. I tasted myself, my own cum, mixed with the salt and hot from his fingers, and oh my God, it made me ravenous. I wanted to devour his whole body.

"Fuck," he breathed, pulling them from my lips and rubbing them between my breasts, down my belly, to my swollen, pulsating clit.

I panted, arching my back, pressing my ass back against him.

Gripping my hips in his big hands, he lowered himself behind me, fucking faster, and I tried to reach behind him to claw his ass so I could feel it flexing as he pounded into me, but he held my wrists in one hand, trapping them between our bodies behind me. He wouldn't let me touch him, and I whimpered and pulled my wrists. Not because it hurt. I wanted to feel how tight he held me. I liked it.

I liked that he wouldn't let me move.

From this angle, he hit the spot inside me that was practically an on-button for my orgasms. It had always been that way. He knew just how to make me come, and he would do it all on his own. I didn't need to move. It was what he wanted.

My head fell back against his chest, my hair sticking to his sweaty skin while he rubbed and rubbed in circles, fucking up into me like he never had before, then reached with his fingers down between our bodies, to feel himself moving in and out of me again. He liked that and it made him shake harder. He moaned and breathed into my ear, and the sound, his desire all around us, took me over the edge.

"I'm coming. Dean!" My body contracted around him—I felt it, my core grasping and pulling him deeper inside—and he fucked harder, hissing in my ear. My whole body jerked as he thrust up into me one last time as we came, and I screamed his name again as he breathed mine.

"Jules?"

"Oly? What time is it?" Jules yawned through her cell phone.

"I dunno."

"What's wrong? It's the middle of the night."

"Oh, it's nothin'. I'm… fine. Never mind. Go back to sleep."

"You're lyin'. Spill."

I sighed. I'd forgotten how nice it was to be able to call Jules any time of day or night. Not that it mattered now since I was indeed calling her in the middle of the night, but we used to have to schedule calls because of the time difference in Cambridge. I'd really missed her.

I opened my mouth, and a whole slew of words tumbled out in a jumbled wad.

"We had sex and it was amazing, but then he left. He didn't say anything, and I'm so confused, and I want him, and I feel ashamed."

Jules laughed.

"It's not funny!"

"No, I know. Sorry, it's just you're not usually so, umm, what's the word? Forthcomin'? Especially about sex. Okay, back up and slow down. We're talkin' about Dean, right?"

"Yes, Jules!"

"He was parked behind me when I left your house tonight. Did he come in?"

"Oh, he came all right."

"You screwed him but now you're confused?"

"Jules."

"What? You didn't screw him? Wait, you've been havin' sex with him since I left? That was hours ago."

"I know! I'm so fucking confused."

"Carolyn Masterson. You never cuss. What did the man do to you?" She laughed again, the phone rustling as she sat up in bed, and I wanted to kick her shins and hug her.

I growled at her.

"Okay, okay. Why are you confused?"

I sighed. "It was— Oh God, it was so hot. Primal. We... *fucked*," I hedged. I was so embarrassed to say the word, but I knew she'd understand. "We didn't make love. Know what I mean?"

"Yeah. Big difference. Not like I've ever been in love, but I can imagine. I can totally picture me and Finn as he f—"

"Jules. Focus."

"Sorry."

"It was like last time. But more… raw. I never— I've never wanted it like that before. But I did tonight. I was so angry with him. I told him I wanted it like that. God, I practically begged him. It was the best sex of my life, but then he… he just got up and left. We didn't talk. I mean, not even one word."

"Ooo. You didn't say anything either?"

"No. I couldn't. My brain hadn't caught up with my body yet."

"Why was it the best sex of your life?"

"What? What do you mean?"

"I mean, what made it different than the other times you guys slept together?"

"He was different. He didn't kiss me. I kissed him, but he wouldn't kiss me back. It was all… physical." Wasn't that what I thought I'd wanted?

"No, it wasn't."

"It was, Jules. Isn't that why he just got up and walked out after? Why else would he do that?"

"Oly. C'mon. You know the guy's got issues. You think the Marines made that *better*? He's a freakin' sniper. He's killed people."

"I know. I mean, he hasn't said anything about it but…"

"Yeah, well, he's a guy. Look, you went to college. He went to war. He hasn't spent the last seven years playin' the field. And as far as I know, he hasn't dated anyone since he's been home. He still loves you. I'd bet my life on it. He's loved you since we were five years old." Jules was quiet for a minute. "But you said you feel ashamed. Why?"

"I dunno."

"Oly."

I sighed. "No snarky comments, got it? No judgement. This is a judgement free zone."

"Okay. I promise."

"Dean has always looked at me like I'm a princess. Like I'm a breakable little girl."

"Mm, I think you're wrong about that."

"Jules."

"Oh, sorry. Zippin' my lips."

"Fine. Maybe *I've* always seen myself like that. And now that I'm done with school, and it's time for me to be… grown up—a big girl," I scoffed at myself, "I need more. But it's not just in my professional life that I… want *more*."

"Want more what?"

"Well, like at work, I need to be confident. I need to be in charge. People look to me for answers. I know what I'm doin'. I know the answers, but sometimes, I doubt myself. Sometimes, I act like I don't know the answers. Or that I don't know what to do or what I want. And I kinda feel that way… in bed too."

"I don't understand."

"I know what I want, Jules. In bed. Sex. But I'm afraid to say it."

"Why? What do you want?"

"I want— I don't want sweet."

"I still don't get it."

"I want— ahh. Are you really gonna make me say it?"

"Isn't that the whole point of this conversation? At two in the mornin', I might add."

"Dang it. Fine. I want… hard sex. A little pain. Ughhh. Why can't I say it?"

"Oly. You and I are never gonna have sex. There's nothin'

to be embarrassed about with me. Just say it. You already know I'm weird. I'm totally attracted to Principal Nevins and he's, like, sixty-five years old. And I have that weird arm hair thing. I don't think anything you tell me will be weirder than that."

"I want to be dominated." There. I said it.

"Is that all? Who doesn't? Are we talkin', like, 'yes sir, no sir, may I lick your feet, sir?' kinda domination or—"

"No, Jules. Just, like, I want Dean to boss me, I guess. Hold my arms down, blindfold me, maybe. I dunno. I like a little… pain. I want him to lose himself inside me, like he did before. I want him to fuck me so hard it hurts. But it's not just that. I want to do those things to him too. But I'm so confused. I get so mad when someone tries to tell me what to do. Especially Dean. I act all tough. So why do I want the opposite?" I sighed. "Maybe I don't know what the hell I want."

"Ols, you're an intelligent, independent, strong woman. You can want whatever you want. Even if it doesn't make sense. If it's what you want, and it's consensual—and safe—it's okay."

"But I don't think *Dean* wants it. This is what I mean. I think it's why he left without sayin' anything tonight. He's so careful with me. He tries not to hurt me, but tonight, it was like he was a different guy. Like he couldn't control himself."

"That's so hot."

"Yeah! But I don't think *he* thinks it's hot."

"Oh-oh," she laughed, "trrr-ust me, he does."

"No, I'm tellin' you, he doesn't. Or he thinks it's bad somehow. It was just like last time. The sex was mind-blowing, but after, he got weird."

"Maybe he thinks you don't like it."

"Oh."

"Mmhm."

"Huh."

"Yep." She popped her lips.

"You think he thinks—"

"That's what I'm sayin'."

16

DEAN

I drove by Oly's house in the mornin', just to make sure things looked okay, and watched her climb into Yola's old Ford Bronco. It killed me to leave her last night after… But I hadn't known what to say. For the second time, I'd used her body to ease my pain, and I felt like a lecherous cur. She hated me. She had to.

I hated me.

But I couldn't have stopped myself. I'd needed her so much my whole body shook. I couldn't think. All those nights I lay alone, all the countless hours on rooftops, wonderin' if I'd make it home alive, if I'd be the one at the end of some other guy's gun, or an IED, or if my Humvee would be blown up, helicopter shot down—every single time, it was Oly's face in my mind. Her voice in my ears. Back then, I swore I could feel the sweet, soft texture of her skin on my fingers, even though I hadn't touched her in years.

It was her disappointment I feared.

And last night, all that fear and longin' and heartache, it all just exploded inside me, and it had to come out. I didn't know how to stop it.

I didn't think she could've either. She wanted my body. Nothin' else. Part of my mind, the part always doubtin' my own intentions, wondered if maybe she knew what I'd done. She couldn't know the details, but maybe she knew, could sense, the bad in me. The shame and guilt.

She still wanted me, but maybe it had only been physical, and she'd just needed the release.

I couldn't think about it because my pulse raced just rememberin' how she looked, standin' on her bed, arguin' with me. It had been the first time I'd felt real happiness since... well, a long time. I couldn't remember the last time. Seein' her so mad at me, gettin' up in arms, like she used to when we were kids, it healed a little bit of my broken soul.

Probably a pretty normal reaction for any guy, but I felt dizzy when I thought about her in my arms, touchin' her. The battle in my mind between the good parts of me meetin' the bad parts, of Oly bein' able to see 'em warrin' with each other —the world started goin' black. My heart pounded, and I felt that clenchin' thing in my chest like I had at Manny's before I passed out.

Maybe I needed to stop by Doc's clinic. Maybe I'd developed high blood pressure. Or maybe I really was havin' panic attacks. Anxiety attacks. I didn't know.

I pulled up outside Bigsy's house and rolled down my passenger-side window.

"Hey, Dean. How are you?" Annie, Bigsy's eerily patient and understandin' wife, asked.

"Okay, Annie, you?"

"I'm great. I don't have to work today, and I get the whole house to myself. I'm going to light some candles, take a bubble bath, and read a good book." She sighed dramatically. "Thanks for taking this one off my hands."

Annie winked at me, and Bigsy scowled, tossin' his

crutches in the back of my truck. He shoved a backpack up into the front seat and climbed in. Maneuverin' himself in and out got easier for him every time.

"Whatever, woman. You'll be lost without me. Go 'head, read your smut books. You haven't seen Dean's sister-in-law. She's like a short, white, freckled supermodel. Hmph."

I snorted. "Yeah, well, better not let my brother hear you say that, or I'll be bringin' minced meat home to Annie."

"Mind your manners, Marcus." She chuckled. Shuttin' his door, she pushed up on her toes as he leaned out the window to kiss her. "Have fun."

Just that tiny gesture had my heart in my boots. It reminded me of so many nights with Oly, droppin' her at home and gettin' a last minute kiss through the window. We weren't that way with each other anymore.

"Yeah, right. Have you seen this guy?" Bigsy jabbed his thumb in my general direction. "He's a barrel of laughs. Bye, baby." She waved as we drove off.

"What's in the bag?"

"Oh, just my horse-riding outfit," Bigsy said, and I could feel him smilin' like the Joker next to me.

"Uh, you know you can just wear jeans?"

"It was a joke, dumbass."

"Oh."

"So, what's up your butt today? There's a vein ticking over your eye."

"What? No, nothin'. I'm fine."

"You're a terrible liar."

"You know, every damn time you step foot in my truck, I feel like I'm bein' forced into therapy with a tiny black bully," I snapped, annoyed at his ever-present insistence at tryin' to get some kinda touchy-feely shit outta me.

"Ha! You made a joke! Call the town council. They'll

throw a parade." He snorted. "Every time you pick me up, I feel like your white-bread cowboy ass is gonna infect me. Next thing you know, I'll be drinking Jack Daniels from the bottle and chewing 'tobaccah.' I'll be calling Annie darlin', and she'll tie me to our bed with wranglin' rope."

"I will never unsee that image."

"Just wait till you see what I got in my trusty government-issued pack." He lifted his camo backpack and let it fall back onto the seat between us.

"Jesus. I'm scared."

"Seriously though. You sleeping? You look like shit."

I sighed.

"You know, you could just talk to her. I mean, I know it's a novel idea, but it might work."

"I saw her last night."

"Ahh, hence the ticking vein and bloodshot eyes. Broody strikes again. Well, you talk?"

"Not exactly."

"Ahh, you fucked." He didn't ask. He stated, like he knew already. Like it had been easy to guess the difference.

"Jesus, Bigsy."

"What? You didn't fuck her? Ohh, you made *love* to her." He dragged the word out sarcastically.

"No. We— I... fucked."

"Why you say it like that? Like fucking is a bad thing. Two consenting adults can do whatever they want."

"It's not that. It's just, it's... complicated."

"Why?"

"It just is."

"Why?"

"Dammit, Marcus. You're like a three-year-old. Drop it."

"No. Why is it complicated?"

"Fuck off."

"Just tell me. Ain't gonna hurt you. You obviously need to talk about it if you can't sleep. I'm right here. So talk."

"Because… Because I love her. She used to love me, but I pushed her away. And last night, it felt like… It felt like an end between us. I couldn't stop myself. I couldn't hold back. I probably scared her. She was angry with me. I-I gave her what she wanted, or I tried, but it felt like I left my soul inside her body, and I ain't ever gonna get it back."

"Damn."

"It's what I wanted. For her to move on. Find someone better but…"

"Your life is a fucking country song."

"Well, you asked!"

"Did she come?"

"Marcus," I warned.

"Well, did she?"

"Yeah. What's that got to do with anything?"

"If you'd scared her, she probably wouldn't have."

"Yeah, I don't think that's true, and it's not the point."

"How do you know she doesn't love you anymore? She say that?"

"She told me she hates me."

"That's different than 'I don't love you anymore.' Were you doing something douchey when she said it?"

"Possibly." I winced.

"What'd you do?"

"Never mind."

"A'ight, well, all I can tell you is, in a mature, committed relationship, marriage or not, if you don't talk to your woman about how you feel, you will be, at the very least, in the damn doghouse. And at the most, single."

"Look who's talkin', Mr. 'I'm worthless, so what's the point?'"

"That's different."

I snorted. "How's it different?"

"It... well, it just is." He scowled out the window for a minute. "Fine. I'll talk to mine if you talk to yours."

"Fine," I said, thinkin' it would be easier said than done.

"Fine. Dick. But you know, talking about sex often leads to more sex, so there's that little incentive. I'll just drop that right here. You can pick it up if you want."

———

I managed to get Bigsy up onto Sammy's back. Jack reluctantly offered his horse for our little experiment. He had been pretty skeptical, especially after Bigsy shut himself in the tack room to change into his "horse wranglin' attire." He'd come out in an old brown-and-blue plaid shirt with white pearl buttons he said he picked up at the Goodwill, a red bandana around his neck, and leather chaps—and no fuckin' jeans! His black ass reflected the sun like two tiny, round moons in an eclipse, and Kevin spit coffee all over Finn who fell to the ground laughin' so hard, he kept sayin', "I'm gonna pee! I'm gonna pee!"

Bigsy crutched himself over to Mad Max's stall and said, "Okay, how am I supposed to get on this motherfucking monster? He's black and he's the biggest one so I know you're saving him for me."

After changin' back into normal clothes (though he kept the damn bandana), Finn and I helped him onto Sammy and led him around the arena a few times. I asked him to pay attention to how his body responded to the horse, the way his core muscles responded to Sammy's gait, and how his thigh and leg muscles controlled his movement.

But then Jack made him get down. He said it was important for Bigsy to get to know the horse he intended to ride. He needed to start with brushin' and feedin' the animal. So that was what we did. And I showed him all the different tools we used to groom, the bits and bridles, and the saddles.

I looked it up online, ways to improve muscle strength after an injury, and I had a lotta ideas about what we could do to help Bigsy. But like anybody else I'd ever met, just bein' around the horse was good for him. He could be a snarky, sarcastic son of a bitch, but around animals—total pushover. And the foals? The guy was a goner. He couldn't stop talkin' about bringin' Annie out to meet 'em, and he asked if I thought he could keep one in his backyard.

He bet Finn he couldn't jump the paddock fence on Gertie, so of course, Finn had to prove him wrong, and it turned into a competition. Even Jack got into it, racin' Finn and Kevin.

Bigsy and I sat on a bale of hay, watchin'.

"You keep saying your lady deserves someone better. What does that mean? I don't wanna get weird, but I think you're a pretty stand-up guy. Your whole family's pretty dope. Taking in some jackass like me, taking time out of your workday. So, what's so bad about you?" He stared at me and it did feel weird.

"I dunno."

"Bullshit."

"This is weird. You're makin' me feel weird."

"Whatever, man. I'm tryin' to be real with you."

I sighed. "She comes from money. I ain't got any."

"Hmm. And you think she's shallow enough to care about that kind of thing?"

"No. She's not shallow."

"Then why does money matter?"

"Fine, maybe it's not about money." I plucked at the hay

between my legs. I wanted to tell him, to say it out loud, but it felt so big in my mind. And I wondered what he'd think of me if he knew what I'd done. He knew some of it, but he didn't know the worst of it.

"You thought about that group I told you about? I think you should try it."

"I really don't wanna sit around talkin' about my feelin's with a bunch of guys. I can handle it. There's just some things I'm not real proud of."

He nodded real slow and pursed his lips. "I did things I didn't ever want to tell Annie about. Things I thought she could never see past." He looked at me, but I kept my eyes on my brothers, out playin' in the fields.

"I did tell her though. After a while. It was eating me up inside, to keep it in. I told her all about getting shot. She kept begging me to tell her, and I kept saying no. I didn't think she could handle it. But it had more to do with *me* not being able to handle it.

"When I told her, it felt like the weight of the world had been lifted off my shoulders. And that thing, you know? That thing we feel, that shame and disgust about ourselves, even though we fought for our country, did the right thing? That thing went away after I talked to Annie."

"It's not just about all the stuff I did with the military. You don't— I didn't tell you everything."

"Mm. Well, I think the theory still applies. What'd you do? Murder puppies?" I flashed him a sour look. "I'm just fucking with you. Look, if you love her like you say you do, you owe her the chance to accept you. All of you. The bad and the good.

"Is it hard? Fuck yeah, man. Is it scary, putting yourself out there like that? Bet yo white ass. But, Dean," he said and waited for me to look at him. I stared into his deep brown eyes, seein' all the men I'd served with, the ones who'd died and the ones who didn't. I saw my brothers in his eyes. I knew I could trust him. I knew he'd understand. "Is she worth it?"

"She's worth everything."

17

CAROLYN

"Well, Oly, whatcha think? You been here a few weeks now. Is vet life all you thought it was cracked up to be?" Yola asked as she, Doc, and I finished our lunch in Doc's office. Mike Williams had returned my truck to me with new tires, and I'd just come back from a farm call to help a nanny goat deliver two kids.

"Yeah. Better. And actually, I didn't think I'd like working with smaller animals as much as I do. I liked it in school, but I was always more excited to get my hands on the horses. But I don't mind the dogs and cats. Hedgehogs, ferrets, birds—they're so fun. I love horses, of course, but you know me. It's the science. I love science." I laughed 'cause I'd always been such a science nerd.

"I'm glad to hear it. You're doin' a great job, Oly. The clients love you," Doc praised. "Though, if you want more horses, I won't complain if you wanna take more farm calls. You know what you're doin'. Now it's just about gettin' the experience. Puttin' in the hours. And we just signed on ten more ranches and farms. Everybody's heard I got some help finally, and they don't wanna wait around for those over-priced city docs."

"Really? That's great, Doc."

"Yeah, it's great for the business, but it ain't gonna be great for your social life. I was thinkin', maybe we oughta hire another new vet."

"Do you have someone in mind?" I asked, thinking I knew the perfect person.

"No, I thought I might call over to Casper College. See if they got anybody lookin' for a job."

"Actually, I might know someone. He went to school with me but graduated earlier. He's in Denver now, workin' with another guy we went to school with, but he hates it there. I might be able to talk him into comin' here."

"Why would somebody with a fancy degree wanna come here?" Doc laughed.

"Hey. I came here. My degree is just as fancy as his."

"No offense, Oly, but you're from here, so you don't count," Yola joked, standing to collect our sandwich wrappers and empty chip bags. "We really need to eat healthier 'round here. No more chips, Doc, or your wife's gonna kick my butt."

"Please, Yola, like anyone could," Doc countered. "Where's the maneater I know and love?"

"Last time I checked, your wife ain't a man. And if anyone could kick my butt, I'd put my own money on Lucinda. Don't you make me choose sides, ol' man. You won't win. I'm puttin' my foot down. You're gonna eat the damn carrots and celery Luci packs for you every day that you throw in the trash. And no more ham, bacon, and salami. You'll eat the turkey or chicken she packs too. That's all you get. No more diner food for lunch. I can't even imagine how much money you waste on all that uneaten food. And I'm cuttin' the coffee off at eleven every day. You got enough caffeine in your system to power a nuclear sub, hear me?"

"Fine, party pooper. But don't come cryin' to me when you find my attitude lackin'." Doc looped his arm over my shoulder and whispered as Yola left the office. "She talks tough, but she's a pushover. Besides, sometimes you pick up our lunch. *You* won't force me to choke down turkey, will ya?"

"Oh, I am so not getting' between you, Luci, and Yola." I laughed. "You're on your own, Doc."

He clicked his tongue. "Dammit. Fine. Go ahead and call your friend. I couldn't pay him fancy city wages. Fifty bucks says he tells you 'no way.' Some young stud vet. He's probably got all kindsa offers."

"He's great. You'll love him. He was top of his class, an amazing vet. He grew up on a dairy farm in the Netherlands, so he knows animals."

"Oh yeah? Okay, well, bring him out here, but don't get your hopes up, Oly. Most people don't grow up here want nothin' to do with such a small town."

"I dunno. I think you might be wrong."

"Bet?" He shoved his hand out in front of us.

I shook it. "Fifty bucks."

"Ha. Easy money."

As soon as I got home from work, I called Luuk.

"Lookie Loo?"

"Carolina! I have missed you." He laughed. "How is it going? How is your new job?"

"I miss you too."

"Well, I cannot blame you. I am wonderful."

I really had missed him. Just the sound of his voice, with his Dutch accent and his tendency to mess up easy American colloquialisms, took me back to Cambridge, where everything had made sense. I'd missed home, my parents, but I'd excelled in vet school. I'd been happy, and Luuk and I had so much fun together.

I laughed. "Yes, you are. So, um, remember how you said you wanted to come up to visit me?"

"*Ja*. Remember how you promised me cowboys?"

"I do." Oh, if he only knew. "Actually, there's a guy from my high school I'd love for you to meet. He's not a cowboy though. He's a lawyer. But I'm not talkin' about just a visit."

"What do you mean?"

"Doc P—that's my boss—he's thinking about hiring another vet. Want a job?"

"I have a job."

"You said you hate Denver."

"*Ja*. I do. Well, I don't hate it. I just don't like it."

"You also said you hated all the guys there."

"*Ja*. I did. Ugh," he groaned. "I do not like dating. It's ridiculous. All these guys want is to— Well, they want nothing more than sex. It's not a bad thing, but I have already done that. It's not good for me. You know? I've gone on a few dates, but nothing is sticking. It is all so superficial."

"I think you mean 'nothin' stuck.' Actually, I think that's the wrong thing to say altogether." I giggled. "But why don't you come up here? My parents would love to see you, and you could meet Doc P. See whatcha think of him, of the practice. You love cows. We got tons of cows around here. Do you have plans for Christmas?"

"I do. I've been invited to a Christmas holiday in Aspen. Very exclusive. The family I have been working for owns a chalet there. It sounds nice."

"Oh, okay. Bummer. What about New Years, doin'
anything then?"

"*Niets*. I am off work. I will be by myself."

"Then it's settled. You're comin' here. I can't promise a
big party, but you won't be alone."

"Emm… Okay. *Prima*."

I was so excited to see Luuk. He had been a lifeline for
me at Cambridge. We met on my first day there at a farm call
in Horningsea, UK. Luuk had performed a C-section on a
cow in the middle of a dairy barn. It was amazing. I'd been
reeling from moving across the world and from The Night
with Dean and all the things he'd said back then.

Dean had undermined my confidence that morning. He
reinforced the doubt I had about myself that I was immature
and sheltered. I felt like I had no business being a vet because
who would ever listen to anything some spoiled little girl
from the middle-of-nowhere Wyoming had to say?

Luuk's friendship had helped to build me back up again.
He helped me believe in myself. He'd become family. His
parents had died in a horrible car accident when he was
fifteen, and since then, he'd been searching for a home.

That was how I knew I could win Doc's bet. If Luuk liked
Wisper, and people got to know and love him—which I knew
they would because everyone did—he might stay. He had
become an amazing veterinarian, so smart and resourceful
and not afraid to work. And if he met Brady, and they liked
each other, who knew what could happen?

But where would he stay? I only had my one bedroom
and the tiny room off the kitchen. I laughed out loud thinking
of his long, tall body trying to fit in that itty-bitty room. But I
could sleep on my couch, and Luuk could take—

A knock on my front door interrupted my musings, and I
walked toward it without thinking.

Or maybe I could rent my house out again, and Luuk and I could find a bigger one. Jules could move in too. They hadn't met yet, but I bet they'd get along really well—

Too distracted to check the window before I opened the door, I was surprised and stunned into silence when I opened it and Dean stood in front of me. I hadn't been expecting him.

"Hi."

"Hi," I breathed and my cheeks heated, remembering what we'd done a few nights before—his hands all over me, binding me, his tongue in me—

"Can I come in?"

"Yeah." I swallowed loudly.

Opening the door further, I stood back to let Dean pass by me, and he stepped into the living room. He stood in front of my couch. He wouldn't sit until I did, of course. Always ladies first.

I sighed. "Sit, Dean." I knew I was being stubborn, but sometimes, his chivalry made me mad. He didn't sit, so I did, and he lowered himself but wouldn't look at me.

"Oly, I um… I wanted to talk to you."

"I'm sorry about the other night." I hadn't meant to say anything, but it just sort of rushed out.

"Sorry? Why would you be sorry?" He shook his head. Still, he wouldn't look at me.

"Because it was unfair to you."

"Unfair. Oh, I see."

"You see what? Dean, will you look at me please?" He turned his head, and his eyes were stormy gray skies. He looked so hurt. But my landline rang, so shrill in the silence between us. "Sorry, I have to get that. It could be an emergency."

"Yeah."

I jumped up and ran to the kitchen. I couldn't believe he

was actually sitting in my living room, willing to talk to me. He'd come on his own. Could this be progress?

I lifted the ancient portable phone from its cradle on the wall. "Dr. Masterson."

But there wasn't anyone there. Or at least, they didn't say anything.

"Hello? This is Dr. Masterson. Can you hear me?" Walking back to the living room absentmindedly, I listened for any sign of the person at the other end of the line. "Look, this is gettin' old. If this is a joke, cut it out. This line is for veterinary emergencies."

Dean stood and stomped over to me. "Gimme that phone."

I held my hand up in front of his chest. "Alright, listen up, if you call again, I'm callin' the sheriff," I warned, my down-home, Wisper accent coming out. "I'm gonna have him trace your number, and you'll be in big trouble." Hmph. Let's see how they liked that.

But apparently my threat wasn't very scary. Whoever breathed into my phone growled. It made the hairs on the back of my neck stand up.

"Get out," they said.

Dean must've noticed my reaction, the look of discomfort on my face. He stole the phone from my hand.

"Who is this?" he demanded in his deep voice. "They hung up," he said, switching off the phone and pulling his cell from his back pocket. He shoved my phone at me then clicked on his cell's screen a few times and held it up to his ear. "How many of these calls have you had, Oly?" His eyes narrowed in suspicion.

I shrugged. "Dunno. A few. It's probably just some kids." Although, that voice, it hadn't sounded like a kid. I couldn't tell if it was a man or a woman. Whoever it was disguised their voice.

"Hey, Carey," he said into his cell. Oh, great.

"Dean, I do not need you to deal with this. I can handle it on my own. You're not my father. I'm twenty-seven years old." I reached for his cell, but he stepped away from me, looking at me. "It's just some stupid kids." It was a lie. I didn't really think that anymore, but I was mad at Dean.

"Can you come to Oly's house?" he asked and waited while Carey spoke. "No, but she's been gettin' prank phone calls. More than one." He eyed me and I looked at the floor. "*Many* more than one." *Ughhh*. Dang him for knowing me so well.

Great. Now the stupid sheriff would come. I stomped into my bedroom to change out of my dirty work scrubs, grumbling and complaining under my breath as I yanked my clothes off.

"Stupid bully. Whaddya think, you're my freakin' fixer? I'm not a baby. I'm a freakin' doctor. Ugh."

"Yeah, you are, but this doesn't feel like just a prank, and you're not takin' it seriously," he said, leaning against the door frame.

I spun around to face him. "Nobody asked you, Dean. I coulda called Carey myself."

"Yeah, but you wouldn't have."

"You're right because it's just some dumb kids."

I hadn't yet covered my chest, and Dean, very obviously, didn't look. He stared into my eyes, and a vein pulsed over his temple.

Finally, I pulled a sweater from my drawer and yanked it over my head. No bra. Ha. Dean could kiss my butt. I'd worked all day. I was tired, and he and Carey didn't deserve any kind of polite societal normalcy. I didn't care if it made them uncomfortable.

"Oly. I came here to talk to you. I'm sorry, I—" He shook his head. "But this isn't funny. People just don't go around slashin' other people's tires. Not around here. This could be a stalker, or... I dunno. I got a bad feelin' about it." He stepped toward me. One step, then two more.

"Fine. But you can leave. I'll talk to Carey on my own."

"That's not happenin'."

"You know what? *This* is your problem. You make decisions for the people around you. For me. Without askin'. I don't need your help and I don't want it. I'm not some damsel in distress." I pushed past him, shoving his arm when he reached for me. No. I thought he'd come to talk to me finally, to open up to me, let me in somehow. It had been what I'd wanted all this time. But he hadn't changed.

I opened my front door and stepped onto the porch so the winter air could cool my boiling blood. Carey would be pulling up any moment. Bein' best friends with the county sheriff guaranteed quick front-door service.

Well, fine. Just freakin' fine.

18

DEAN

Carey showed up a few minutes later with Frank Sims, one of his deputies, followin' behind in his patrol car. They looked around Oly's house, checked out the property, but didn't find anything suspicious.

"So, Oly, I think it might be a good idea if you stayed somewhere else for a little while. Just till we can figure out what's goin' on."

"I will not. You wouldn't be sayin' this if I were a man. And you wouldn't be sayin' it if Dean wasn't your good ol' boy."

Carey sucked his teeth. "Well, guess I can't force you to stay somewhere else, but I really think it's the prudent thing to do."

"I am absolutely fine. Everybody's takin' this way outta —" Oly froze as she heard a commotion outside her front door, and both her parents barreled into the house. She turned to glare at me. And I mean, she stared *daggers* right into my eyes. "You. Called. My. Parents?"

"No, I… texted 'em," I said, just a little bit abashed. "Sorry." I really did feel bad about textin' her parents, but I knew she was mad at me, and I knew she wouldn't listen to me. She'd be mad at Carey, too, by association.

She punched my bicep with her tiny fist and pushed me, then threw her arms up in the air. "Fine," she growled, turnin' and stompin' off to her bedroom again. Her mama followed.

"Dean, would you let Oly stay with you a few days?" Mr. Masterson asked, runnin' his hand through his hair. He was worried. "I've got work. I won't be home much this next week."

"Yes, sir." Actually, I had just been about to suggest it.

"What do you think's goin' on, Carey?"

"I really have no idea, Glen. I mean, she could be right, could just be kids. I don't think kids woulda done that much damage to her tires though. And... the neighbors two doors down noticed a sedan sittin' out on the side of the road the other night. Said somebody parked there a while, watchin' the house." He'd told me when I called him, which was why I'd texted Oly's dad.

"What? You didn't tell me that," Oly accused, appearin' in the hallway, draggin' a suitcase behind her.

"Well, you haven't exactly given me a chance." Carey turned his hat in his hands, clearly uncomfortable dealin' with Oly's... feist.

"Okay. Okay. You all win. The little lady will go to mommy and daddy's house. For two days. I'll give you two days. I've got a life, you know? A job." She scoffed and shook her head.

"Actually, Oly, um, I think you should stay with Dean, at the ranch," her dad said and winced 'cause he feared her retaliation.

"No. Oh, oh no." She laughed, clearly not amused. "I put up with this matchmakin' crud, all your little comments here and there about me and Dean. But there is no me and Dean. Are we clear?"

"Ols, I'll be at work. I've got meetings all week that I can't get out of. The bigwigs are comin' in, and I won't get home till late every night. Your mama isn't gonna feel comfortable with just you and her in the house."

Ooo. Now I winced.

"Seriously?" she squeaked. She looked hurt, and her eyebrows crumpled in incredulous disbelief. Oh boy. Mr. Masterson had just landed himself in a heap a' trouble, makin' Oly feel guilty about her mama's safety like that.

"Honey," Mrs. Masterson nudged, "we just want you to be safe. Plus, I'm gonna be helping Mrs. Jacoby this week. From church? She just had surgery. I probably won't be home much either. Please? Do this for us? I won't push. I promise."

"Ugh," Oly growled, mad as hell, and yanked her suitcase to the door, mumblin' all the way. She swiped her work bag from a side table as she marched out to the porch, stormed down to her truck, and threw her suitcase into the back seat. She climbed in and stared straight ahead while she waited to follow me home. No one else said a word as we watched her.

Oly's dad turned to shake my hand. He had a weary look on his face, and I had a hard time keepin' a straight one. Oly mad was just about the most adorable thing I ever saw.

"Thank you, Dean. Tell your family thank you."

"Yes, and I'll bring food and toiletries for her tomorrow. I don't think she grabbed any of that stuff," Mrs. Masterson added.

I nodded, and Carey said, "Okay then. I'll see if I can trace these calls and talk to the other neighbors, see what they know. If there was anything to see, you know Mrs. Wilson saw it."

"Hi Oly," Evvie chirped when Oly pushed past me, draggin' her suitcase into the kitchen in the middle of dinner. "Are you st—"

"Where am I goin'?" Oly demanded over her shoulder, interruptin' Evvie, and Evvie cringed, clearly pickin' up on Oly's sour mood.

"Uh, my room, I guess," I said.

"No. I'll sleep on the couch." She lifted her nose into the air a little.

"Take my room, Oly," I spoke a little louder, more firmly. "I'll sleep on the couch."

"Hi, Mrs. Mitchum. I apologize. Sorry to interrupt y'all's dinner," Oly said as she stomped past Ma. Ma looked at me and I shook my head.

"Finnie, run, go get me a phone," Ma whispered. The Wisper gossip tree would be lightin' up like Christmas tonight.

I followed Oly up the stairs to my room. She hefted her suitcase onto my bed and rounded on me in the doorway.

"You said I could have your room."

"You can."

"Okay. Then go away. I'm goin' to bed." I looked at her, cheeks flushed with anger and irritation, hair all messed up 'cause she kept runnin' her fingers through it. "Buh bye," she said and slammed the door in my face. I wanted to bust through it and make her listen to me, but I knew she didn't want that, so I went back downstairs and answered every-body's questions.

Carey had called Billie, a hacker he knew from Oregon. She'd helped us when Evvie had been in trouble a couple months ago. Carey trusted her, and we all knew she was good

at what she did. But all she found about the person callin' Oly
was that they used a disposable cell, untraceable. She spoke
to Oly—Oly had allowed Evvie into my bedroom to deliver
Carey's phone—and Billie looked through Oly's laptop and
tablet remotely but didn't find anything nefarious.

Carey waited for Oly and Evvie to come downstairs, but
when they didn't, he went up and I followed.

Carey spoke to my door. "Oly, can you open up?"

The door creaked open, and Evvie stepped back to invite
Carey in. I stayed in the hall, outta sight. Oly probably
wanted to strangle me, and I understood why, but I just didn't
feel right not bein' near her.

"What can you tell me about the phone calls?" he asked.

She sighed. "There's nothin' to tell. There've been, I
dunno, five maybe." She winced. "Okay, maybe more like
fifteen. But they never say anything. Except… well, except
tonight, they… growled."

"Was it a man or a woman?"

"I'm not sure. All they said was 'get out.' I don't think it
was a teenager. The voice wasn't familiar, but they disguised
it. Kinda like a growl. I dunno. I think they just wanted to
scare me."

I knew there was a reason her face turned all ashen when
she'd gotten that call.

"'Get out?' That's all they said?"

"Yeah."

"Have you had any problems with a client at work?"

"No. Everyone's been really nice."

"Well, what about… maybe, did you piss someone off at
the grocery store, cut someone off in traffic?" Carey asked,
tryin' to come up with some kinda explanation for the calls
Oly'd been gettin'.

"No, Carey. Not that I know of."

"Well, this is an investigation now, okay? This isn't just me bein' a 'good ol' boy.'" I heard the humility in Carey's voice. "I'm gonna look through the clinic's phone records too."

"I'm sorry I said that. I'm sorry I got so upset. I guess I am kinda scared. And there's some stuff with Dean. And he called my parents. Like I'm—" She huffed a breath. "I just got really frustrated."

"I understand. It's not a problem. But call me, okay, if you think of anything else I should know?"

"I will."

Carey left the room and rolled his eyes when he saw me still lurkin' out in the hallway. Evvie got up to shut the door again, but just before she clicked it shut, she winked at me and smiled. What did that mean?

Confoundin' women!

19

CAROLYN

Shuffling downstairs the next morning, I was showered and dressed and wearing pink scrubs and wet hair 'cause I'd forgotten my hairdryer, and Evvie didn't have one.

I was freaked out. I had no clue who could have slashed my tires, who could hate me so much they'd want to scare me or hurt me. But I had a job to do, and I intended to do it.

The coffee pot was empty when I made my way into the Cade kitchen. The guys had already downed the stuff—they'd probably downed a few pots—so I made another and filled my favorite extra-large travel mug I kept in my work pack. I didn't look for anything to eat. I just wanted to go to work.

Lingering at the ranch, having to deal with Dean, would not be fun, and he wouldn't talk to me, I knew, especially with everyone around. Best just to get my day started and try to forget how mad I was at him and how sad I felt being in his life, in his world, without his love.

Unfortunately, Dean didn't share the same plan. When I got out to my truck, he was leaning against it with a travel mug of his own.

"Made this for you. Black, right?" he asked, holding it up.

"Yes. But I don't need it." I held up my mug, too, then unlocked my truck and loaded my coffee and pack into the front seat.

"Would you please let me to come with you today? I can take my own truck, if you like. I won't bother you, but I don't think it's a good idea for you to be alone out on the back roads, drivin' to farm calls."

"Aren't you needed here?"

"Well, yes, but they're fine with it."

"I have clinic appointments this mornin'. I'm not goin' on calls till this afternoon so…" I shrugged.

"Oh. Okay," he said, but I knew that wouldn't be the end of it. He'd follow me or jump in my truck at the last minute, once again, deciding what he determined to be best for me.

"Well, I gotta go. I'll be back tonight, I guess," I said and climbed in my truck. He watched me back up, and I caught a glimpse of him in my rear-view mirror, his beautiful ash blond head shining golden in the winter morning sun, walking down the lane while I drove away.

He didn't try to jump in my truck. He'd been trying to placate me by asking my permission. It was what I wanted, and I appreciated the effort it took to ask. I knew, stubborn as he could be, it hadn't been easy for him.

Why couldn't he have done that before he'd joined the Marines? Why had he needed to make the decision to end things between us all by himself? He just assumed, in all his stupid alpha-maleness, that he knew what had been best for me.

He did it now.

Though, if I were honest, he was probably right. There was *something* going on. I didn't want to admit it could be anything serious but…

Almost to the turnoff from Route 20 into town, I noticed a

car following me. There'd barely been any other cars on the road, so it was easy to spot. It didn't look suspicious, exactly, but it made every turn I did and stayed behind me a good distance. It looked like a sedan, four-door. Maybe an older Oldsmobile, but I couldn't tell the color because of all the dirty snow and salt crusted all over it from the winter roads.

I made a couple of unexpected turns, leading me in the opposite direction of the clinic, and the car followed. My heart dropped into my stomach, and I drove quickly to work. The second I locked the clinic door behind me, I called Dean.

"Dean?" I wheezed into my phone after my sprint inside.

"Oly? You okay?"

"There's a car. It's probably nothin' but— Oh!" As I turned to walk through the clinic to hang up my bag and turn on the lights and computers, I gasped. The clinic had been ransacked. There were papers everywhere, the waiting room chairs had been thrown around, and dog food littered the floor.

"Oly? What's wrong?"

"I think someone broke into the clinic. Dean, just please — I need— I'm scared."

"I'm already on my way, duck."

Doc showed up a few minutes after me, and Dean and Deputy Abey Lee both just a few minutes later. Abey took my description of the car, then investigated while Doc followed her through the clinic, pointing out anything that had been messed with.

Dean and I helped Yola and the rest of the staff clean the mess. None of the animals in the overnight kennels had been harmed, thank God, but two dogs had been let out of their cages (or maybe they escaped when they heard an intruder), and they found the samples of dog food by the back door and decided to rip them open and have themselves a feast. I found them curled up together, looking guilty, under Doc's desk.

The medications in the locked cabinet hadn't even been touched. Usually, when a veterinary clinic was broken into, it was because someone wanted to steal the pain medication and sedatives we used on the animals.

After that, I got to work. The animals and the science would calm me down. Abey said Carey was in Jackson dealing with a small rash of break-ins there too, but she said she'd drive by every so often to check up on us. And Yola called Manny, so he had been in and out all morning. Nobody messed with his Yola.

Dean stayed mostly behind the counter or outside, looking around. A few times, though, he'd come to check on me in between appointments and ended up helping me. Once with a Great Dane I had no hope of administering a steroid shot to by myself as the hundred and fifty pound goofball dodged and struggled.

Dean sat on the floor, holding the dog still while I prepared the medication and treated the allergy-ridden gentle giant. He also helped with a feral cat a client had captured and brought in for vaccinations and a spay. The cat ripped his arm up pretty good, and Dean became the patient so I could clean and bandage the bloody gouges she'd left in his arm. He watched my eyes as I worked on him, and I tried as hard as I could not to wrap his arms around my back and let him envelop me into his body.

He stayed outside while the clinic staff, Doc, and I ate lunch and then met me at my truck to go with me on farm calls.

"You okay? What a mornin'," he said.

"Yeah. Thanks for comin'."

"I like seein' you in action. You're really good at this."

"Thanks." I peeked at him as I drove, and he smiled out his window. It was so rare to see him smiling.

We were quiet for a few moments, and it was awkward at first, but it quickly morphed into a comfortable familiarity. I wondered what he thought so hard about as his smile faded and the usual heavy mask he wore returned. I thought about the last few weeks since I'd come home. Something had launched us into this new territory, a place we'd never been to before, a weird twilight full of push and pull. Did he feel it too?

"I'm sorry."

The resonance of his voice reverberated through the truck, snapping me out of my head.

"What?"

"I'm sorry I make decisions without askin'. I didn't really realize I did that till you said it. I'm sorry."

"You didn't realize? How could you not realize that?"

"I dunno. I just didn't. I guess I thought I was doin' what was best for you. I thought I was protectin' you."

Pulling up to the McGuckin's pig farm, I parked and shut the truck off. "There is so much more to talk about after what you just said, but I can't right now."

"I know. I just wanted you to know I'm sorry."

"I, uh… okay."

I stepped out into the cold, dry, overcast winter afternoon, and he slowly followed.

Sorry? For what? Which part, which time? I could've punched him for saying he was sorry two seconds before I had to treat thirteen squealing piglets for parasites and diarrhea!

Once we were back in the truck and I was covered in mud

and pig gunk and about to arrive at another farm, he started again. "I've done a lotta things in my life. Bad things. I thought you deserved better. I wanted to protect you... from me. And I thought, if I let you go, you could find someone better. You could find someone who could give you all the things I can't."

"What can't you give me? What have I ever asked for?"

"Nothin'. It's not what you asked for, but you deserve the whole world. A nice house, a good life. Your career could take you all kinds of places. I'll always be here. On the ranch." He said this as we pulled into the North Pole Taxi Service, a reindeer ranch.

I had been so excited to come on this farm call. I'd never worked with reindeer before. I'd worked on red deer and antelope but never reindeer, and now I just wanted to get it over with so I could at least attempt to process what he'd said, and hopefully, he'd say more.

"What's wrong with the ranch? Are you doin' this on purpose?"

"Doin' what?"

"Making these huge confessions as we drive up to another farm. So I can't respond."

"No." He chuckled. "It just takes me a while to work up the courage to tell you how I... feel."

The farm owner, who looked a bit like Santa himself with a big belly, red puffy coat, and long, scraggly white beard, walked out of his barn and waved at us.

"Okay, but can you hold that thought?" I looked at him and he smiled and nodded, but he looked apprehensive. Worried. "This is really important but—"

"I know, you're Dr. Oly right now. C'mon, let's go wrangle Rudolph."

We did wrangle Rudolph. An actual reindeer named

Rudolph. I also treated Donner and Blitzen. I had been called out to do a herd health check, just a basic overall exam. Some of the reindeer hadn't been eating as much as they normally did, but I didn't find anything wrong with them. Santa and I chalked it up to performance anxiety before they were to be taken on visits to malls and Christmas festivals. We wormed them, petted them, and watched the calves jump and frolic in the snow. Oh my God, the reindeer babies were soooo cute!

Mr. Barone—Santa—gave us a Christmas tree when Dean told him he didn't have one. (His main business was Mr. B's Christmas Trees.) "Well, that's just plain bah-humbug," he said.

We finished with the reindeer and went on a few more farm calls, but Dean didn't say anything else. I tried to continue our earlier conversation, but all I managed to get from him was "I dunno." The moment had passed and it made me so sad. I practically begged him to talk to me, but he'd locked himself down again like Fort Knox.

The rest of my farm calls ran past clinic hours, so we took the Christmas tree back to the ranch in the evening, and Evvie nearly tackled us when we dragged it inside.

"Oh!" she squeaked, literally jumping up and down. "Is that a Christmas tree?"

"Yep. Ugh," Dean huffed a breath as Evvie ran and jumped at him. He hugged her, and I couldn't hide the smile on my face as I watched how he cared for her. All the guys loved her, and having her around seemed to have softened them up, especially Jack.

"Thank you. It's beautiful!" She beamed. Jack chuckled behind Evvie, and I peeked at him, watching him smile. If Evvie was happy, so was Jack.

"Thought you might like it," Dean mumbled, smiling as he lowered her to the floor. As tense and confused as things had been between us, seeing him like this, open and happy, made me feel happy too, even if he wouldn't talk to me.

"I love it. I haven't had a Christmas tree since before my parents died. We talked about getting one this year, but the wedding planning kind of took on a life of its own, and I guess we forgot."

"Yeah, thanks, Oly. I'm sure this was your idea," Jack said. "I'll get a bucket of water. I dunno if we even have a tree stand anymore. All that stuff's probably up in the attic. I'll get up there tomorrow, see what I can find."

"Actually, it was Dean. He talked to Santa today, and when he told him you didn't have a tree, Santa insisted."

"Santa? Oh man, I hope Iggy doesn't try to climb it," Evvie said and laughed, referring to her precocious black-and-white cat. "Hey, Oly, can I talk to you for a minute in private?" Evvie eyed both of the guys, flashing them a mock-stern look.

"Sure?"

She grabbed my hand, dragging me behind her up the stairs to Dean's room. When we were behind the closed door, she turned to face me.

"Did you and Dean talk today?"

"Well, we did a little. There's so much more to say, but I had a ton of work."

"Oh, well, I'll distract everybody, and you can take Dean up to the love nest."

"The love nest?"

"Oh yeah. The foaling room above the barn? You and Dean never used it?"

"No. Before I left for school, their dad was still around. He was always in the barn. Alright, well, I'm starving. Who's cookin' tonight?"

"Kevin. But I brought you up here to ask you something."

"Oh, I'm sorry." I laughed. "What'd you wanna ask me?"

Evvie smiled apprehensively, opened her mouth, and a bunch of words rushed out. "I know it's so last minute, and with everything going on, it's probably the last thing you want to do, but would you please be my maid of honor? We moved the wedding up to New Year's Eve because we want Ma to be able to enjoy it. But I'm gonna need some help. Probably a lot of help. I've already ordered a dress, and I know basically what I want to do but… help? Please?" Dropping down to her knees, she clasped her hands together in front of her chest, like a little girl praying.

"Oh my God, Evvie, of course I will. How exciting! Oh, and I'll call my mom. She's a decorating genius. And an organizational one too. She'll whip this weddin' into shape in no time."

"Really? Oh, thank you so much."

I pulled her up and hugged her. "Don'tcha worry. This'll be the best quickie country weddin' ever. Now, show me your dress."

20

DEAN

Christmas came so fast.

When Oly didn't need to be at the clinic or out on farm calls, she was at the ranch, helpin' Evvie with weddin' plans.

Turned out, between Mrs. Masterson and Ma, they had access to all kinds of resources. People had been droppin' stuff off for the weddin' all week: chairs and tables, huge potted pine trees (though I had no idea what in world they could be used for), extra Christmas decorations, and more.

Bigsy came often, usually in the evenin's, so we could continue with his ridin' lessons. He'd even driven himself one night. It had been the first time he'd driven since his injury. Annie came with him that night, and man could she cook. She'd made a big pot of jambalaya with shrimp and andouille sausage. She'd had a Cajun upbringin', and she and Finn talked all night about étouffée and gumbo.

Oly and I had fallen into somewhat of a routine. She slept in my room and I slept on the couch, still, which was awful since I was nearly a foot longer than the old piece of junk. I swore every mornin' my back was broken. I coulda slept in the barn, but after what happened with Evvie in October, I didn't wanna be so far away from Oly at night.

Then, in the mornin's, I'd go with her to work if she had farm calls. It put a strain on my brothers, especially with all the weddin' stuff goin' on every day, but they understood. Well, mostly. Kevin complained a little, but Jack told him to shut his cake hole. He understood; if it had been Evvie in danger, he woulda done the same thing. In fact, he had two months before.

Oly and I talked a little more. I still really hadn't told her anything. I wanted to, but the words just wouldn't come. I knew she was frustrated with me. I felt the irritation comin' outta her every time I tried to talk to her and failed. We kept gettin' interrupted, though, or I'd lose my nerve.

Everything felt all jumbled up and confused because, besides her irritation and my anxiety, we were so drawn to one another. It was torture, bein' so close to her every day and every night, not bein' able to put my hands on her. She watched me all the time, stared at me when she didn't think I knew, and if she wasn't gawkin' at me, I gawked at her.

We didn't touch each other at all, not unless it was absolutely necessary when I helped her on a farm call, and then it felt awkward. I didn't think she wanted me to touch her.

But everything changed on Christmas Eve.

We'd gone on two calls, a cow with pneumonia and a horse that had slipped on ice and sprained his knee. Oly ultrasounded it, treated the horse with pain meds and a cold compress, and lasered it. She looked so confident, so happy, doin' what she'd always loved.

When we arrived back at the ranch, she said she wanted to check on Mad Max so she wouldn't have to do it on Christmas, and she wanted to look in on little Ruby. The foal had healed beautifully and was fine, prancin' around back in the nursery stall with her mama.

Mad Max, on the other hand, had resisted the antibiotics we'd given him and still struggled with infection so he needed another shot. Oly administered it, and I watched in awe while she contended with the horse, calmin' him in her usual way. I remembered a few weeks ago when I'd imagined her doin' the exact same thing before everything had erupted between us.

"You amaze me. You know that?"

"I do?" she asked, surprised, steppin' outta Max's stall in front of me. I followed and slid the door shut quietly.

"Yeah. He's one ornery beast, four times your size, and you never showed fear. And you're not afraid to work. For weeks, I've watched you get right in there, contendin' with the animals, gettin' dirty, shovin' your hands in places they should never be."

"What does *that* mean?"

"What?"

"Why should my hands never get dirty?"

"That's not what I meant."

"Thank you for the compliment, but yes, it is. It's exactly what you meant. Like I'm a princess, like I'm too good to get my hands dirty. You do realize bein' a vet's pretty much all about poop, pus, animal sex, birth, and goo? It's like you have some messed up view of who I am. You put me on a pedestal."

"No, I— Well. I guess I do. It's where you belong."

"That's just"—she clicked her tongue—"well, that's just bull."

"Why? It's bad that I think so much of you?"

"Yes, it's bad. I'm not a princess, Dean. I'm a regular person. Just like you. Just like everyone. And makin' me out to be so much better than you gives you the excuse to push me away. You tell yourself you're not good enough, successful enough, to be with me, and you take away my choice in the matter completely." She scoffed, shakin' her head. "It's a self-fulfillin' prophecy, and it's utter *bullshit*. It was bullshit after high school and it's bullshit now." She grabbed her pack from the floor beside the tack room and turned. "I'm goin' inside. Merry Christmas."

"Oly, wait."

Stoppin' at the mouth of the barn, she turned to face me. "No. I'm tired of this. You're right here in front of me. After all this time, you're here. It's all I've ever wanted. But I can't touch you. I can't talk to you. So, what's the damn point?"

She walked outta the barn, and I couldn't move. I wanted to go after her, but I felt stuck in place.

She was right.

She'd been right every time. I did make decisions for her. All kinds, like whether she should drive to the clinic. If she should sleep on the couch. I brought her lunch 'cause I decided she needed to eat, not 'cause she asked for food. Those were all small things, but it was the same thinkin' that made me end things between us. I decided she should have somethin' different, and I didn't ask what she wanted. Ever.

I didn't trust her to make the right decisions for herself.

And if I convinced myself she was so much better, then it did make it easier for me to push her away. I could tell myself it was all for her, but it wasn't. It was for me. So I never had to face myself and all the things I'd done that I was ashamed of.

I wouldn't have to face how I really felt about myself, that I didn't deserve to be loved or happy.

If I didn't tell her about all those things, the things that kept me up at night, then she'd never have to choose. I'd never give her the chance or the option to choose me or not.

I looked up from the spot I was starin' at on the floor when I heard movement. Oly stood outside Gertie's stall with her hands on her hips and her bag on the floor. Legs wide. She expected an argument.

"And another thing. I don't want you to come with me anymore. I know it's not safe, but I'll take Jay or Finn or somebody. You can stay here."

I barely heard what she said. I felt like I had tunnel vision —my heart raced and my hands sweat, but I stared right at her, marchin' toward her. Her eyes grew huge, like an owl, eyebrows arched high.

"I don't wanna take your choice away," I said and lifted her up.

"What are you doin'? This is kinda the exact opposite of not takin' my choice away, and it didn't work out so well for us last time, remember?"

"What? What didn't work out?" She wrapped her legs around me, not as adverse as I thought to bein' manhandled without her permission.

"Sex."

"That's not what I'm doin', and I'm about to explain all that, so just hold your horses."

I carried her outside, down past all the aisles to the last, and up the stairs to the little room over the barn. She wrapped her arms around my shoulders and examined me the whole way, squintin' her eyes in doubt.

"Explain what? Is this the love nest?" she asked, lookin' around as I carried her into the little room and shut the door with my boot.

"The what?"

"Evvie calls this room the 'love nest.'"

"She oughta call it her den of iniquity 'cause that's all they use it for." I placed her on the bed, and she scooched back against the wall and pulled her knees up to her chest. "So, you're right," I said, steppin' back a couple feet.

"Yeah. But about what, specifically?"

Pacin' in front of the window, I tried to figure out how to start.

The snow had begun to fall again. It came down pretty fast, sparklin' against the dark in the moonlight. I had so many thoughts runnin' through my head and things I needed to tell her. Things I'd never told anyone. Things I'd hid from her on purpose. It felt wrong now to want her to know my secrets, but I knew, if I didn't let her in, I'd lose her forever. And she would go out and find some other man, some other life.

I'd been given a second chance, and somehow, she still wanted me.

"I... I've killed a lotta people, Oly."

"Dean, that was your—"

"No. Don't you forgive me yet. Not till you know everything. Just let me get this out."

She pressed her lips together and watched me pace the room.

"I killed a lotta people, and I don't feel good about it. Sometimes, I hate myself for it. I dunno about any god or whatever, but sometimes, I think I'm goin' to hell. I just did what I was supposed to. I did my job, fought for my country. But I killed 'em. They were evil. The shi—the stuff they did to us. It was— But that... that's not the only thing. That's not what's so hard to say.

"I'm sorry. I'm sorry I made all those decisions for you, and you're right about the self-fulfillin' prophecy thing. I never thought about it like that but you're right. It's just... I did somethin' real bad, and once you know what it is, once I tell you—"

I stopped pacin' in the middle of the room at the end of the bed, like I stood on a stage in front of her. The only thing missin' was a spotlight. "Once you know, there's no goin' back and that scares me. Terrifies me. But I know I gotta tell you. It's not fair for me to keep makin' decisions about you, involvin' you, without givin' you all the facts."

This was it. I would tell her and it would finally, and permanently, be the end of Oly and me. But Bigsy was right. I needed to let her choose, or I'd never know for sure if she could truly want me, and she'd never know... me.

I looked in her eyes and the Oly I'd loved since the first day of kindergarten, the one I couldn't live without, with her kindness and forgiveness, her strength and love, she sat before me with patience and acceptance, waitin' for me to tell her this thing I'd held inside me, the thing I'd kept from her. And I could tell she'd already forgiven me.

But she didn't know yet.

Pushin' up onto her knees, she reached for me. "Dean, whatever it is, you can tell me. I love you. There's nothin' you can s—"

"I killed my mama."

She dropped her arms. "What?"

Closin' my eyes, the breath I'd been holdin' in rushed out. I sat on the bed, facin' away from her. I couldn't look at her face while I admitted the thing that would take her away from me.

"This past spring, I was sent to Colombia to work with some Marines doin' reconnaissance and intel gatherin' there. I saw her. I saw my mama there. She lived there. And I… I said some things to her, some pretty awful things, and I left her there, even though she begged me not to." I pushed on my chest. My heart felt like it would pound right through my skin. "Is it hot in here?"

"No." Oly crawled off the bed and came to kneel between my legs. "Dean?"

I looked at her and I cried. Nothin' coulda stopped the tears. All this time, all this weight on me—once I started, I couldn't stop. She wrapped her arms around my back and held onto me, restin' her cheek against my chest.

"Your heart's beatin' so fast." Reachin' up to swipe the

tears from my cheeks with her fingers, she whispered, "Take slow, deep breaths."

"No, I, I'm f-fine." I tried, but my breath kept hitchin' and jumpin', like a little kid's. Maybe I was a little kid in the moment.

A kid who'd killed his own mama.

"Dean, lie back, c'mon," she murmured, and I let the sound of her voice wrap all around me.

She had the most calmin', nurturin' voice. It was the same way she talked to the horses. I'd missed her so goddamn much. Her love. Her patience and kindness. Forgiveness. And her fierce loyalty. My best friend.

She pushed my shoulders and I fell back on the bed. I wanted to feel her body draped over mine. It was the only thing in the whole world that coulda made me feel even the tiniest bit better.

I took a deep breath and then another, and she crawled up next to me. We lay facin' each other and I was so afraid. Time was countin' down. She wouldn't be able to accept what I'd done, and she'd finally give up on me. She'd leave me this time. It was what I'd been afraid of all along. But I couldn't live with myself if I didn't come clean.

She deserved the truth.

"I've never told another soul, Oly. My brothers don't know. When my dad was dyin', he asked me to find my mama. He wanted her there at the end, but I lied to him. I told him I would look for her. But I lied. I didn't look. But she found me, or I guess, we kinda found each other a year later."

She lifted her hands to my face, strokin' my cheeks with her thumbs, and I took a deep breath and started talkin'.

"I was workin' one day with my buddy, Ox. He'd been assigned as my watch while we surveilled some women who hung around with these thugs from the Muñoz cartel. The women sat, eatin' and drinkin', in this outdoor café kinda place.

"We had audio, and we were supposed to listen for any intel on some big shipments these men had comin' in and goin' out. They'd been increasin' their activity in Miami and Texas, and the White House wanted somethin' to be done. They wanted results. It was an easy assignment, you know? Just listenin'. Not a lotta danger.

"We'd set up on a rooftop across the road, and I had my sight trained on the women. When one would talk, I'd focus on her, so I could connect the voice to a face. Ox had planted a microphone near their table, and I had an ear bud in. Only one woman sat with her back to me, so I couldn't see her. And she hadn't spoken the whole time we'd been watchin'. The other women didn't really speak to her, though she was clearly included in their group.

"You know I took Spanish in high school," I said, and Oly nodded, grabbin' hold of my hand, "and I'd gotten a little better at it while we were in South America, but still, some-times, I had to ask Ox to translate—he was fluent. But when this woman finally spoke, the one I couldn't see, I didn't need any help. Her voice rang in my ears, and I thought I might be havin' a hallucination or somethin'. It was my mama's voice."

Oly gasped. "Did you— Are you sure it was her?"

"Yes. But I didn't see her face that day. She never turned so I could see her, and I freaked out. So many times, I'd been in that same position, watchin' people, and I was always good about stayin' in the moment, not lettin' my mind wander, you know? But when I heard her voice, it was surreal. I thought for a minute, maybe I should call for my relief. I thought maybe I had sun stroke or somethin'. But I saw her the next day. I spoke to her."

"How? I mean, well, what did you say? What did she say?"

I closed my eyes, rememberin' that day, rememberin' my mama's face, her voice, her smell…

"This has been the easiest fuckin' gig. Whaddya say we get some cervezas from the cantina? The one where the pretty mamacita works?" Ox wiggled his eyebrows, makin' a rude gesture with his hands and hips in the air.

"Oh yeah. The one with the bottomless brown eyes?" Denny fell back into his chair. "Man, I could fuck for days lookin' into those eyes."

"You'd fuck into anything, Denny, as long as your crinkly little dick fits. Maybe even if it don't," Kyle joked and sniggered. "You'd rub and rub till your prick got raw. You'd give yourself dick burn." He snorted at his own stupid joke.

"Ha ha, Mendelson. Well, who's gonna go get it? I vote for Wyoming. He's the most polite. He should go. I might create an international sex scandal." Denny panted like a damn dog.

"Yeah, I'll go," I said. "Wouldn't mind the walk anyway. Ox, scout me?"

I also wouldn't have minded the chance to look for my mama before I left the little town we'd been in for two weeks. I was sure it had been her voice. I hadn't heard it since I was eight, but it was her. I would never forget the sound of my mother's voice.

"Yep."

"That all you want, just beer?"

"Ooo, no, get us some of those tamales from that little old lady on the square. Oh! And a couple bags of the little fried cheesy fritter balls and some fried green bananas. What are those fuckin' things called? Gomez brought some back the

other day, and I thought I'd died and gone to green-fried monkey heaven."

"You are a green-fried monkey, Denny, and you got cheesy fritters for balls," Mitch said over her shoulder. She sat cross-legged on the floor of our current rundown, makeshift command, dismantlin' and packin' away some of her audio surveillance gear.

"Plantains?" Ox rolled his eyes. "They're called pata-cones, Denny."

"Yeah! Get a lot. You bitches'll eat 'em all before we even make it outta town."

"Mitch, any requests?" I asked her.

"Naw, beer works for me, too, Wyoming."

"All right, rest of you finish packing up. We're leaving in two hours," First Sergeant Graves ordered and threw a bunch of coaxial cables at Denny's head.

"Yes, sir."

I walked the mile to the cantina. The booths with food were near the town square, but Ox had scouted ahead for me and said there'd been just a little too much activity goin' on in town that day, so Denny would just have to keep dreamin' about his green-fried monkey balls. Beer would have to do. The activity hadn't been anything concernin', but best to be safe.

I'd dressed in plain clothes. Not like it helped me blend in. I shoulda scouted for Ox. With his dark skin and dark hair and eyes, he woulda raised less suspicion, but we hadn't had any problems the whole two weeks we'd been on mission. It had been an easy gig. Almost like a vacation.

Until I'd heard my mama's voice.

I remembered the last time I'd seen her, in our kitchen when I was a little boy. I remembered her hair, and I remembered the lines in her skin around her mouth when *she told me she had to go, and the way her eyes had darkened.*

I also remembered the look of betrayal on her face before she walked out the door and never looked back.

I didn't give a shit why she was in Colombia. She'd been with the wives and mistresses of the cartel scumbags. That was all I needed to know. Those people were the most disgustin' human bein's I'd ever encountered.

She'd been with 'em, so that meant she was one of 'em.

I hadn't said anything to Ox, and I knew I'd never tell my brothers I'd seen her. That she was alive and well, and— What would I tell 'em? "Oh, by the way, saw Mama. She's livin' in Colombia, suckin' the dick of the head of the Muñoz drug cartel." Yeah, that was never gonna happen. The woman had done enough damage to my family.

I wouldn't help her add to it.

Part of me hoped I'd see her. I wanted confirmation it had really been her. I wanted to know why. Why'd she'd left her five children. Her husband. Why, after I'd found her that mornin' with one foot already out the door, why did she do it? How could she do it?

Why did she leave me to feel guilty my whole life, thinkin' I coulda done somethin' more to make her stay? I'd held that secret, and it made me feel like a failure. A bad son. The worst brother.

But the other, bigger part of me hoped I didn't see her, 'cause then I could try to convince myself she wasn't a drug whore.

When I'd heard her voice, after the shock and heart wrenchin' realization I hadn't been wrong about what I'd heard, I wanted to call Oly. I wanted to tell her I'd found my mama after almost twenty years, and I wanted to hear her voice as she told me I'd be okay.

I didn't feel okay.

I didn't know what I felt, but whatever it was, okay didn't come near to describin' it.

The sun blazed down on me and sweat dripped down the middle of my back by the time I arrived at the cantina. There were a lotta people in the small open restaurant surrounded by palm trees and thick, dark green vegetation. I saw a couple tourists but mostly locals.

Pickin' a spot by the little thatch bar, I waited for the server to see me. It took a few minutes, but she finally did, and I asked for my beer in Spanish. I had twelve of the brown bottles with the bright green label, a local brew, in a box in my hands, ready to walk back and enjoy a cold drink with some of the best people I'd ever met.

I'd forget I found my mother. I hoped to never think of her again.

But just as I was about to walk out, I heard the timid, raspy sound of her voice again. She tried to fuckin' seduce me.

"Well, hello, big man." She spoke in English, apparently assumin' from my colorin' and blond hair I was probably an American. I wore a hat, but still, it hadn't been hard to tell. "You're not from around here, are—"

I turned, locked my eyes on hers, and waited. Would she even know me?

She did.

She gasped, staggerin' back, and it seemed like she shrank a few inches. I couldn't help the look of filthy fuckin' disgust on my face. I had my confirmation. I didn't need anything more. I left the cantina and walked back the way I'd come.

She followed.

I knew she followed. It hadn't been hard to hear her

*clumsy movements and footsteps, even over the deafenin'
thuddin' of my heart.*

*Finally, in a tiny alley between two ancient adobe
buildin's, she spoke, and I hoped Ox had already gone on
ahead of me. I didn't wanna have to explain. I didn't want my
mama to get in the way of my job. I didn't want her to blow
our cover.*

*"Dean? Is that you? It's me. It's your mama. You
know me."*

*I stopped in my tracks and slowly turned to face her. My
anger did a good job of distractin' me from noticin' too much
that she looked the same. She seemed so much smaller
though. Weaker. She still had the same eyes as Jack, and I
missed my brother somethin' fierce as I looked in 'em.*

*Nothin' else had changed about her. Her hair was the
same. Her skin. Her clothes were different, fancier, but everything else seemed the same. She had a few age lines around
her eyes and her mouth, but she was still beautiful, still that
ethereal, dreamy vision of my mama I'd remembered all these
years.*

*But she wasn't a dream. She was real, and she looked like
she'd been well taken care of, hadn't had a hard life. Hadn't
struggled.*

*I laughed, and she gasped when she saw the look of
contempt on my face.*

*"I know you're angry. I-I... But, please, take me home?
I've missed you so much," she whined, layin' her country
accent on real thick, and her words came out in a rush. "Your
brothers. Please, I wanna see 'em. Your daddy. I wanna go
home. I've been stuck here. You don't understand. The man—
I— Please, he won't let me—"*

I didn't hear a word she said.

"I don't know you, lady. I knew a woman once who

looked an awful lot like you, but she left her family in the dust. She lied and walked out the door, leavin' her son to blame himself his whole fuckin' life. I don't know her anymore, and I sure as fuck don't know you. You ain't my mama or anybody else's for that matter. You never were."

"Please, listen to me, please, I—"

"Here," I said. Holdin' my box of beer in one arm, I pulled all the money I had outta my pocket and tossed it at her feet. "This is what you really want, isn't it? You can't whore yourself out to the American tourist, so you'll just take his money instead? There ya go. Buy yourself somethin' nice, or maybe you already got everything you want."

I heard her cryin' as I walked away, and I felt nothin' but seethin' anger as I thought of my brothers when we were just little boys, rememberin' the looks on their faces that mornin', when everybody'd woken up to find her gone. And I'd known. I'd watched her go and hadn't done anything to stop her. I remembered my little brothers cryin' for her. I'd cried for her, too, in the meadow, alone where no one could see. Till Oly found me there and changed my whole world.

An hour or so later, we'd packed up and driven our old beat-up cover vehicles to the edge of town when the world blew up. We heard explosions and gunfire, and the little cantina blew up next to us as we passed it. All the windows in the car blew in at us in millions of pieces, slicin' through the skin on my face and arms. My ears rang and my heart thudded.

Denny had been drivin' one of the cars, and I looked back to make sure they were all okay, my brothers and sister, but he'd pulled off to stop at the cantina, probably for more beer, or to stick his tongue down the throat of the sexy waitress before he beat feet outta town.

The car he'd driven burned. Big flames and smoke.

He was dead. Mitch was dead.

Sergeant Graves raced us back to town, and we shot and fought and tried to save the townspeople. The whole place burned. A rival cartel wiped that whole town off the map that day. They blew up homes, businesses.

People.

Somebody up the line hadn't done their job properly, and we'd missed out on intel that coulda prevented the massacre, or at least prevented our men's deaths.

Ox died that day, in my arms, shot, tryin' to save the little old lady in the town square, the one sellin' tamales.

We learned later every single man associated with the Muñoz cartel had been killed. I saw my mama's face with the head of the cartel, Rodrigo Muñoz, in a photograph included in some of the reports we'd received after the explosions. His home, everything he owned, had been blown up too. Razed to the ground, left in rubble. His entire family, women and children.

Which meant my mama had died too.

22

CAROLYN

"I can't even think about tellin' my brothers. I betrayed 'em. My dad."

Oh my God. I'd had no idea. For months, he'd blamed himself for killing his own mother?

"Dean, what? Why?"

I couldn't figure out what to say first.

"It's okay, Oly. I knew you... you wouldn't— You're such a good person. This is why. This is why I ended things between us. You're everything good. And you had your whole life in front of you. I didn't want you to throw it away for me. I've been bad my whole life."

He kept his eyes closed, wouldn't look at me as he confessed this thing, but he was so wrong. He rolled over and sat up facing the window.

"Would you just stay here at the ranch for now? Until we figure out what's goin' on, and then you can go back to your life. I won't bother you anymore." The despair was so clear in his voice.

I couldn't let him hurt like that for one minute longer. I

couldn't let him believe he wasn't a good man for one second more.

Silently, I moved to the edge of the bed and walked around to stand in front of him. When he looked up into my eyes, the pain and guilt and regret I saw in him stole the breath right out of my lungs. I dropped down to my knees between his legs.

"Dean. You are not a bad person. You didn't do anything wrong." He hung his head, and I pushed it back up with my hands on his jaw. "If this is what's kept you from me all this time, you didn't have to do it. I love you. There's nothin' to accept or forgive.

"That woman put you and your family through hell. She deserved your anger. You didn't kill her, and there's nothin' you coulda done to make her stay. You were eight years old. It's not your fault." My words came out in a growl. The pain his mother had inflicted on him—it made me furious.

Tears fell from his eyes, dripping down onto the floor between us, his face contorted with pain and shame.

"I love you. So much. I always have and I always will. There's nothin' you can say to change it. Do you hear me?" I crawled up into his arms, and he hugged me to his body, sobbing. "Why do you doubt me?"

"Oly."

I wanted to say more, but I couldn't. The words stuck in my throat. So I showed him how I felt. I kissed up his neck to his cheek.

"Oly. There's— You need to think about—" I shook my head against his, and he lifted his hand into my hair. "This isn't just about—"

"No."

"Dammit, Oly. Listen to me. I'm not good. I can't trust

myself around you. I took advantage of you. I hurt you. Doesn't that matter to you?"

"Is that why you walked out?"

"What?"

I pulled back, looking at him. "At my house, when we— when I asked you to— Were you afraid you'd hurt me?"

"Yeah, I did hurt you."

"I'm not so fragile."

"I know that. That's not what I mean."

"*Do* you know that?" I asked, bracing my hands on his chest.

"Maybe I'm the one who's fragile." He looked down.

"No, you're not. You're the strongest person in the world."

"Now who's got rose-colored goggles on?"

"I know who you are," I promised as he looked back up into my eyes.

"I love you. More than I can ever tell you, duck. But I'm different. I'll never be…"

"What? You'll never be what?"

He gently pushed me off his lap and stood. "I'll never be what you need. You're not listenin'. I'm not the same person I used to be. I killed a child, Oly. Yes, it was my job. Yes, he was a threat. A big one. But he was fucking child. And I killed him. I have to live with that. I won't make you live with it too.

"And I won't trap you here. You wanna forgive me, but at some point, you're gonna realize who I am and you'll leave. Or you'll resent me and I couldn't handle either."

"Trap me?" Like his mother. We had finally come back to that. I laughed as the anger came back. "I can understand why you could think I wouldn't wanna share your life. It's completely untrue, but I can understand it. But Dean, I know who you are. I know your soul. Don't you dare tell me I don't.

"You didn't kill anyone out of malice or because you're a bad person. I'm so sorry you had to go through that, but you need to hear me. You are not now, nor have you ever been, responsible for your mama's actions. For her leavin' or dyin'. *She* left *you*. It's her own fault she ended up down there in the position she was in, with those bad men. You didn't owe her anything. It's the opposite."

"But—" he said, trying to protest. He still thought himself beneath me, and he still thought I'd leave him like his mother.

"Nope. It's my turn now. I'm so sorry. I would give anything to be able to take your pain away. I wish I could. I wish you hadn't had to go through that. Thank you for tellin' me.

"But I wish you woulda told me this years ago 'cause I coulda saved us both the heartbreak. Have I ever given you any reason to think I wouldn't want a life here with you? We talked about this. Don't you remember? We talked about me comin' back here after school, openin' a horse clinic."

"That was just kids dreamin'."

"Not to me. We talked about all kinds of things like that, startin' our own ranch someday, buildin' a house out overlookin' the mountain. I wanted to be wherever you were. I still do. I know you think I shouldn't, but I'm tellin' you, I do. I wanna raise a family here. My parents are here. I've always planned on livin' my life here." He stared at me and I stared right back.

"Dean…" I closed my eyes and took a deep breath, holding it for a minute. "Why do you think I came back here? I spent the last seven years longin' for you, wantin' you, and hopin' you could forgive me for leavin' *you*. There's no one else for me. There never will be. Understand? You're the only one I want. Rich or poor, broken or not, I want you."

"Oly, no."

"What do you mean 'no?'"

"I mean you just graduated. I'm sure you've applied to work at plenty of clinics, and if they call wantin' to hire you, I don't want you to feel obligated to stay back here just to make me happy.

"You've worked so hard, little duck, and I'm so damn proud of you, but there's a million different things you could do. I don't wanna hold you back. You're sayin' all this now, but in a year, or five, when your friends are doin' amazin' things, you'll still be stuck here, lookin' at the same old land every day and wishin' you'd made a different choice. I won't trap you here. I won't do it. You deserve more."

I had to count to ten in my head, so I didn't bitch-slap him with my words.

"First of all, what about you? You deserve the same thing. And second, didn't you hear anything I *just* said?" Oh, I was so freakin' mad, I could've breathed fire! He was making decisions for me again. Not letting me choose. I took two steps toward him, hands on hips. "Do you think I'm unintelligent?"

"What? No." He backed against the wall, scared of little ol' me.

"Do you think I'm shallow or that I don't know myself?"

"No, 'course not."

"Do you think I'm a liar? Or that I'm so blinded by your magnificent... *dick*"—his eyebrows shot through the roof when I cursed—"that I can't see anything else, that I'm some stupid girl who just wants a man to make her happy? Is that whatcha think of me?"

"No, duck, I—"

"Don't you 'duck' me. If you walk away from me again, and lemme just inform you now, if you walk away, there will be no comin' back. Ever. Do you hear me? What I *deserve* is for you to have the guts to stand by me, even though we don't know exactly what the future will bring. Nobody gets a guarantee, Dean, nobody! Why should you be so special?

"I have planned on bein' a vet my whole life, and I have always known I would come back here. And from seven years old, I knew you would be a part of my life." Clenching my fists, I could feel my face turn red and heat in anger. My words came faster and faster.

"You're right. I did apply to lots of places 'cause I need experience. I'm not ready yet to open my own clinic, but in a few years, I will be, and it has always been what I planned to do. I could make a phone call right now and have two or three vets hoppin' planes to get here, to work with me, Dean, in horse country, 'cause that's where we live. Fuckin' horse country! Where the hell else would I wanna be?

"In a few years, with or without you, I will open my own clinic. I'd rather it be with you, but I guess that part's not up to me." I breathed hard after my rant, huffing and puffing.

"So, you need to decide. Are you gonna keep wallowin' in your damn self-pity, or are we gonna have a chance at a life together? And by the way, if you chose self-pity, you should know, you're lettin' that woman ruin your life. You and your brothers picked yourselves up and brought this ranch back from the brink of death, but if you don't let her go, you're lettin' her win."

I took a deep breath, released my fists, and turned on my heel to storm away from him, but I stopped at the door.

"I'm gonna let you ruminate on that for a bit. It's Christmas Eve, and my parents are stoppin' by. I'm so mad at you I could... spit!" His eyes were as big as baseballs, watching me. He'd never seen or heard me so mad. "And FYI, I liked it when you *fucked* me. I liked the pain. I *loved* it. I wanted it. You don't scare me. The only thing you can do to hurt me is this"—I motioned between us—"this stupid thing you're doin', pushin' me away? It ain't for my own good, Dean. It's for yours. You're actin' like a coward."

I stormed out of the room, slamming the door shut behind me.

Christmas Eve passed in a blur. I was grateful to be able to spend it with my parents, Evvie, Ma, and the guys. It wasn't what I pictured when I thought about coming home after so long, but I did my best to get into it and be happy, even though I knew Dean was still out in the barn, sulking or… whatever he was doing. I made Evvie sleep in Dean's room with me so she could stop me if I got up in the middle of the night to go to him.

I *yearned* to go to him. To hold him and comfort him after everything he'd told me. It was physically painful to not go to him. But he needed to figure things out. I couldn't make the decision for him. He had to forgive himself.

Or I would have to let him go.

For good.

I barely slept. I fought with myself all night. All I'd wanted to do was hold him. He'd looked like that eight-year-old little boy last night as I'd yelled at him after he'd confessed his perceived sins to me. I finally fell asleep but only got a few hours, and I woke at eight on Christmas morning to a call.

"Oly?"

"Yeah, Yola? Farm call?" I yawned.

"Yes, but... Oly, Doc had a stroke."

"What?" I jumped out of the bed.

"Oly? What's wrong?" Evvie rasped, sitting up and rubbing the sleep out of her eyes.

"Doc had a stroke," I said to Evvie and asked Yola. "I-I... Yola. Is he—?"

"He's alive. He's in the hospital, but that's all I know so far."

"Thank God."

"Look, I'm sorry, but that means you're in charge. Don't freak out. I'll help you. And we're gonna have to get another Doc out here, at least temporarily."

"My friend's comin'. He'll be here for New Years. I'll just have to convince him to stay."

"Okay, well, that's somethin', at least. Alright, but right now, there's a stuck calf at the Johnson's farm."

"Okay. Um, but what about Luci? She must be freakin' out. I mean, how long will Doc be in the hospital? Will he ever be able to come back to work?"

"I don't know," she admitted, and for the first time ever, I heard Yola's bravado slip.

"Oh, Yola. I'm so sorry."

"It's gonna be okay. It's gonna—" Yola's voice cracked, and she tried to hold back her fear. She and Doc were practically joined at the hip. She was like his daughter.

"It *is* gonna be okay, Yola. I've got this. You don't have to worry about the clinic. I won't let you down. We can do it."

She took a deep breath. "Thank you. Okay. God, I'm sorry, Oly. It's Christmas."

"No, thank you for callin'. Call me when you hear anything, okay? I'll head to the Johnson's."

"Okay."

I shoved my hair into a ponytail, brushed my teeth,

dressed, and hurried to my truck, chewing on my lip and worrying about Doc the whole time. I reassured Yola, but I had no freakin' clue how to run a clinic.

Dean heard me and followed.

"I gotta go. I'm just goin' to the Johnson's. It's literally right down the road. I'll be fine."

I stood in front of Dean, hip cocked, dressed in thermals, snow boots, coveralls and a negative-thirty-degree work coat.

"Oly, I should c—"

"I am not a child. If I need help, I'll call."

"Fine, but can you text me when you get there?" It looked like it physically hurt him to concede to me, if the ridiculous grimace on his face was anything to go by.

"Fine."

"Just… be careful."

The heifer was small, but I had been able to adjust the calf in the mama cow and pull him without even needing a calf jack. The feeling after pulling a live calf or foal, goat kid, or piglet never got old. I felt like I could rule the world. I wanted to call Doc to tell him about it, but then remembered I couldn't.

Mrs. Johnson brought tins of Christmas cookies out, one for me and one for Doc P. Somehow, they'd already heard about Doc's stroke. I didn't tell her he probably couldn't eat them. God. Could he still eat? Was he conscious?

I decided to go back to the ranch, shower, and head to the hospital. If nothing else, I could provide some comfort for Doc's wife, Luci. I figured I should call Luuk too. He should know the chaos he'd be walking into.

"Merry Christmas. How's Aspen?"

"*Vrolijke Kerstfeest*," Luuk said through the phone. His

warm voice instantly made me feel calmer. "Aspen is cold. I don't really like skiing."

"Well then get your butt to Wisper. I really need you. There's a lot goin' on. I'll tell you when you get here but—"

"Tell me now. I'm sitting in a ski lodge on the middle of some mountain, trying to look like I'm enjoying doing absolutely nothing so I don't have to go back out there. Have you resolved things with your cowboy? Please tell me you're having raunchy sex again, because I am not, and I would like to live viciously through you."

"Vicariously."

"*Ja, dat,*" he said, chuckling at himself.

"No cute boys at the ski lodge?"

"Oh no, there are many, but they are... ughhh." He groaned. "You know how men, especially some gay men, try too hard? Well, these men are all overachieving. They are just not for me."

"Well, when you get here, I'll introduce you to Brady. He's really cute and normal. At least, I think he is." I scrunched my face, thinking about Brady, trying to remember if I'd noticed any weird quirks to warn Luuk about.

"Please, do not sit me up. Honestly, I'm just looking forward to being alone and being comfortable in my own skin without every man in a ten-kilometer distance hitting on me while trying to seem uber-cool at the same time. If I am forced to discuss the local IPA flavors once more, I will scream."

"Set you up." I sighed. "And, yeah, pretty sure you won't have to worry about that here."

"Well, so hot cowboy sex. Please, describe in detail. But not your gooey girl body parts. Only his. Hard and straining. Leave nothing to my imagination."

I laughed. I'd missed him. I could not have been more

excited to see him. He'd helped to keep me sane at Cambridge. He always made me laugh, and he was the kindest person I'd ever met. I needed his steady and calming influence right about now. And he was an outstanding vet. There wasn't a person or an animal he wouldn't help, and I was seriously counting on that particular personality trait.

"Luuk, Dr. Prittchard had a stroke. He's in the hospital. And now, I'm on my own. I've never run a clinic before. I'm freakin' out."

"Oh no. I'm so sorry, Carolina. I know how you admire him. But you will be fine. You were born to do this."

I took a deep breath. "Thank you, but now I really need you to consider workin' here. I know you said you'd check it out, and I'm sure Wyoming is the last place you ever thought you'd find yourself, but... Luuk?"

"I'm on the way. As soon as I can figure out how to get off of this snow-coated, gay-mixer mountain."

As I headed back to the ranch, I passed a woman on the side of the road. Her car was smoking a little, and she was bent over the open trunk. I drove by and thought I should call Carey. Maybe he could send a tow or someone to help her.

"Oh, that stinks."

"What?" Luuk asked. "Are you okay?"

I clicked my tongue. "There's a woman on the side of the road. Looks like she's havin' car trouble. I was gonna call the sheriff for her but— You know what? I'm goin' back. It's Christmas."

"Carolina, are you sure this is a good idea?"

"This is Wisper. We help people here." I slowed my truck and pulled a U-ey. And as I drove back to offer my help to the woman, I saw another car had already stopped. "See, someone already stopped to help her."

I clutched the steering wheel to turn back around to head

south again, but a man stepped out of the second car, and the woman backed up. She looked scared.

"There's a man," I said, squinting through my dirty windshield. The man took his hand out of his pocket, and whatever he held flashed in the bright light of the early morning. "He has a gun!"

"What? Carolina? Who?"

"I don't know who he is. Oh, no you don't!" The man pointed his gun at the woman, and she ran into the trees along the side of the road, but I revved my engine and made a beeline straight for him. He jumped out of the way, and I rammed into the back end of his car.

"Carolina? What was that noise? What's going on? Are you okay?"

"Luuk. Hang up and call nine-one-one. Tell them Route 20, in Wisper, Wyoming, between Cade Ranch and Johnson Dairy Farm."

"Carolina, I don't want to hang—"

"Luuk, do it! We need help."

I backed up to ram the guy's car again, but he jumped in and tore out of there, squealing his tires and whipping his car around, and he took off toward Wisper. I tried to see his license plate, but I'd kinda crumpled it with the front of my Four-Runner.

I parked and climbed out of my truck. There was no one else around. Not one car on the road. I looked at the front of my truck and winced. Dang. Now *my* engine was smoking.

I didn't see the woman. She was probably hiding in the forest or she ran.

"Hello? Are you there?" I called out for her and took a few steps toward the tree line. "The man is gone. I chased him off. Hello? Are you okay? Are you hurt?" Following her footprints in the snow to the edge of the trees, I called out, "Ma'am?"

"Are you okay, Carolyn?"

She stepped out from behind a tree. She had brown hair poking out under a black beanie, and she wore an oversized winter coat. No gloves. Tennis shoes. Her feet had probably been soaked by the snow. She looked in the direction the man had gone.

"You know me? I'm so sorry. I— You look really familiar. Please forgive me, but have we met?" I stepped closer.

"A long time ago. I remember the first day he met you. He came home from school and said, 'I'm gonna marry Carolyn Masterson. Will you call her mama and ask if I can marry her?'"

That's when I noticed her eyes. I'd seen those eyes before, the shape, but the color—it was unmistakable.

I gasped.

"You're— Oh my God."

23

DEAN

After Oly left for her Christmas mornin' farm call, I went back up to the room above the barn and replayed last night in my head over and over. She hadn't reacted the way I thought she would have when I told her about my mama and about the people I'd killed.

I guess I'd known all along she'd forgive me. The problem was, I couldn't forgive myself.

I wanted to. I wanted to deserve Oly.

I was desperate to be worthy of her love and forgiveness, but I just couldn't figure how I ever could be. She made it sound so easy, but I killed my *mother*. Who comes back from that? How was I ever supposed to be okay with that?

"Dean! Where the fuck are ya?" I heard Kevin's voice down in the barn.

"Here. I'm comin' down."

"What the hell did you do to Oly?" he called up from the foot of the stairs, leanin' on the wooden railin'.

"Nothin'. None of your business," I said, closin' the foalin' room door behind me, and headed down the stairs. It was Christmas, but there was still work to be done.

"The fuck it ain't. She's been in a fine mood." He laughed. "You managed to piss Ma off too. She says you better get your ass in the house. Well, she didn't say ass. I added that. But I thought you and Oly worked things out."

I eyed him as I stepped off the last stair.

"Whatever, man. All I'm gonna say is you're fuckin' stupid. Don'tcha see she loves you?"

"Yes, Kevin. I know that."

"You sure? 'Cause you're actin' like a fool. You're so fuckin' lucky, and you're throwin' it all away. For what?"

"I'm not throwin' her away."

"You know, I get it. We all got our bullshit. Maybe the Marines fucked you up a little, but you found your person. Seems to me you oughta just get the fuck over your shit and love her. Ever heard the expression 'don't cut off your nose to spite your own face?' Don't do that."

I scoffed. My brother, always so tactful. "Really? It's that easy? So when you gonna get over your own shit then? Huh?" The second I said it, I wished I could take it back.

He glared at me and shook his head once, like he couldn't believe I would say that to him, but our mother had fucked him up too. She'd fucked us all up. Both of our parents had.

Laughin' bitterly, he said, "Do whatever you want. I don't give a shit. Go 'head, push her into the arms of some other guy. Fuckin' serve you right."

"Kev, I'm sorry. I'm just—"

"Fuck off, Dean. Merry fuckin' Christmas." He stomped outta the barn.

"Dammit."

Inside my house, the Christmas celebration had already begun. Evvie opened gift after gift while Jack sat next to her, rubbin' her back. Evvie had T-shirts made for us that had curse words on the front, "F#ck," and "A$$," and on the back they said, "Sorry, Ma." Ma acted mad at her for it, but I caught her grinnin' when Finn put his on.

Finn had given Evvie a guitar sized to fit her small body, a stack of new piano books, and a buncha different kinds of those little coffee pods—gourmet flavors—and a coffee pod machine, but she smacked Finn's arm, complainin' about the little plastic containers fillin' up landfills. She kissed his cheek, though, and admired the box when he looked away.

Jay gave her a tablet and new books to read, and she and Ma both got candy from some fancy candy shop in Jackson from Santa (Finn).

Kev and I bought a saddle for Evvie, and he decorated the leather with an intricate filigree pattern, usin' some of our pop's old leather workin' tools. He'd designed a big "EDC" on the seat jockey under the seat.

Jack made a new piano bench for Evvie, usin' some of the wood from the barn refurbish after the fire in October. He'd had Kevin help him engrave her parents' names into it to honor their memory. They'd burned the names in with brandin' letters. Evvie was sittin' on it, playin' Christmas songs on the piano in the den, when I walked back into the livin' room.

Ma sat in her chair, listenin' with the happiest look on her face, until she saw me, and then she scowled.

I looked at the clock on the wall. Nine forty-two. Not much time had passed since Oly texted from Johnson's farm, but how long did it take to pull a calf? I didn't suppose too long unless she'd run into complications, but I was gettin' nervous. Yeah, I knew the farm was less than ten miles down the road but—

"Merry Christmas," Ma said, archin' an eyebrow. "What'd you do to Oly?"

"Nothin', Ma. We just…" I sighed.

"Oh, Dean," she said, clearly disappointed in me. "Well, her mama left a few gifts for her. And there's somethin' there from me to you." She pointed toward a handful of gifts under our weird Christmas tree.

We'd found our old decorations, but most of 'em had been broken or just plain ugly. So Evvie'd gone around the house, swipin' little items here and there to tie string to, and she hung 'em from the branches. Toothbrushes, apples, a banana, forks and spoons, pens and pencils, DVDs, and tons of paper snowflakes she forced Finn to help her make. She surrounded the rusted tree stand with old horseshoes, like a metal tree shirt, and Jack found some lights at Bob's Feed and Tack, so at least they looked nice.

We all vowed to buy her real ornaments for next Christmas. The damn tree looked like a well-fed homeless man's version of the Charlie Brown tree, but she hadn't cared. She loved the tree, her first since her parents had been killed.

Iggy had climbed the tree and currently hid halfway up the thing with her head pokin' out through the branches, lordin' over the present-openin' ceremony like a queen on a dais. She didn't knock any "ornaments" off, though, stealthy vermin that she was. No doubt she'd be covered in sap.

"I'm sure she'll be back soon. She's gonna have to handle all the emergencies till Doc comes back to work." I looked at the clock again. "She's probably already on her way back."

"I was thinkin' I'd have you take me to church while she's out, but I'm not sure I feel like trudgin' through all that snow.

But maybe we oughta head over to the hospital. Give Luci some support. We could take her somethin' to eat."

Sittin' on the arm of the couch, I was gettin' more nervous by the second. I stood again, walked to the fridge, opened it, looked at nothin', then closed it and walked back into the livin' room, lookin' at the clock again. The naggin' bad feelin' I'd felt before had settled back in my gut, and I wasn't at all comfortable bein' away from Oly.

"Dean? What's the matter with you? Looks like you got ants in your pants."

"I think I'll head over to the Johnson's. See if Oly needs some help. It's been a while. She's probably havin' a hard time gettin' the calf out. Maybe a little muscle will help. I'll be right back. Somebody shovel so I can take Ma over to see Luci when I get back."

Jay stood and stretched. "I'll do it."

"Okay, Dean, but be careful. The snow stopped, but I'm sure the roads are a mess."

"Yes, ma'am."

"I'll come with," Finn said, hoppin' up to get his coat.

My phone rang as I pulled away from the ranch onto Route 20, and I sighed in relief, then felt a pang of fear when I saw Bigsy's name on my screen instead of Oly's. I turned on speaker and set my phone in my dusty cupholder.

"Hey, brother, Merry Christmas."

"Merry Christmas. How's it going over there? No more creepy phone calls or knifed tires?"

"No. Things've been quiet. You and Annie good? Have a good Christmas?" I looked up at the gray sky through my windshield. The snow had stopped fallin' for the most part, but little flurries whizzed by my truck as I picked up a little speed on the highway. I had snow chains on my tires, but still, if the roads had frozen over, they weren't a slide-free guarantee.

"Yeah, it was good. I gave her this purse/bag thing she wanted. She gave me a trip to Hawaii."

"Sounds like you got the better end of the deal there, Bigs."

"Yeah." He sniggered. "Her sister lives there so we don't have to pay for a hotel."

"Nice," I said, squintin' against the bright, overcast sky reflectin' off the endless sea of shock-white snow all around.

"Looks like an accident or somethin'," Finn said, peerin' out the windshield at the flashin' lights half a mile ahead of us. We got a little closer, and I thought the white truck on the side of the road looked—

"That's Oly's truck!" I sped up.

"What's wrong?" Bigsy asked.

Another call beeped through on my phone. "I gotta go."

Slammin' on my brakes, almost slidin' into Oly's truck, I threw my phone to Finn. "Answer that."

I got out, lookin' everywhere for Oly, but the only person I saw was Abey Lee.

"Abey, where's Oly? This is Oly Masterson's truck."

The truck had clearly been in an accident. The front end had been smashed in, and there was another car, a tan sedan, but it didn't look like it had been hit.

"Yeah, she's with Carey. Didn't he call you?"

"Dean," Finn said my name through his open window. "It's Carey. He wants us to come to the station."

"Oly's okay?"

"Yeah. But Dean, he wants us all to come. He said, 'bring *all* your brothers.' He said it's important." Finn lifted his hands in a "I don't fuckin' know" gesture.

"What's goin' on, Carey?" Finn asked when we stomped into the sheriff's station, knockin' the snow from our boots on the entrance rug. The main county station was in Jackson, but we had a small outpost here in Wisper, in the middle of downtown. Carey used it mainly as an office.

"Where's Oly?" I demanded.

"Her parents are with her." Carey looked into my eyes, and I saw worry in his. "She's fine, Dean. I just... I wanted a little privacy. Just wait for a minute. I sent Abey to fetch Ma and Kevin, and Jack's followin' in his truck with Evvie and Jay."

"Carey. *What* is goin' on?"

Carey shook his head. "Please, just be patient."

My anxiety was through the roof. I couldn't figure out why one of my best friends in the world—my brother, really —wouldn't tell me what the hell was goin' on. But Ma, Evvie, Kev, Jay, and Jack walked in finally, and Carey cleared his throat.

"Everybody come with me," he said, and he led us down the hall from the front desk inside the sheriff's station. There was a conference room at the end. The door stood open, and I could see it was empty except for one person.

A woman.

She sat at a small conference table, facin' away from the door. She wore a dark blue, oversized winter coat, and she had brown hair that looked familiar somehow.

Carey stopped in the doorway. "So, um... this is... uhh... the..." He winced and ran his fingers through his rusty red hair as my entire family followed him, lookin' from him to the woman. "Uhh, yeah, I dunno how to say this. This is—"

The woman turned at the sound of Carey's voice as we all piled into the little room, and as soon as I saw the side of her face, my knees turned to jelly, and I staggered to the wall behind me, ploppin' down into a hard-plastic chair.

Finn blurted, "Holy *fuck*!"

24

DEAN

What was it I'd just said about fate? About believin' in it?

Finn stepped back, bumpin' into Evvie, and she grasped his arms to steady him, lookin' from him to the woman and back to Jack in confusion.

"What? Who is it?" Kevin asked, squintin' at the woman.

"Kev, you need glasses. How many times I gotta tell ya," Jay said, chucklin'.

"Well, I'll be good goddamned," Ma said under her breath, and Jay and Kevin looked at her.

"Ma!" Jay laughed.

"Is that—" Takin' one step toward the woman, Kevin's face turned back into the sad little boy he'd been his whole life, but the look disappeared in half a second, replaced with his usual anger, but turned up to eleven on a ten-point scale.

"Yeah, Kev," Jack said, "that's our long-lost *mama*." He spat the word, and Jay gasped, jerkin' his head to look at her. He didn't even know who she was.

But she couldn't be our mama. Our mama was dead. I'd killed her.

Well, kinda.

It all seemed a little ridiculous 'cause I was lookin' right at her.

"*You* ran Oly off the road?" Kevin said through clenched teeth. "That's your Christmas gift after twenty fuckin' years? What the fuck, lady? You haven't done enough damage, you thought you'd try to kill our friend?"

The woman—the mother—*our* mother—sobbed once, coverin' her mouth with a shaky hand.

"Oh, you lemme at her." Ma squabbled with Jay while he wrapped his arms around her, tryin' to hold her back, and I laughed. It was such a fucked-up reality—our mama sittin' in front of us, alive after all this time, and I'd thought I'd been responsible for her death, and little ol' Ma tryin' to break free from Jay's grasp to get at her. Like a sitcom.

"Ma," Carey coaxed, "c'mon. Let's give 'em a minute."

"I'll go with Ma. Stay calm," Evvie whispered to Jack. I looked at my brother and saw hatred comin' outta his eyes like lasers. Evvie kissed his cheek, and he closed 'em, breathin' deep, like if he concentrated hard enough, he could soak her goodness in through his skin.

I wished it could work with Oly and me.

They left the room, Ma lookin' behind her from my brothers and me to our mama till Carey pulled her through the door. He came back a few seconds later, shut the door quietly, and stood on the other side of the room, just watchin' the fucked-up reality show unfold.

I stood.

"You were dead. I saw you there. There's no way you coulda survived that explosion."

"Saw her where?" Jack demanded. "What explosion?" It hadn't even occurred to me to warn my brothers. I just reacted. I walked to my… mother… and she stood from the table as I approached.

"The woman, the one you ran off the road? That's the love of my life." I towered over her, clenchin' my fists at my sides. "You coulda killed her, and right now, the gun in Carey's holster is the only thing in the world stoppin' me from stranglin' you." She blinked up at me with fear and trepidation in her eyes.

"I'm so sorry," she whispered, eyes shinin' with unshed tears. "She stopped to help me. My car broke down, but then he showed up and she saved me. Please, I'm so sorry. I think he wants to kill you."

"Who's that now?" Carey asked, perkin' up at the mention of people killin' other people.

"His name is—"

"Wait just a fuckin' minute. What do you mean you *saw* her?" Jack asked. He stood next to me, starin' at the side of my face, demandin' my attention.

Closin' my eyes, I took a deep breath, expandin' my lungs as far as they would go, and turned to face him. My brothers stood behind him, implorin' me with their eyes for an explanation. The pain and betrayal on their faces felt like it could rip a hole clean through my gut.

"I saw her in Colombia. When I was there with the Marines."

Jack's eyes narrowed and bored into mine. "That was, what, six months ago?" I nodded. "You saw... her," he said, inclinin' his head in our mother's direction but wouldn't look at her, "six fuckin' *months* ago and didn't think that was somethin' we might wanna know?"

"I'm sorry. I just— I didn't know how to tell you what I'd found. Who she... was. Who she'd become."

Outta the corner of my eye, I saw my mama hang her head.

"You gotta be kiddin' me. Is this a fuckin' joke?" Jack

laughed and shook his head. He clenched his jaw, hard. "I can't believe this." He turned to walk away from me, and she tried to stop him. She reached with her hand for his arm, but he rounded on her. "Don't you fuckin' dare touch me, woman." He stepped in front of her, less than a foot from her, starin' down into her eyes. "Don't."

Carey chose that moment to interrupt. "Sit down, Jack. Please."

"Fuck you," he snapped and stepped back several feet.

"Guys? Everybody sit down. Jack, please?" Carey prodded.

Jack walked around the table, as far from our mama as he could get, pulled a chair from under the table, and sat.

"This is— The situation is obviously pretty charged. Let's all just calm down. Dean, guys, please?"

My brothers sat near Jack, but nobody could take their eyes off the woman sittin' across from 'em. Except me. I watched their faces as I sat next to our mama, with one chair between us.

"I think it's best if you start talkin', Miss... Cade."

"There ain't nothin' she can say to excuse her absence over the last twenty years," Jack said to Carey, but to her, he said, "but you go 'head. Give it your best shot." The apathy comin' off his body permeated the stale little room.

"I... I don't... um..." Her voice sounded so small, and I remembered seein' her in Colombia like it was yesterday. She'd said somethin' about a man that day, too, but I'd been too pissed off to listen.

"Why don't you start with the man you were just talkin' about. I assume he's the other driver?"

"Oh. Yes. Okay. Um..." She took a deep breath. "His name is Santiago Muñoz. He's the son of the head of a drug cartel. Well, he was." She sniffled, wipin' her nose with the back of her coat sleeve. "His father is dead. He thinks Dean killed his father. That I conspired with Dean, with the US Military, to have his father and their business... associates killed."

"What?" I laughed, a little crazed, lookin' at her. It was the most ridiculous thing I'd ever heard. "We had nothin' to do with those people bein' killed."

She turned in her chair to face me. "When I saw you that day in the cantina, Santiago was there. Santi. That's what his father called him. He saw me talking to you. I don't think he put two and two together until recently. That you were my son."

She took a shaky breath. "I need to back up. I'm sorry. I just can't believe you're all here sitting right in front of me." She looked around the table at all of us. Jack glared at her, and Kevin crossed his arms over his chest, smilin' at her, but with *so* much disdain. It dripped from his face. I could almost reach out and touch it.

She took the hint, and her eyes dropped to her hands on the table. For the first time, I noticed there were scratches and a little blood on 'em, and she had a cut on her forehead.

"I met his father, Rigo—Rodrigo Muñoz—three years ago in Paris."

"Nobody gives a shit what your boyfriend's nickname was. Get to the fuckin' point," Jack ordered.

"Right. I-I didn't know who he was then. He... duped me, I guess. I believed he was just a businessman. A year later, I moved with him back to Colombia. I thought we would... Um, I guess that's not important." She shook her head. "I learned pretty quickly he was not who I believed him to be. And six months ago, after I'd seen Dean, Rigo was killed in an explosion. The very same day. All of the men involved in the cartel had been targeted, their homes blown up. No one survived. Except me, and well, Santi."

"What in the actual fuck are you talkin' about?" Finn laughed. "Are we on some kinda hidden camera show? This is— Are you off your rocker? Or you just makin' shit up so we'll, what, feel... bad for you? So you have a plausible excuse for walkin' out on your family?" He scrunched his face in confusion.

"No, sweet—" she started, but Finn cocked his head, warnin' her with his eyes at her almost-use of an endearment for him. "No, Finnigan. This isn't a joke. I'm not crazy."

Finn stood from his chair to pace. There wasn't much room for it, but he never had been able to sit still.

"'Scuse me, but there seems to be a lot missin'. I don't think we quite understand, Ma... uhh, ma'am." Jay scratched his head. "Yeah. I don't get it." He didn't look angry. He looked confused and sad.

"Lemme clear it up," I said, lookin' in my mother's lyin' eyes. It was insane how much they looked like Jack's. "Our mother was the wife, mistress, girlfriend—whatever you wanna call it—to the head of a powerful drug cartel in Colombia. That's what I didn't know how to tell you." Her face crumpled with shame, and I looked away.

I faced each of my brothers and then looked at my mama again. "She knew what those men had been up to. She knew it and she stayed. But a rival cartel moved against 'em. I lost brothers that day." My voice cracked as I remembered Denny and Mitch. And Oz.

"We tried to help the people in that town, and I lost half of my team in the gunfire between these two cartels. We didn't start the fight. We'd only been there doin' surveillance. I thought she died in the explosion. I never saw a body, but... I didn't think anybody coulda survived those explosions.

"That whole town was razed to the ground. I thought I killed her. I thought— She begged me to bring her home. She cried and moaned, but she knew who they were. And she stayed. I left her there, and we never woulda heard from her again, but her bank account got killed that day. Isn't that right?"

"Dean, no," she said, desperately. "There's so much more to it. I-I know you're all angry. You have every right to be, but this about your safety. Carolyn's safety. I didn't know he was looking for you. I didn't know. Until a few weeks ago, I thought he was still in Colombia or anywhere but here. But I saw an article online about"—she looked at Jack—"about Everlea. Her mother, the musician, she was a big deal in South America.

"I came home. I came home and I-I was trying to work up the courage to come to you." Tears leaked from her eyes, and she wiped 'em away with her fingers. I remembered those fingers caressin' my forehead when I was a little boy, when I was sick, or when she'd put me to bed at night. I remembered 'em clutchin' my shoulders the mornin' she left.

"I was in Jackson, but then I saw him. I think he saw the same article I did. It talked about Everlea and Jack and the ranch. There was a picture of all of you. It was one of those tabloid websites, and it talked about Everlea's mother, how she'd been having an affair with that man. It's just gossip nonsense, but it talked about me and how I'd— how I left you.

"Oh, God. I'm so sorry. I'm not explaining this right. There's so much more, but I saw him in Jackson. I couldn't believe he'd found me. You. But I followed him, and he watched her, Dean." She turned toward me. "He was watching Carolyn. I think he wants to hurt you both. As payment for killing his family. I tried. I tried to lead him away. I tried to scare her so she'd go to you. So you could protect her. But she's so stubborn!"

"You slashed Oly's tires? Made all those prank calls?" I asked and she nodded. "Why would you break into the clinic?"

"No, I-I didn't break into the clinic. You mean the animal clinic?"

"Yeah, someone broke in—" I said, but Kev interrupted me.

"So, lemme get this straight," he said, sittin' up straighter in his chair. "You expect us to believe these people held you hostage for two years, and then they all just conveniently died, and it took you six months to make it home? That's the stupidest shit I ever heard." Kev snorted and rolled his eyes. "What about the sixteen years *before* you met your drug lord lover?"

I looked at Carey. "Where's Oly?" Standin' from my chair, it scraped across the floor, makin' a screechin' sound that pierced my eardrums.

"She's in my office, I think. I asked her to stay here till we can figure out who this man is, where he is."

I didn't say anything. Openin' the door, I walked calmly from the room. Ma and Evvie both called my name when they saw me, but I just kept walkin'. When I knew they couldn't see me anymore, I leaned against the wall to catch my breath—maybe more like fell against the wall.

My mind raced round and round in circles, and nothin' made sense. I owed my family a better explanation, but I couldn't think. This man targeted Oly because of me, and I couldn't leave her exposed. I had to get back to her. I needed to be there to protect her. The rest would work itself out.

I hoped.

25

CAROLYN

I paced the waiting area of the Wisper sheriff's office.

Carey asked my parents and me to wait in his office, but I needed to see Dean. I didn't want to interrupt them though. I heard raised voices in the conference room, and I knew Evvie and Ma waited outside of it. I heard their voices, too, but I couldn't talk to anyone. I just needed Dean. My parents had grilled me already, but I couldn't concentrate enough to answer their questions.

Daisy Cade was alive? And she had come home? I mean... what the fuck?!

Dean was freaking out. He had to be. He thought he'd killed her. All this time and she was alive? And now she was here?

My mom stepped out of Carey's office. "Oly, honey, please tell us what's going on."

"Mom, I really don't know."

"Are you sure you're okay?" my dad asked.

"I'm fine."

"Okay, I'm gonna call Mike about your truck."

"Dad, it's Christmas. Don't worry about the goddamn truck."

"Oly!" my mom scolded me.

I looked up from my pacing. "I'm sorry," I said, realizing I'd cursed at my dad.

"It's okay, Ols." He hugged me. "C'mon, Susan, let's give her a minute. I could use some fresh air." My dad pulled my mom outside, and I continued my pacing.

Four minutes later (I counted), I heard a door open in the hallway, and one minute after that, Dean appeared in front of me. When he saw me, he stopped walking.

"Dean? Have you seen her?"

Oh. He looked in my eyes, and I saw eight-year-old Dean in front me, not the hard, disciplined Marine. He reached his hand out to steady himself against the reception desk but then just crumpled down to the floor.

I ran to him.

Holding and rocking him, I didn't say a word and neither did he, but I felt his heart hammering in his chest. I leaned back against the side of the tall reception counter, pulling him with me.

"Dean? Talk to me. Are you okay?"

Finally, he looked back at me. "I didn't kill her. I didn't kill my mama."

"No." I shook my head. "No. You're good. You're a good man. I never thought anything else. It was never your fault," I promised, caressing his scruffy cheek with my fingers.

He trembled and cried silently in my arms, and I shushed him and rocked him more, until we heard his brother's voices as they left the conference room and entered the hallway. Jack, especially, didn't sound pleased.

Dean looked in my eyes. "I need to get outta here."

"Okay. We can go to my house," I whispered.

He nodded. "You still got your gramp's shotgun and shells?"

"Yes. My dad keeps it up."

"Okay. Let's go."

We escaped and I brushed my parents off. I told them I'd explain everything later, but I knew my mom would get the gossip from Ma. Dean drove us in his truck to my house really slowly, and when we pulled into the driveway, he shut the truck off and pulled his cell phone from his back pocket.

"I need to make a call. Stay with me?"

"Of course."

He hit his screen a few times and held the phone to his ear, but he reached for my hand and held it, looking in my eyes.

"Bigsy? No, Oly's okay. It's a long story, but I wanted to ask you somethin'. Do you know when that group meets? The one you told me about? I, uh, I think it might be a good idea for me." He listened for a minute while Bigsy talked. "Okay. I'll call you tomorrow. Thanks, brother. Merry Christmas."

Clicking his phone off, he dropped it into his jacket pocket.

"Group?"

Taking a deep breath, he released it slowly. "Yeah. I've been havin' anxiety, about a lotta things but... about my service. About my mama. And about the kid. I... I think I need help. I need to talk to someone about it. I get these... attacks. Panic attacks. At least, I think that's what they are."

I threw my arms around him, plastering my body to his. "Thank you for tellin' me. I'm so proud of you."

He sighed, burying his nose in my hair. "Thank you, duck." We breathed together for a moment. "Let's get inside. It's cold out here, and I bet we won't have much time till my brothers or Carey or someone shows up, knockin' on your door."

"Okay."

When we were inside, Dean found my grandpa's gun and loaded it, then we sat on the couch and just stared at each other.

"What did she say?" I finally whispered.

He shrugged. "Dunno. A lotta things. She says that man, Muñoz, he's after us. He thinks she and I had somethin' to do with killin' his family. I didn't, but I don't think he much cares about anything I have to say.

"But it was my mother who slashed your tires. The prank calls. She thought you'd run to me for protection. She tried to scare you." A slow sly smile spread across his face. "She said, 'I tried, but she's just so stubborn!'"

He laughed, and when I saw the smile on his face, I did too. I crawled into his lap, and he wrapped his arms around me, holding me against his chest, and I tucked my face into the crook of his neck.

"I told you. I've been tellin' you for years. You're a good man. There's no one better."

"Oly."

His body became stiff, and I pulled my head out of his neck to look at him. "This is where you push me away again, isn't it? You're gonna say you're broken, you're damaged. Not good enough." I sighed and crawled off his lap.

Right on cue, there was a knock on my door.

"It's fine. It's… whatever." Taking a deep breath, I stood and shook my head. "It's for you. I don't wanna be rude, but I need a minute. Invite whoever it is inside. I'll go make coffee."

"Oly, I—"

"Don't, Dean. There's nothin' more to say. Just get the door."

Instead of the kitchen, I ducked into my tiny second bedroom. I closed the door, slid down the wall, and cried my eyes out. I heard Carey's voice and Daisy's. I really had no business going out there. How freakin' uncomfortable. It was my house, but they needed to talk.

But after a few minutes, Daisy knocked and spoke through the door. "Carolyn? Are you in there?" *Crap*. I stood, smoothed my sweater, wiped the tears off my face, and opened the door.

"Mrs. Cade. I'm sorry. I don't mean to be rude but—"

"Just call me Daisy, and Carolyn, you're not being rude. *I'm* sorry, sorry to intrude. I just wanted to apologize. Clearly, I went about this all wrong." She stepped in the room with me and shut the door. "I was afraid. Afraid to face the boys. I should have gone straight to the police."

"It's okay. I think I understand."

She smiled, reaching for my hand. "It's so weird seeing you all grown up." She caught my eye. "I remember you when you were five. And you're being so gracious. Thank you. This might be... inappropriate, but I've spent a very long time hiding and not telling the truth. I don't want to do it anymore."

Wiping a runaway tear from my cheek, she said, "It looks like I've interrupted something between you and Dean. This is probably going to sound creepy, but since I've been watching you, I've noticed the... difficulty between you two. And I, in *no* way, can claim to know what's going on with him, but it's clear to see he loves you still. He's loved you your whole lives."

I shook my head. She was right. It was inappropriate and I felt weird. I felt like being nice to her betrayed Dean.

"I know," she said. "This is weird. It's just, I don't know if he's told you, but that day in Colombia? It couldn't have been easy for him, for so many reasons. But the death he saw that day? It had to have caused him pain. You love him too. You always have. You know how empathetic he can be. How much love he has. Watching those people die— Some were his friends…"

It felt so bizarre. Most of my life I'd hated this woman. Dean and his brothers held so much animosity for her, but seeing her like this, as she talked about what Dean had faced that day, I saw all the love in the world in her eyes. Pain. Regret.

She hurt for him.

If she'd never cared about him like he'd always thought, she wouldn't have said those things to me. She wouldn't look so tortured.

"I know. He told me a little."

She nodded. "I'm sorry. That's all I wanted to say. I'm sorry you've been dragged into this." She turned to leave the room, but I stopped her.

"Why'd you do it? Why'd you leave? You broke their hearts. All of them. He blamed himself his whole life."

"I— It's not— I-I can't." She looked all around my little room. "It's not something I can talk about right now." Her eyes dropped to the floor.

I felt like such a brat. Who was I to demand answers from her? Dean wasn't my boyfriend. He was barely my friend at this point. As mad as I was at her for all the pain she'd caused him, I still felt sorry for her. She seemed sad and scared, and I couldn't imagine coming back after twenty years to face five angry adult sons.

"I'm sorry. I shouldn't have said anything. It's not my place."

"No. It's not that. This is your house. It's just not such an easy subject. And I think I should talk to the boys first."

"Right. Of course."

"I think Carey would like to speak with you."

"Okay," I said, and I followed her to the living room. Dean stood in the middle of it, looking lost again.

"Hey, Oly," Carey said. "I just wanted to let you know we think the man, Santiago Muñoz, has left the area. His car was found south of Yellowstone. The state police were able to identify it because of the makeover you gave the back end." Carey smirked. "I'd still like you to stay with Dean, just until he's found. The FBI thinks he'll head to Canada, but he could double back. So just be alert. All of you."

"Thanks, Carey," I said.

"Alright, I'll uh, I'll talk to you both later. Mrs. Cade, c'mon with me."

"Wait. Where are you takin' her?" Dean asked Carey. Then to his mother, he said, "You're leavin'? Again?" He sounded confused, hurt, and angry.

"No, Dean." She shook her head. "I'm not leaving. I'm staying in Wisper."

"Then you should come to the ranch. I mean, I think it's a good idea if everybody sticks together."

"No. I've already ruined your Christmas. I'll be in town. Sheriff Michaels said he knows a place I can stay. I think it's probably a good idea if I give you boys some time. But thanks for, I don't know, hearing me out, I guess." She walked to the door but turned and looked at Dean. "I am so very, very sorry." It was painfully awkward, but I didn't think anybody knew what to say. She walked onto the porch quietly and closed my front door.

"Carey—" Dean started.

Carey put his hands up in front of his chest. "She's stayin' with Abey tonight. That way we know she's protected. I think José's little apartment over the diner is for rent. Abey said she'll drive Daisy over to talk to him tomorrow. I dunno what her financial situation is, but the apartment is cheap."

"That's fine, I guess," Dean said.

"Okay, well, try to salvage whatcha can of Christmas. I'll stop by the ranch later for our annual Christmas whiskey."

"How'd it end?" Dean asked. "After I left the station."

Pressing his lips together, Carey scratched the beard on his chin. He sighed. "Not well. It was like just now. Awkward." He flashed a weak smile and shook his head a little.

"Thanks, Carey," Dean said, and they did that macho "hug your brother but beat him on the back at the same time thing," but Carey didn't let go.

"I didn't know you lost your team. Dean, I'm here, man. You can talk to me anytime. We're brothers, you and me. Hear me?" Carey pulled away, looking at him.

Dean nodded, but I saw so much emotion simmering behind his eyes.

A few minutes later, Daisy and Carey left, and Dean and I stood there just looking at each other again until I realized it was pointless. We could want each other till the cows came home, but if he was determined to be miserable, to continue to hate himself, as much as I wanted to, I couldn't change his mind.

"Okay, well, I'm gonna grab a few more things to take back to the ranch. I'll just be a minute," I said, turning to go, but he grabbed my wrist and held tight.

I turned back. "What? What is there left to say? If you won't—"

He clasped his hand over my mouth to stop me, but then caressed my face, wrapping his fingers behind my neck.

"Stop. I heard whatcha said to my... to Daisy. My mama. I dunno what to call her." He squeezed my wrist, then released it. "I heard you defendin' me. You've always been my defender. My fighter. I know you're mad at me 'cause you put your heart out there last night, and I kinda shot you down. I'm sorry. But you were right. You're always right and I'm done not listenin'.

"What you said was right. I underestimated you, I didn't trust you, and I'm guilty of wallowin' in my own self-pity for far too long." He dropped his hand from my neck and took one step back, like he feared retribution for what he'd just said.

"That is not what I said."

"Not word for word, but that's what it all boils down to, ain't it? I didn't trust you enough to tell you my fears, and I didn't believe you when you told me you loved me and wanted a life with me. And I acted like a fool, walkin' around feelin' sorry for myself while you were out there hurtin' and workin' hard to make your dreams come true.

"And you were right last night when you said I was lettin' my mama win. Jesus, how ridiculous does that sound? I thought I was a grown man. And now that she's here, it's all just so... stupid.

"I never wanted to deny you. I never turned it off, but I convinced myself you were better off without me. That you would move on, that you should. I expected to live without you, in pain for the rest of my life. I built this wall inside my head. Whenever it hurt too much, I dropped the wall. Hid behind it. It kept everyone else out, but it didn't do much to keep you out. It couldn't. You're inside me. Inside my soul."

"Why, Dean? I'm not better than you. I don't deserve more happiness or success than you do. I want those things in my life, but I don't want them without you. I could never love anyone the way I love you. Don'tcha know that?"

"I know it now. But Oly, all my life I felt like a failure. I felt like I shoulda done somethin' more to make her stay. If I'd said somethin' to her that mornin' or if I'd done somethin'. If I'd been a better son. If I could've spared my brothers their pain, my dad. I thought I was the worst son in the whole world. The worst brother.

"I thought I didn't deserve your love. Even before the Marines. And when you were in California, you grew so much, experienced so much, matured, and, duck, you blossomed. You came back so strong and smart and ready to take on the world. I thought I would hold you back. College was never for me.

"I guess my resolve started fallin' away when Evvie showed up. And then I saw Jack losin' her, and I saw how much he loved her. I thought about you every goddamn minute of every day. And then, a month later, there you were, two feet away from me.

"But, Oly, don't you ever hold back, okay? Not for me. If there's somethin' you wanna do, or need to do, or somewhere you wanna go, you do it. You go. I don't ever wanna be the reason you don't reach for your dreams."

"I promise if you promise too. There will be things I wanna do, places to go, but Dean, I want you to go with me. Someday, we'll have babies, and then they'll come too. Would you do that? Do you want that?" I stepped closer, lifting my hands to hold his face between them, and he covered them, holding my hands in place with his.

"That's all I want. I want you. Wherever that takes me, however I can have you."

"So, we're done fightin'?" I asked, and he tried not to smile.

"Yeah. We done."

"I like it when you talk cowboy."

"Oh yeah? I like it when you curse at me. When you yell at me. You're a lot feistier than I remember. Also, have you noticed your accent gets thicker with your anger?" He chuckled.

"Yeah, well, I've been pissed off and horny for a long time."

"Well now, s'pose we oughta do somethin' 'bout that," he whispered, releasing my hands and gripping my hips, digging his fingers into my skin.

I moaned when it hurt. When I felt the desperation in his body.

"What was it you said about pain? About likin' it?"

I licked my lips slowly and bit the skin, hard.

"I didn't mean for it to hurt, but it's so hard for me to talk about how I feel. Maybe I can get better at that. I dunno. I hope I can. But I can *show* you. I can show you how much I love you, how *hard* I love you. That's what I was doin'. I needed you to know what I felt inside. I just couldn't say it."

A wicked grin spread across my lips, and I gazed up at him though half-closed lids.

I arched a brow.

"Do it again?"

26

CAROLYN

Dean seemed to like sex a little on the rougher side, too, but he especially liked it when I ordered him to bite and suck and pinch. He liked to hold me down. He wanted to possess and own every inch of me, and I *loved* it.

I craved it more and more.

The word "harder," when it came from my mouth, had become a personal invitation for him to find new and swoonworthy ways to make my body sore for days.

I'd never felt so free. So confident.

And Dean had never expressed himself to me more than he had in the last week. It was the night before Jack and Evvie's wedding, and Dean and I had holed ourselves away for a break from wedding prep in the little room above the barn.

He'd discovered he liked to torture me a little.

As he pounded into me over and over and over, I clutched his stupid sexy arms, attempting to hold onto him as he bucked me up off the bed. But when I was seconds coming, he pulled out and slid down my body, the sweat from his skin slicking mine, and I writhed and begged him to make me come as he held my legs open, as wide as they would go, and feasted on my body.

If I touched him, he stopped licking, stealing his fingers from my weeping core and tsking his tongue in admonishment. But I couldn't help myself, and finally, I grasped his hair between my fingers and yanked, and he growled and raised up on his knees. He flipped my body and yanked my ass in the air, spread my legs to the sides, and pinned my wrists to the bed with his hands.

"Don't move."

"Mmng." It was the only response my brain would allow as he held me captive and ate my pussy, hands-free, from behind. Oh my God, just thinking those words made my core clench and squeeze in emptiness without his cock to fill me. Arousal dripped from my body, and he lapped it up, moaning and groaning and rocking the bed with his urgent thrusts, fucking into thin air because he wanted back inside my body so badly.

I wanted him inside just as bad.

"Dean, please. Take me, *fuck* me," I begged, pumping my hips, seeking any contact. Anything!

Growling, he stopped all movement, and I whimpered and panted and tried to press my ass back into his face. I felt movement behind me, but I couldn't see what he was doing.

Oh, I was a wanton hussy now, and I felt *no* shame.

Finally, he released my wrists, and I rolled them to restore a little blood flow. He backed away from me; I couldn't feel the heat from his body anymore.

"No," he said, and I scrambled up to my knees, turning to see him relaxing back onto his elbows at the end of the bed. He arched one beautiful blond eyebrow, and his sexy gray eyes lured me in. "You fuck me."

Oh God, his cock throbbed and practically stood straight

up in the air. It glistened, wet and ready, in the moonlight coming in the window. And the lust on his face, the trust, and impatient longing—I climbed up his body so fast, like a cracked-out Komodo dragon, and impaled myself on his cock. His head fell back, hanging off the end of the bed, and I fucked him silly.

Leaning down, I licked and sucked his chest, his nipples, and he lifted back up to watch me pleasure myself with his body, thrashing and moaning and owning it. He gripped my ass and shoved me down as hard as he could with every single voluptuous swoop of my hips. I swore I felt his thrusts in my lungs.

Clawing his chest and ribs with my fingernails, down his legs, I left trails of reddened scratch marks. He hissed at the pain but fucked up into me harder, and I moaned and pulled his hair again, leaning down to kiss him.

The kiss was consuming, possessive. I used my whole mouth, my breath, my tongue and teeth. I rubbed my face against his beard and my breasts against his chest. His hair abraded my skin as I rode his slick cock in and out of my body, and I loved it.

I loved the scratch, the pinch and pain. The burn.

I loved it because it was his body and mine, his angst and frustration with life, his pain and mine, crashing together. Releasing each other.

"Fuck, Oly," he whispered into my mouth, reaching up to cover my breasts with his hands, squeezing and rolling my nipples between his fingers and thumbs, pinching hard. I cried out and came and strangled his cock with my pussy.

He yanked me down one last time, connecting our bodies together desperately, as he drove into me as hard as he could. I exploded all over him, and his head fell back again as he grunted and growled and came inside me.

I moaned in satisfaction, draping my body over his. Den of iniquity, indeed. "How are you feelin'? After meetin' with the guys and your mom?"

"Are you kiddin' me?" he choked and sputtered. "After *that*, you wanna talk about my mama?"

"Yeah."

He contracted his abs and rolled me, pinning me to the bed and pumping slowly as we came down from the high.

He kissed me and untangled his body from mine, sighing. "I dunno. Jack's still pissed at me. I don't expect him to get over that too quick." He worked to catch his breath, pushing my sweat-soaked hair away from my mouth. "But I think he understands why I never said anything. Kev is just pissed at everybody, as usual. And Finn and Jay, they're dealin'. I think. It's just— It feels weird, her bein' back. And I guess... I'm relieved. I didn't kill her."

"Of course you didn't. Did she really say she'd been held against her will? Do you believe her?"

"Yeah, that's what she says." He rolled onto his back. "I dunno what I believe. If what she says is true, it had nothin' to do with why she left when we were little. She won't say why. But yeah, she says that Rigo man kept her there, in his house. She tried to escape a couple times, but they beat her. After that, she stopped tryin'. She gave up. She said she always had a guard—the man the authorities mistook for Rigo's son, Santi, when they looked through the wreckage for survivors. It's why nobody knew he was alive."

"They beat her?" I whispered.

"Yeah," he whispered, too, shuddering. "Those men, they were the most disgustin' human bein's. They lived like kings while most of the townspeople suffered in squalor. I don't doubt they woulda done it. And I—" He sighed again, hiding his eyes with his forearm over his face.

"What? Hey. Talk to me."

"I didn't listen that day, when I saw her down there. I barely heard what she said when she begged me to help her. If I had, I mean, I coulda— maybe she—"

I sat up, pulled his arm away from his eyes, and held his hand. "Dean, you can't do that to yourself. You had no reason to trust her. Maybe what she said is true, but there's still a lot missin'. Where's she been for twenty years? She only met that guy a few years ago."

"I know. It's just, I keep thinkin' it goes against my character. Or what everybody tells me my character is. You know? I remember her tellin' me I had so much love, that I was 'a lover not a fighter.' But I kinda became the opposite after she left. If I hadn't, maybe I wouldn't have pushed her away in Colombia. If she hadn't left us, maybe I never woulda chosen to join the military at all. I dunno. It's just a lot to think about. My head's spinnin'."

"Well, I think you're both. You do love big. You always have. Why do you think I couldn't let you go? I knew no one could ever love me the way you did. Your love spoiled me. Ruined me for all other men." I purred the last bit in my best Scarlett O'Hara accent.

"Oh, you better not be jokin'. Since I'm both, I'll fight anybody tries to win you away." He rolled again, planking himself above me.

"That's my point." Winding my arms around his neck and my legs around his waist, I hung from his body like a spider from a web. "You love hard and big, but you'd die to protect me, your brothers. Your family. And you've always fought for the underdog. Your fight is *part* of your love. The best part."

"Dunno about that," he said, lowering us back to the bed, "but I'm gonna fight for you every day of our lives. But let's be clear, you are no underdog. You're a fighter too. Thank you for fightin' for us when I didn't. Thank you for never givin' up on me, stubborn woman." He smiled, and his eyes twinkled molten chrome as the little lines around them crinkled. "I love you."

"I love you too." He kissed my neck in soft little pecks, then rubbed his beard against my tender, over-sensitized skin, and I shivered. "But Dean?"

"Yeah?" Lowering his head, he nuzzled his nose between my breasts.

"I believe her. Your mom."

He pulled back to look at me. "You do? Why?"

I shook my head and sighed. "Christmas day at my house, after we left the sheriff's station—she was overwhelmingly sorry. There was so much pain in her eyes. I can't describe it. It's just a feelin', but I think she's been through a lot. More than she's tellin' you." I reached up to push his hair out of his eyes. "You didn't see the look on her face when she talked about you and your brothers." He rolled away from me and sat up facing the window. "I don't know why she left you, but I don't think she did it because she's a bad person. There's more to it. I'm sure of it."

"So, what, Oly? Are you sayin' I should just forgive her? 'Cause I can't do that. We don't even have kids yet but think about it. If we did, can you even imagine leavin' 'em? Walkin' away and never lookin' back?"

"No." I crawled over to him, climbing up to press my body around him. I laid my cheek against his back. "No. That's not what I'm sayin' at all. I'm just sayin', I dunno, maybe just try to keep an open mind?"

Laying his hand over mine on his shoulder, he pulled until I crawled around into his lap.

"I will. Because you asked me to. Duck, I've been broken

without you. I don't ever wanna be that way again. If you're here with me, by my side, I can face anything. I trust you. I trust us. So I'll do it, or… I'll try."

"Thank you." I held his face between the palms of my hands, kissing his lips so softly. He smiled, and they became soft pillows under mine.

"Mmm. Thank you," he whispered and kissed my nose. "But Jay's enamored with her. That concerns me."

"Why?"

"'Cause he don't remember her leavin' or the sadness that clung to the ranch for years. He was so little. He looked at her the other day with awe. Like she was some answer to his prayers."

"He's never had a mother."

"He has Ma."

"I know but—Ma's wonderful, please don't misunderstand me—but there's somethin' different about your own mother. You know? Jay's never had that. I'm sure there's a pull there for him, a desire to be loved by her. He can't help that."

"The problem is he doesn't know the damage she can cause. The pain she can inflict. I don't want her to hurt him. She can do whatever she wants to me, to Jack, Finn. We can take it. Maybe even Kev, but she can't fuckin' hurt Jay. I won't let her."

"Hey."

"What?" He sighed, looking in my eyes.

"You are such a good brother. A good man. I love you." I kissed his lips again, this time not so softly.

"I love you too," he breathed into my mouth. "I can't tell you how good it feels to say that to you finally."

"Are you worried about the man? That Santiago guy?" I asked, 'cause I was worried.

"The FBI thinks he might already be in Canada. They're still lookin' for him."

"What do *you* think?"

"I think… he'll be back. If he really believes I killed his family, he'll come back for me." He looked in my eyes. "But he won't like what he finds when he does."

"What do we do?"

"We keep our eyes open. I'm gonna be stuck to you like glue, and Manny will be at the clinic a lot. I've already spoken to him. And when he can't be, Bigsy's volunteered for the job."

"Really? I like him. He's good for you."

"Bigsy?" He chuckled. "How?"

"I dunno." I shrugged. "You help each other. Seems like he helps you get out of your head."

He snorted. "Yeah, 'cause he's relentless. What about your friend? Luuk? That guy's somethin' else. He just barreled in here." He laughed. "I got no idea what he's sayin' half the time. It's nice, though, him agreein' to stay, to help you at the clinic while Doc's out."

"Yeah. He's takin' farm calls for me tomorrow so I can be here for the wedding even though he has no idea where he is, doesn't know the area, the clients. He's a really great friend. But… did you see the way Luuk looked at—"

He interrupted me, his eyebrows raised to the ceiling. "Did you see the way *he* looked at *Luuk*? Have I been missin' somethin'?"

I giggled. "I think so. I missed it too. Brady noticed. Or he guessed."

"He did?"

I nodded. "Mmhm. You okay with that?"

"Well, yeah. I mean, if that's what makes my brother happy. It sure would be nice to see him smilin' for a change."

"It's just, I know your dad was…"

"What? Intolerant?"

"You said it. I was gonna say mean."

"Yeah, well, he could be both. But he's gone. His opinion don't matter anymore." Wrapping his arms around my back, he pulled me against his chest. "Maybe his opinion never shoulda mattered in the first place." He rubbed his chin along my shoulder, and my whole body became one big goose-bump. My nipples pebbled and poked his chest, and he moaned.

"Can I ask you somethin'?" I smirked, peering up at him through my eyelashes, rubbing his scratchy cheeks with my fingertips.

"Anything, duck. I'll do anything for you."

"Will you grow this beard out? I like it."

"You do? Really?"

"Oh yeah," I purred and he laughed. God, I loved when he laughed.

"I thought I kinda resembled a scraggly bum," he said, stroking his beard with his fingers.

"Oh no. I love it. I want it between my thighs."

He growled and kissed me.

"My feisty duck."

The End
For Now

If you liked the book (or loved it, I hope), please leave a review—even just a few words would help—wherever you buy your books, on Amazon, Goodreads, or Bookbub. We self-published indie authors rely heavily upon reviews to get our stories out to the masses. And thank you. I know it takes time to do this. I appreciate the time out of your day and the effort.

Read on for an excerpt from Kevin's book… Busted.

BUSTED

Chapter One
Kevin

I watched from the back of my horse in the front paddock under a gray winter sky (yeah, right, like I was my brothers, all broody and whiny—gimme a break) as a big blue GMC Sierra raced up the lane to stop right smack-dab in front of my house. My family had been a little on edge, so it was no surprise to me when my older brother, Dean, appeared on our front porch with a shotgun aimed at the driver of the unknown truck as he emerged from the cab.

I was too far away to see or hear what the blond-haired, sexy-bodied man said. Yeah, so maybe I needed glasses, but I still had a pretty good view of the shape of his body 'cause he wasn't wearin' a coat. Tall, lean, invitin'—fuckable, if he happened to swing that way, which he wouldn't 'cause this was Wyoming—but he raised his hands in front of his chest and advanced slowly.

After a few seconds, my brother lowered his gun, and his girlfriend, Oly Masterson, emerged from the house in her pink pajamas and snow boots, squealed (I heard that), threw her arms up into the air, and ran down the porch stairs toward the stranger. She jumped into his arms, and he hugged her close.

My brother and Oly had just gotten back together after a long time apart, like, literally a couple days ago, so I was a little confused as to why Dean didn't pummel the guy into the snow. To my surprise, the guy released Oly, and she grabbed his hand as they climbed the porch stairs, and all three of 'em went into my house like they were BFFs.

The guy looked hot and I was curious, so I fed Classic some hay and left him happy in his stall and stalked up the gravel lane leadin' to my house to investigate. I still had an air cast on my right leg from a break three months before, and I had to cover it with a stupid rubber boot and eight damn socks so my toes didn't freeze off. I hobbled a little like an idiot, but I finally made my way to the front porch.

When I pushed the kitchen door open and barreled in like I always did, my whole body was assaulted with the sounds, scents, and sights of my nightmares. Or my dreams.

I couldn't fuckin' decide.

I heard my brother introducin' the guy to my family.

"… and this is Ma." Dean stepped away, and I saw the sexified stranger extendin' his hand to my best friend, my surrogate mama.

"*Hallo*, Ma. Pleasure to meet you. Luuk van der Wouden." It sounded kinda like he said Luke Vandervowden, like he described himself as lukewarm, but he wasn't. He was hot AF. I hadn't seen his face yet, but his body… *Good grief.*

Ma held out her small hand and he clasped it gently, givin' it the tiniest of shakes.

This had to be Oly's friend from veterinary school. She'd been expectin' him.

"Luke?"

"No, *mam*, Luuk. Think of it as L-E-U-K. But you can call me whatever you like. My English friends call me LV. Except Carolina." He turned his perfectly coiffed blond head to the side to smirk at Oly, and I choked on my own spit. Just the side of his face, with his dimple and his full lips—oh my

God. And the sound of his voice? Pure fuckin' sex, even with the weird accent.

"Well, aren't you a charmer," Ma cooed, sittin' back in the old brown recliner in the livin' room. "LV? Sounds like Alvie. Maybe that's what I'll call you." She laughed. "Well, Alvie, this is Jay, Dean's youngest brother, and have you met Carey?" She motioned to the two dumbasses sittin' on the floor.

"*Hallo*, good to meet you, Carey. Jay, it's nice to meet you as well."

Jay and Carey stood to shake the guy's long-fingered hand.

"We spoke on the phone," Carey said.

"We did?"

"Yeah, I'm Sheriff Michaels. We talked when you called about Oly's accident the other day."

"Oh, *ja*, of course."

Carey relaxed back on the floor into the ridiculous bean bag chair he'd previously occupied, and the guy smiled, lookin' a little confused, probably at the *super* professional image of the Sheriff of Teton County perched in a bean bag chair. Man, we really needed to invest in some new furniture.

"Good to meet you, Luuk," Jay said. "You hungry? We got enough food to feed an army this mornin'."

"Sure, sure, *ja*. I'm actually starving. I have been on the road all night."

"Luuk, you drove all the way here?" Oly asked. "I thought you flew. That's not a rental?"

"No. I bought it a few weeks ago. Did I forget to tell you? And *ja*, I drove straight here. Carolina, I thought you had been highjacked."

I snorted.

"Carjacked. I tried to call, Lookie Loo. I'm sorry."

Lookie Loo? What a stupid nickname.

"*Ja*, but by then, I was somewhere in the middle of—Where am I?" He laughed, and all the blood in my head rushed to my dick when the silky sound of his voice entered my bloodstream through my ears. "I spoke to your parents, but I lost my cell signal. It's okay. I'm just so relieved you're not hurt."

"So, Alvie, where you from?" Ma asked. Jay came into the kitchen and looked me up and down, standin' in the middle of the room, frozen, hard, and stupid. What? So maybe I didn't get out much. I couldn't remember the last time I'd seen a guy so hot, though I hoped Jay couldn't tell what I was thinkin'. I sat at the kitchen table, unlacin' my boot and removin' my stupid cast.

"Eh, originally I come from Oudewater, a small farming town, but also we lived in Amsterdam for a short time. In the Netherlands."

"Have a seat, sweetheart," Ma said. "Oh, I bet it's beautiful there. I've always wanted to travel. I just never really had the chance. Do your parents still live there?"

"No, *mam*, they passed when I was fifteen." He sat on the couch next to my almost-sis-in-law, Evvie, and she smiled and patted his leg.

"I'm so sorry. Please forgive me."

"No, no, Ma, please. It was a long time ago." He smiled a little awkwardly, like maybe he didn't really wanna talk about his family, but he also didn't wanna make Ma uncomfortable.

"Oh, honey. Well, who raised you then? Do you have brothers or sisters?" I could hear Ma adoptin' him in my mind. She kinda tended to do that. Ma—our lady of lost boys.

"No, it's just me. I stayed in boarding school until I graduated. Then I went to university and then to vet school, where I met Carolina."

"Oh, you poor dear," Ma said and he smiled at her, but somethin' sad flashed across his face, or at least the half of it I could see. "Well, congratulations on your graduation, honey. What an accomplishment."

He tilted his head a little. "*Dank je wel, mam.*" He sounded completely taken back by Ma's praise.

"Boardin' school, what was that like?" Jay asked.

"It was pretty boring. I got into trouble a lot. I guess you could say I had a habit of trying to make my own fun."

Carey snickered and Jay laughed, walkin' back into the livin' room. He shoved a huge plate of food into Luuk's hands, and Luuk thanked him. God, that voice. Like a low, relaxin' hum.

I took the opportunity to walk in there to get a better look at the guy, and when he saw me, he choked on his first bite of bacon and eggs! Hm. Interestin' development. Did he like what he saw? I sure did.

He was sexy as shit! Blond hair, blue eyes for days, dark eyebrows, and his jawline coulda cut through leather. Two-day scruff covered it, framin' a smile to die for. 'Cept, he didn't smile. Somethin' dark and... intense hid behind his eyes. He stared up at me, slack-jawed, and I arched an eyebrow. Oh man.

Catch, *fuck*, and release.

"Luuk, this is Kevin," Oly said, and he glanced at her for half a second before lookin' back at me.

"*Hallo*, nice—" he lifted his arm to cough into it, clearin' his throat, "nice to see you, Kevin."

I didn't respond. I just stood there like an idiot, lookin' at him. I kinda felt like I was stuck in a trance—I couldn't look away from his aqua-blue eyes.

Finally, Sheriff Dickwad reached over and yanked on my pant leg, and I lost my balance. I tipped over but regained it before fallin' on my face in front of, literally, the sexiest man I'd ever laid eyes on. I pounced on Carey, took his ass down, pulled his arm around his back, and shoved his face against the wood floor.

He rolled me off him and sat up. "Quit bein' a jerk. Sit down and join us," he said, grabbin' a ridiculously large bucket of popcorn from the floor, shovelin' a handful in his mouth.

"Fuck you, Sheriff. Did you really get elected, or did the other guy just *die*? And why you eatin' popcorn at nine in the mornin'?"

"Kevin Christian Cade, watch your mouth in front of our guests, or I'll wash it out with soap."

"Yes, ma'am. Sorry." Yeah, okay, I wanted to be cool in front of Dutch Hot Guy, but I couldn't be rude to Ma.

"Nice, Kevin," Jay said, and Carey smacked the back of my head, causin' my hair to fall in my face, and I coulda sworn I saw Luuk, outta the corner of my eye, watch me push it away. He licked his lips.

"We're havin' a movie marathon. We finally talked Evvie into somethin' other than Christmas movies." Carey leaned closer to me. "So fuck you too," he whispered, thinkin' he'd be the one to get away with a little profanity.

"Carey Michaels, you may be the sheriff, but I'll still tan your hide," Ma scolded. "Show a little decorum, would ya? Jeez-o-pete, what's the matter with y'all? Buncha hooligans."

Sexy Luuk chuckled, and I turned away from Carey to face the TV, tryin' to act like the hottest guy on the planet wasn't sittin' right behind me. I felt pretty confident from his physical reactions to me. He thought I was hot, too, and I planned on takin' full fuckin' advantage of that.

Contrary to what my brothers believed, I hadn't had sex

with anybody in a *long* time, and by sheer coincidence, I'd just found the guy to break that unlucky streak.

I sat with my back to him, flexin' my shoulders while I pretended to watch whatever stupid movie played. I knew he watched me. I felt it, like he had lasers in his eyes and aimed 'em right between my shoulder blades.

A lotta people liked watchin' me. I'd never had a shortage of admirers. Mostly women, unfortunately, but I knew I looked good. I still felt his eyes on me while he ate, and everyone else casually asked questions about his life and work, and I listened to his every word, plottin' how I might get him on his knees in some dark, secret spot.

"So, you're visiting with Oly for New Year's?" Evvie asked.

"Em, yes. Well, actually, I'm going to work with her at the veterinary clinic. I was supposed to interview with Dr. Prittchard, but now, I will full in to help Carolina while he recovers from his stroke."

"Fill in, dear," Ma corrected him. "Isn't that sweet of you. I'm sure Doc will appreciate the help." She swooned and I rolled my eyes. Dude sounded like a goody-two-shoes to me. A hot-as-fuck goody-two-shoes, but still.

"Seriously, I can't thank you enough, Luuk. You are totally savin' my butt," Oly said. "I have no idea what I would do if you couldn't help me. I've been a vet for five minutes. I can't do this by myself."

"Of course you can, Carolina. But I'm happy to help. Denver was not really working out for me. I much prefer a mixed practice, and the clinic there is strictly small animals. I miss cows and horses."

"You're in the right place then," Jay said, chucklin'. "Here, Luuk, lemme get your plate." He stood and stepped toward Luuk.

"No, no, please, relax. I need to stretch my legs." The couch creaked, his clothes rustling when he stood.

"Alright, well, make yourself at home then. Grab a soda or there's coffee, if you like," Jay said.

"Dank je wel. Can I get anything for anyone?" he asked, and finally, I sprang up from the floor in one lithe movement and turned to him.

"Yeah, but I'll get it. Sit, Doc." I took his empty plate from his hands, makin' sure to touch my fingers to his, and looked right into his eyes. He kinda fell back down onto the ugly plaid couch, and I smirked but schooled my expression quick. My brothers didn't know I liked guys, and I wasn't about to broadcast it.

I wondered if everyone in the room could hear my heartbeat. It pounded in my chest like a bass drum while I stared at him, imaginin' chasin' him into the kitchen and takin' him up against the ancient fridge.

WANT MORE?

Become a Wisperite!

Join my newsletter for exclusive stories, Wisper news, and The Cade Ranch Sexcapades—naughty little interludes for my subscribers ONLY! Jack and Evvie's wedding scenes are there!

Join for the first FREE short story, Wild Heart: Welcome to Wisper.

Sign up on my website

gretarosewest.com

You can find me on the usual social sites, but I mostly hang out on Instagram, Facebook, and Goodreads.

Join my Team!

Wanna be an ARC reader? Receive an advanced review copy of my next book. Join my Street Team, a wonderful group of people who help get the word out when I release a new book!

Sign up on my webiste

gretarosewest.com

ABOUT THE AUTHOR

Greta Rose West was a floundering artsy flake until Jack showed up, knocking on the door of her brain, and then pounding on it, and then he just plain kicked it down. She lives in NW Indiana with her husband and her two precocious kitties, Geoff Trouble and Sally Mae Midnight. When she's not writing, she's reading and devouring music. She enjoys indie films no one else likes, and her favorite food is Aver's Veggie Revival pizza.

facebook.com/gretarosewest
twitter.com/gretarosewest
instagram.com/gretarosewest
goodreads.com/gretarosewest
bookbub.com/authors/greta-rose-west

Made in the USA
Middletown, DE
26 November 2022